REDEMPTION

A LOVE STORY

NAOMI BROWN

FOREWORD

PROLOGUE

The garden withered slowly. One by one, each vine shriveled and turned to dust. Each crystalline stream stopped flowing, and the pure, life-sustaining water evaporated as if it had been lapped up by the thirsty tongue of a vengeful god. Soon the lush and fertile valley He gave them became as useless and barren as the womb of a ninety-year-old woman. So, it behooved Adam and Eve to leave their garden paradise and search for new land, but they knew nothing of the world beyond the perimeters of their home. Fear crept into their consciousness, like a thief creeping into a fortress, and it was fear that made them aware of their sin. It was fear that strangled the vines and fear that poisoned the ground, and it was fear that bound them to the past and to a way of life that was no longer fruitful. A whole undiscovered universe awaited them, but fear chained them to the garden. With only bitter fruit and stagnant water for sustenance, their bodies became addled with disease. Like the garden, they withered slowly.

PART I
STORGE

"When my father and mother forsake me, then the Lord will take me up."— Psalms 27:10

CHAPTER 1

*I*t never mattered that Andi wasn't my real daughter. I loved her as purely and intensely as though I had carried her in my womb, nursed her at my breasts, and sang lullabies to her while I gently nestled her in my arms. The truth was I met her when she was eight years old, already a fully functioning human being with independent thoughts and a wit sharp enough to challenge Einstein himself. I casually dated her father, but it was Andi who knocked on the closed door of my heart and gained entrance into that secret place inside me where few people were welcomed.

It rained the first day I met her. Trey promised to take me to an art exhibit downtown, but he didn't mention he was bringing a pint-sized chaperone. I lowered my umbrella and crawled into the cab of his bright red Dodge Dakota, surprised when my hand landed on soft human flesh in the seat beside me. That's when I saw her. Two dark brown French braids dangled to her shoulders, and a set of almond-shaped brown eyes widened, either in curiosity or apprehension, at my touch. I was usually pretty good at reading facial expressions, but those two confused me.

I glanced over at Trey in the driver's seat, whose arm the child clung to tightly. He smiled that goofy, crooked grin I fell so hard for six weeks earlier when he was the responding officer after I called for police assistance in removing three children from a dangerous environment.

"Emily," Trey said in a deep masculine Texas drawl. "I'd like you to meet my daughter, Andi Scoggins. Andi, this is Emily Kirk, a good friend of your daddy's."

She smiled sweetly but tightened her grip on her father's arm.

"Well, hello, Andi," I extended one hand. She brushed my fingertips with her own, but promptly pulled out of the handshake.

"Trey, you didn't tell me you had a daughter." It was meant more as a question than a reprimand.

Why wouldn't he have told me about her? Did he think I wouldn't accept her? I was a social worker, for Christ's sake. I related to kids, especially kids from broken homes, which I assumed Andi was.

"Well," he explained, still sporting that irresistible jackass grin. "We haven't really known each other that long. I figured I'd tell you about her when the time was right."

I nodded, perhaps a tad condescendingly. "And you thought the time was right now? While she is sitting right here between us?"

He laughed. "Honestly, I didn't expect Andi here until sometime this summer." He tousled her hair playfully. "She usually lives back east with her mother. A few days ago, I got a call from her mom. She told me she was putting our daughter on a plane and said I needed to keep her for a while. Said there were some things she needed to take care of."

I decided against asking what things were so important they justified putting a little girl on a plane by herself and flying her halfway across the country in the middle of a school year.

THE EXHIBIT WAS a collection of works by local artists, sculptors, and photographers. Some of it I thought was quite impressive, especially for a town the size of Ashford. I'd lived here for many years and never knew such talent existed in our little community.

These artsy affairs don't generally draw big crowds in small southern towns. Besides the three of us, half a dozen or so septuagenarians milled about, sipping bargain basement merlot from disposable wine glasses and talking pretentiously about the huge galleries they had visited in Dallas or other cities. Trey seemed bored. He kept checking his phone for sports scores and rolling his eyes at the anatomically accurate sculptures.

For a moment, I felt selfish for dragging him here. Surely a rugged policeman and his displaced offspring would be more comfortable at a McDonald's, or in a darkened movie theater, watching cars transform into robots. I was about to suggest leaving when I realized Andi was completely enthralled by her surroundings. She stopped at every display and quietly mulled it over.

I continued down the narrow corridor until I came upon a stunning masterpiece. It was a painting of a woman with a giant apple protruding out of her mouth, the fruit held in place by electrical tape. Long flowing auburn tresses covered her upper torso; her hands were bound by barbed wire and placed strategically, shielding her more sacred region. Her legs ended, not with feet, but with a globe. Instead of the names of countries, this globe was marked with words like "famine," "war," "poverty," and "disease." The exquisite artwork was provocatively titled "Eve, Still Chained up in Eden."

I wanted to linger and contemplate the profundity of the artist's message, but I feared Andi might start asking awkward questions. How could I explain such poignant symbolism to a child? What could she possibly understand about the systematic silencing of women's voices by a creation myth that laid the blame for all the world's ills at the feet of a solitary woman?

It turned out I worried needlessly. It was another portrait that caught Andi's attention. This one depicted a Marilyn Monroe likeness sashaying down a spiral staircase, wearing a crimson dress with matching stilettos and elbow-length gloves and a white scarf draped loosely around her flawless neck. The glorious train of the gown flowed seamlessly behind the woman, carpeting each stair in elegance. I noticed it was not the painting itself that captivated my young companion. She stared at the tiny square of paper in the bottom right hand corner that identified the work by its title, "She Walks in Beauty."

Andi ran a bony index finger over each word, then spoke softly, "I like that poem."

Holy cow! I thought. *How did this pre-pubescent little marvel know about Lord Byron?*

"How did you know that is the title of a poem?" I gasped while giving into the sudden urge to touch the frizzy end of a braid.

"My mom read it to me. She loves poetry, and she reads it to me all the time. I just like the way it sounds."

A kid who appreciated the cadence of classic poetry? I was duly impressed.

"Oh, really? Who's your favorite poet?" I asked, half expecting the answer to be Dr. Seuss.

"Emily Dickinson," she replied.

"She's mine too!" I gushed, feeling like I was conversing with a lifelong friend and not a child I'd just met. "What's your favorite Emily Dickinson poem?"

She drew in a deep breath and thoughtfully replied, "The one about I've never been to the ocean, but I still know it's there."

Absolutely incredible, I thought. Most of the adults in my life didn't know Lord Byron from Lord Calvert, and they were only passingly familiar with Emily Dickinson. Now here was this prodigy as knowledgeable of both the famous poets as most kids are of their favorite nursery rhymes. I laced my fingers through hers. This time she showed no trepidation at my touch. We explored the rest of the exhibit hand in hand. We'd long since lost Trey when he ducked outside to take a phone call. As we prepared to leave, I asked her what she thought about our local artists and their works.

"They're okay," she conceded, "but I like the ones I saw when my mom took me to The Met better."

I smiled at her honest assessment. She had been to one of the most celebrated art museums in the world, so she was understandably under-whelmed by the amateurish offerings of rural artists.

"You know what, Miss Andi Scoggins?" I asked her as we walked outside and scanned the parking lot for Trey's pickup. By now, the rain had subsided, and all that remained was a few fat drops falling from the eaves and slithering down our backs. "I have a feeling you and I are going to be great friends."

CHAPTER 2

*B*efore The Incident, things were very different. I didn't live with my imperturbable boss, Connie, and her menagerie of overly indulged pets. I had my own apartment where I cooked fabulous meals that even the most discerning epicurean would have appreciated. In the springtime, I entertained guests on my balcony that overlooked a resplendent courtyard garden. Flowers in a variety of shapes, sizes, and hues permeated the air with a heavenly scent. In the winter, I locked the doors, curled up on the sofa with my cat, Bronte, and drowned myself in hot chocolate and classic literature. I cherished my alone time, but now I was lucky to get five minutes alone, with the way Connie hovered over me, and I could forget about cooking. I wasn't even allowed in the kitchen.

After Andi came into my life, she spent many nights at that apartment with me. Trey worked a lot of double shifts. I think he was grateful he met me when he did. Otherwise, finding a babysitter willing to work the graveyard might have been difficult. I usually only saw him when he dropped his daughter off or picked her up, but I didn't mind. I didn't feel taken advantage of. In fact, I considered it a privilege spending so much time with such a delightful child.

She and I baked sugar cookies that we decorated with blue or pink icing squeezed from a tube, or we played Scrabble for hours. She always beat me and accused me of letting her win. I assured her I was far too competitive for any of that nonsense. She became my sparring partner. We debated such hot button issues as gun control, global warming, and whether *Hello Kitty* was a zoomorphic girl or an anthropomorphized cat. Sometimes we went to separate ends of the couch, and I read Charlotte Bronte while she read *Charlotte's Web.* Those were the best evenings of all.

One night, Andi and I stayed up until after midnight, binge-watching Lizzie Maguire reruns and devouring the puff pastries we'd worked on all day. It was spring break for her, and I was used to getting by on very little sleep. Shortly after my charge drifted off on the living room floor, and I lovingly covered her with a light blanket, my phone rang. I deduced from the ringtone that it was my supervisor, Connie Parsons.

"It's the Detwiler kids again, Em." Connie always spoke with a syrupy sweet southern accent, even when she was angry or scared. Right now, she was both. "The boy is at the ER. This time his scumbag father almost killed him."

"I'm on my way." I hung up the phone without saying good-bye.

I found one neighbor still awake. I knew elderly Mrs. Whitten well, so I recruited her to sit with Andi while I rushed to Mt. Olive Memorial, our town's only hospital.

Thomas Detwiler was a seven-year-old boy with an affinity for mischief and Ninja Turtles. His three-year-old sister, Harper, gave magical bear hugs that made sadness disappear. In the past six months, I had been called out to their house five times. A teacher noticed Thomas had worn the same clothes every day for an entire week. Harper showed up at pre-school with headlice and a black eye. Thomas fell out of a tree and broke his arm—on two different occasions. Their pediatrician spotted bruising on both children that was inconsistent with their parents' explanations.

As soon as I burst through the automatic sliding doors of the emergency room, the physician on duty, an African-American woman with kind eyes and a warm smile, greeted me and guided me into a room where a sweet-faced, blonde-haired boy was stretched out on a gurney. One side of his face was stained the color of grape Kool-Aid, and there was a deep laceration above his right eye.

His mother sat in a chair next to him. If the universe had been a bit more kind, she might have been beautiful, with golden blonde hair and green eyes, but a lifetime of injustices left her visibly marred with pock marks and premature laugh lines. Her mouth twitched uncontrollably, and her neck jerked spasmodically. I immediately recognized the tell-tale signs of severe methamphetamine addiction.

"What happened to Thomas?" I asked bluntly as I took a seat in the only other chair in the room, glaring hostilely at the woman across from me and mentally berating her for her failure as a parent.

"Fell out of a tree," she lied. Her husband had hospitalized her before too, once when he kicked her in the side and ruptured her spleen, so I understood her reluctance to tell the truth.

"It seems to me your son falls out of trees a lot. Maybe you should stop letting him climb them."

"I told him not to go up there," she protested.

"Rose," I felt familiar enough with Mrs. Detwiler to address her by her first name. "You and I both know Thomas didn't fall out of a tree. Not this time, nor the times before. What did your husband do to Thomas?"

She hesitated for a moment. Then sniffled, "Hit him with a vacuum cleaner."

Here was the part of the job that never got any easier—listening to the details. I trained myself not to wince at the bruises, black eyes, and broken bones. The bodily injuries were all the same. It was the details behind the physical wounds that changed, each story a little worse than the one before, and it was those stories that made me weep for humanity. Every time I thought I had witnessed the worst thing anyone could do to a child, somebody upped the ante and did something even more horrendous.

"Thomas wasn't doing his homework," Rose continued. "He said it was too hard. Luke looked at it, and he said, 'It ain't hard, you little retard. It's just adding and subtracting.' Well, anyway, remember how the last time you came to my house you said I needed to get that place cleaned up? That's what I'd been doing all day, cleaning. I borrowed a vacuum cleaner from the landlady. It was still plugged into the outlet. When Luke got mad, he yanked the cord out of the wall and smacked poor little old Thomas right upside the head with that big old machine. Knocked the wind plumb out of him. I was gonna bring him to the hospital sooner, but I had to wait for Luke to go to sleep before I could even get out of the house."

I bit down hard on the inside of my cheek, hoping the physical pain might mitigate the wellspring of emotional turmoil that threatened to engulf me. Suddenly, a disturbing thought struck me.

"Rose," I asked. "Where is Harper?"

"She's home with her daddy."

"You left her alone with him?" I fought back the urge to add, *Are you out of your ever-loving mind?*

"Don't worry about him. He's passed out drunk," she said nonchalantly, as though leaving a toddler alone with an unconscious alcoholic was a perfectly logical decision.

"We have to get over there." I utilized my most authoritative, but still polite voice, the way a frazzled store clerk speaks to a belligerent customer. I was determined to get the Detwiler kids away from their father, even if it meant strong-arming their mother. "I will make sure the nurses know Thomas is by himself. I am taking you home, and you are going to pack your things. You are leaving that house with me, or your kids are going into state custody as soon as I can file the paperwork, and you will go to jail for failure to protect your children."

"Where am I supposed to go? I ain't got no money," she lamented.

I was already one step ahead of her excuse. "There is a battered women's shelter called My Sister's House. It's in a secret location in another town. I already told them about you. They are willing to take you and the kids, but there are some conditions. First, you have to go to rehab, and then you have to get a job." I stressed the final stipulation. "And, Rose, under no circumstances can you let your husband know where you are."

To me, Rose seemed like an empty shell of a woman, one of those drug-addicted mothers who have been so thoroughly robbed by life and circumstances, they are devoid of even the most rudimentary maternal instincts. It amazed me when she looked at her helpless son, moaning and moving restlessly in his sleep. A single tear snaked down her face, and she sobbed loudly.

"Just get us out of there," she cried. "I'll do whatever I have to. I'm tired of him beating on my kids."

It surprised me how quickly she acquiesced. In the past, Rose resisted leaving her abusive husband; I suspected because he was also her drug supplier. Now with custody of her children on the line, she acknowledged the futility of both her marriage and her habit. Somewhere inside that empty shell of a woman, there still beat the heart of a mother.

CHAPTER 3

The houses stood in parallel rows, an archipelago of wood-paneled Alcatraz Islands. *Prisons. Presumably inescapable prisons*, I thought as I maneuvered my SUV onto the graveled parking lot of the River's Edge Mobile Home Park. Eight rows, five houses per row. Forty oblong prison cells, each one housed inmates convicted of the felonious act of having been born at the wrong end of the American caste system, a brutal social order that does not officially exist.

The sun emerged from its ethereal hiding place and painted the eastern sky with ribbons of orange and pink. Trey and his partner, a diminutive dynamo barely big enough to hold up her own gun belt, pulled up beside us.

"Does he have any guns in there?" Trey demanded of Rose as we waded across the dewy wet grass, tall enough it moistened the bottoms of my pants legs.

"No," she responded. "He had to pawn them a while back to pay the electric bill."

"You two wait out here while we take him into custody," Trey instructed Rose and me. "We'll bring the baby out to you." Then he pounded on the door of cellblock 17 and shouted, "Police! Open up! We've got a warrant for your arrest!"

"He ain't gonna hear you," Mrs. Detwiler calmly informed the policeman. "He's passed out. Here. Take my key. I give you permission to go in." She tossed a keyring to Trey.

The officers left the door wide open, and I could see the violent man lying shirtless on the couch, both arms hung limply over the end of the sofa. While his partner searched for Harper, Trey descended on the suspect with all the stealth and agility of a jaguar pouncing on its prey. Before Luke Detwiler awoke from his drunken stupor, he was in handcuffs.

"What the hell is going on?" he demanded groggily.

Trey informed the captive that he was being arrested for child abuse and child endangerment. Then the officer mirandized the suspect as he pulled him up and dragged him to the door. When Luke saw me, his demeanor shifted from confused to enraged. His eyes narrowed into slits, and he struggled to break loose from Trey's firm grasp.

"Don't make a scene, Luke," Rose warned. "Me and the kids are leaving. We won't be here when you get back. I ain't gonna let you hurt my babies anymore."

The hostile man was impervious to his wife's words. He kept glaring at me. "It's you," he growled menacingly. "I should have known you were behind this, you nosy goddamned bitch! Why can't you just mind your own goddamned business?"

I took a step backward, caught off guard by Luke's verbal assault. Trey shoved him in the general direction of the police cruiser and told him sternly, "Calm down, Detwiler."

The female officer appeared, holding a smiling but filthy little girl. The policewoman quickly handed the child over to the mother and sprinted off to help her partner subdue the irate prisoner. Luke broke free and charged at me.

"You take what's mine, and I'll take what's yours! Sound like a fair trade, bitch? They ain't keeping me in jail forever. I'm coming after you!"

I didn't respond. I couldn't. My body wouldn't move, and my mouth refused to open. I stood there immobile and silent, nervously chewing on my lower lip until my tongue detected the metallic taste of blood.

The officers regained control of the situation and finally got the prisoner in the car. I could still hear him screaming in the back seat, but I couldn't see him anymore. My voice and my mobility returned.

"Let's go in and get your things," I suggested to Rose, partly because I was in a hurry to get her delivered to the women's shelter, but mostly because I would have used any excuse to get away from the crazed banshee threatening me.

I had been in the Detwilers' trailer many times. It was no different than a hundred other homes I'd been in while investigating allegations of child maltreatment. Rose had said she'd been cleaning all day, but I saw no evidence of that. The dingy yellow carpet was stained with dog urine and food spills, and the entire house reeked of stale tobacco, cheap booze, and the tangible stench of poverty. Foam rubber padding peeked out of tears in the seventies-style orange vinyl couch and fist size holes in the walls exposed the shoddy framework of the mobile home. Cockroaches blackened patches of the tattered pea green wallpaper and crawled freely over the dirty dishes left in the sink and on the table. Tiny specks of rat feces dotted the kitchen stove. I followed behind Rose as she shoved random items into an Army green duffle bag. As we made our way to the bedrooms, we stepped over the weaponized vacuum cleaner, still toppled over in the hallway, and I sighed in disgust as we maneuvered around a mound of soiled laundry in the floor. I was glad it didn't take Rose long to pack.

As a matter of protocol, I took a winding and confusing route to My Sister's House. It was supposed to deter abusers from following or tracking down their fleeing victims. The trees along the highway had not yet recovered from winter's savage pillaging. Their grayish hue and their nearly naked limbs created an eerie ambience across the bucolic landscape. Even though I knew Luke was on his way to jail, I still checked my mirrors more often than usual. Any time someone pulled up too close behind us on a deserted stretch of road, I pressed down a little harder on the accelerator.

They say eyes are the windows to the soul, and I believed it.

During my fifteen years with Child Protective Services, I'd faced down more than my share of angry, violent men. When I looked in their eyes, I usually saw something behind the rage. Sometimes it was sadness. Other times it was disappointment or disillusionment, or maybe frustration. On a few occasions, I saw pure evil. When I looked in Luke Detwiler's eyes, I saw the most frightening thing I'd ever seen emanating from a man's soul. Nothing. Absolutely nothing.

"He's really going to do it, you know?" Rose spoke in a squeaky, high-pitched voice that sounded like she had sucked all the helium out of a balloon.

"Do what?"

"Hurt you. Or your family. He's crazy that way. He gets mad, and then he gets mean, really mean."

"Your husband is not the first man to threaten me." I downplayed my own concern.

"I've seen him do it before, you know?"

"Do what?" I asked again, anxiously tapping my thumb on the cloth cover of my steering wheel.

"Hurt somebody. Do something really mean because somebody made him mad. One time, he got fired from his job. His boss was this really old lady, and she had this little yapping dog. You know, one of them little ankle biters. Real annoying little shit, but she loved that thing like it was her kid or something. Anyway, Luke just marched right over there to her house and grabbed that mutt right up and slit its little throat right in front of her. That old lady ain't been the same since."

Every fiber of my being wanted to scream, *Will you please just shut the hell up?* Instead, I changed the subject. "Thomas is being transported by ambulance to a hospital in the same town where you are going." It bothered me that she hadn't even asked about him. "When the doctors release him, he'll join you at the shelter."

I dropped Rose and Harper off at My Sister's House, filled the administrator in on the situation with Thomas, and headed for home. Another social worker would take over the case since the shelter was in another county. I couldn't help feeling relieved that the Detwiler family was now someone else's problem.

WITHIN HOURS, we learned Luke had bonded out of jail. That night Trey stayed at my apartment for the first time. While I made manicotti and cheesecake, he nervously paced around the living room. Occasionally he stopped, parted the blinds, and peered out.

If he had been the first man I'd ever known, I easily could have loved him. Everything about him appealed to me, from his salient smile and pure blue eyes to his protective, chivalrous nature and the tenderness he showed his daughter. Unfortunately, he followed a succession of drunks, drug addicts, and deadbeats, starting with my father.

I didn't like thinking about him, that gargantuan pinkish-skinned man who existed now only as a shadowy figure that haunted my most horrifying dreams. My earliest memory of my father involved him shoving my mother's head under a sink full of scalding hot dishwater and holding it there while her arms flailed wildly and she desperately fought for life, all because she audaciously asked what he wanted for breakfast when she "should have by God known" what he wanted for breakfast. Once, he locked me in a closet for an entire weekend, because he caught me talking to a boy. No daughter of his was going to be a slut before she even graduated junior high. Who knew explaining fractions to a learning disabled classmate made a girl slutty? No matter how he treated his wife and children, he was considered a good man by the community. He was a good man because he was a religious man. He thumped that Bible like a dog thumps its ears when it's scratching fleas. In the reddest of the red counties, in the reddest of the red states, that was the only qualification for being classified as a good man.

He was the caliphate of his own mini-theocracy, handing out edicts and enforcing them with brute strength and terror tactics. Laughter was foolishness, so it must be quelled. Imagination was of the devil, so it had to be suppressed. All expressions of affection had sexual over-tones; therefore, they were strictly forbidden.

When I started dating, almost every man I met rivaled my father for the Psychotic Asshole of the Century award. They violated me in ways I never knew were possible. Then, of course, there were the garden variety lowlifes I encountered on the job. At some point, I started thinking truly good men only existed in women's dreams and romance novels. Now I had a perfectly decent adult male human being right here in my apartment, and I had absolutely no idea how I was supposed to feel.

We finished dinner and Andi excused herself to do the homework she had neglected over the break. Trey and I washed dishes. We play-fully tossed lemon-scented suds at each other until he grew pensive, and a serious expression darkened his face.

"I've been thinking," he began. "Maybe I should get someone else to keep Andi for a while, until this mess with Detwiler settles down. Or I could tell my sergeant that I can't do anymore night shifts, and I can just keep her myself."

"Oh, Trey! Why?" I hadn't realized how dependent I had become on the companionship of a child, but now when faced with the thought of losing her, I was terrified.

"I don't want her getting drawn into any more adult drama. Didn't she tell you why her mother sent her down here to stay with me?"

"I assumed it was because she got tired of being a parent. I see it all the time in my profession." I wiped a glass tumbler dry with my red-checkered dish towel and placed the glass in the cupboard.

"No," Trey scrubbed a stubborn marinara stain off a plate. "It would almost be easier if that was the case, but no. Sarah is a great mother. She loves our daughter with her whole heart. But she married this guy—a real winner. He was Andi's piano teacher. At first, he doted on his prized pupil, until the first time Sarah pissed him off. He blamed Andi for all his and Sarah's problems. He started smacking her around and hitting her with belts when her mother wasn't there to defend her. When Sarah found out about it, she left him. Then one day this guy showed up at Andi's school and tried to snatch her off the playground.

An alert teacher saw what was happening and intervened. The next day Andi found a snake in her backpack. It turned out to be non-venomous, but it scared the hell out of the poor kid. After that, he stalked and harassed them both relentlessly. Sarah is still fighting it in court. She doesn't want to take Andi back home until she is sure it's safe."

It saddened me thinking of Andi in that situation, the kind of situation I devoted my life to protecting children from. Still, I was desperate to convince her father she was safe with me.

"But, Trey," I pleaded as I dried the last of the dishes. "Please don't take her away from me. You're a cop. You must get threatened all the time. That ignorant hillbilly, Luke Detwiler, is no more likely to act on his threats than the thugs you deal with every day."

"I don't know," Trey sighed wearily. "Somehow this just seems different."

CHAPTER 4

*T*hree months passed with no sign of trouble from Luke. I heard an unsubstantiated rumor that he was in jail in another state. Trey got behind on his mortgage and started working double shifts again, and I resumed my role as Andi's primary caregiver.

We celebrated her ninth birthday at one of those kid-centric pizza places with games and human-sized dancing rodents. Andi's mother flew down for the occasion. Sarah was the adult version of her daughter with well-coiffed brunette hair and soulful brown eyes. Despite her gregarious personality, I hated everything about her. It wasn't her relationship with Andi that bothered me. In fact, I found it oddly comforting that mother and daughter still shared a close bond even after a lengthy separation. The problem arose when Sarah draped her arm affectionately over Trey's shoulders. Suddenly, I felt like the dowdy Jane Eyre, vying against the regal Blanche for the affections of the magnificently flawed Mr. Rochester.

My disdain was solidified when Andi tore into her presents. Trey had gotten her a doll, custom designed to look exactly like her. Both Sarah and I had gotten her a book titled *Poetry for Kids: the Emily Dickinson Collection.*

Sarah laughed. "I see my little literary genius told you about her fondness for Miss Dickinson."

I nodded sheepishly. "I'm sorry. I guess I should have asked everyone else what they were getting her."

"Oh, don't be silly," Sarah waved one elegantly manicured hand in the air, as though she was brushing away the negative vibe between us. "She can keep one book at her dad's house, and I will take one with me, so she will have it when she comes home."

Home. From the beginning, I had known Andi's stay here was temporary, but when I thought about her leaving, my heart sank.

"When do you think you will take her back?" I hoped I sounded disinterested. If Sarah suspected I was moving in on her territory with her daughter, she might snatch the child up and leave tonight. I'd seen mothers do it when they thought their maternal role was being challenged

Sarah watched her daughter, now busy playing games with her father and the handful of kids who showed up for the party. "Andi has enjoyed being here with her dad—and you. I've seriously been thinking about moving back to Texas, so she doesn't have to be uprooted again. I still have family in the area. Besides, I could certainly use a fresh start."

Sarah stayed a few more days, and I begrudgingly stepped back and let her enjoy her time with her daughter. Then she went back east to tidy up loose ends in preparation for her big move, and Andi returned to my apartment.

The next day I took her roller blading at the local skate park. I trailed behind barely balancing on the inline wheels while she easily spun around and made perfect figure-eights. When we stopped to re-lace her skates, the sun hit the earth at just the right angle it created a golden halo above her smiling, radiant face. For a moment, I let myself imagine she was mine and only mine, but she had parents who loved her, and it was selfish for me to even think she could be exclusively my child.

THAT NIGHT after a game of Scrabble, which I lost soundly when she spelled out the word "lexicon," our conversation turned serious.

"What is your job, Emily?" she asked as she dug a pair of pajamas out of her dresser drawer and prepared for bed. With her inquisitive nature, I was surprised she had never broached the subject before.

"I'm a social worker," I answered as I folded back the covers on the twin size bed I had bought just for Andi. "Do you know what that is?"

She nodded, "It means you help kids and families. I had to talk to a social worker once. My step-dad was mean to me."

"Your dad told me about that." We sat on the edge of her bed, and I drew her close to me. "How did that make you feel?" I utilized my training in active listening skills.

"Scared, at first. Then sad. But then I told my mom, and we talked to the social worker, and I wasn't scared or sad anymore. I knew the people who loved me wouldn't let anyone hurt me again."

"I'm glad you're not scared or sad now. And you're right. Those of us who love you will always protect you."

"When I had to talk to the social worker, a girl from my class said I was going to get taken away from my mom. She said that's what social workers do, take kids away from their parents. Do you ever do that, Emily?"

That was part of the job I never liked talking about, especially not with children, but I had always been honest with Andi.

"Only when their parents don't love them or can't take care of them," I assured her.

"Why do people have kids they don't love or can't take care of?"

I shrugged. "Well, sweetheart, that's one of those questions that's really hard to answer. It's like asking why the sky is blue."

"I think I read somewhere it has something to do with the sun's rays shining on specks of dust in the air."

"That's amazingly accurate," I laughed, impressed with her rudimentary knowledge of Rayleigh scattering. I knew adults who had no clue what made the sky blue.

"You didn't know that when you were a kid?" she chided.

"I don't think anybody knew that when I was a kid," I defended my childhood ignorance, then I pulled Andi closer to me. I snuggled her gently and caressed her hair. I felt her soft skin and breathed in her sweet smell. She always smelled like cotton candy, and I wanted to savor that aroma forever.

CHAPTER 5

*E*ven though I'd heard nothing from Luke, I couldn't help thinking his insane ranting was more than idle threats. He had overtly threatened me and made a veiled threat against my family, a family that now consisted only of my sister, Janice, and my mother. Janice and I had never been close enough for anyone to harm her to get even with me. I thought about my mother, alone and vulnerable in that God-forsaken shack she refused to leave, and I decided I should check on her.

It had been more than ten years since I last visited my mother in her home, although I talked to her frequently by phone, and she visited my apartment for birthdays and holidays. It was simply too painful for me going back to that secluded, dilapidated house where I was physically beaten and browbeaten for eighteen long years.

I grew up in a farming community twenty-seven miles south of Ashford. Our home was the kind of place that always seemed to have a dark cloud hovering over it. Not a cloud made of moisture, but one made of misfortune and human suffering. Our church gave our family a couple of acres and an old barn somebody had converted into a house, because my father managed to get fired from every job he ever had and we had no place to live. The makeshift domicile looked the same as I remembered—run down and practically uninhabitable. Loose siding flapped furiously in the wind, and the front door moved back and forth, hanging on by one hinge. In the surrounding fields, longhorn cattle grazed mindlessly on the tall prairie grass the way people feed on myths and folklore.

I knocked on the door and instantly regretted it. It wasn't my mother who answered. It was Janice.

"Emily?" she acted as though she wasn't sure she recognized me. "What are you doing here?"

"I'm...I'm...here to see Mom," I stuttered. Something about my older sister made me feel like an insecure child, attempting vainly to appease an austere schoolmarm, and I ducked my head to avoid her disapproving glare.

"It certainly took you long enough to get here." She stepped aside barely far enough for me to pass through. "I suppose you finally got my messages."

"Messages?' I ignored Janice's calls, and I deleted her texts without reading them.

"Oh, I suppose your phone has been broken again." Her accusatory tone dripped with icy sarcasm.

"No," I replied honestly, fidgeting with the strap of my purse. "I've just been really busy."

"Busy shirking your family obligations, as usual."

"Where's Mom?" I demanded impatiently. I had no desire to stay trapped in this hellhole, alone with a woman who made me feel like I still belonged in Pampers.

"If you had bothered reading your messages," she scolded, "you would know she's not here. She's in the hospital."

"Hospital?" I echoed numbly, suddenly overwrought with guilt for not being a more dutiful daughter. "Did her glucose level skyrocket again? I thought she was eating healthier."

Strange how we worried about the nutritional intake of a woman who subsisted on a steady diet of figs, fish, and pomegranates.

"No, Em," Janice corrected me in a condescending manner. "It has nothing to do with diabetes. Mom has cancer."

Stunned, I pressed her for more details. "What kind of cancer?"

She lowered her voice, like she was about to reveal a shameful secret. "She has cancer down *there*."

When it came to biology and anatomy, Janice often spoke in a juvenile code I couldn't fully comprehend. I knew "down there" was a reference to the reproductive organs, so I asked for clarification. "Uterine, cervical, or ovarian?"

My sister, a formidable she-bear of piety and propriety, grimaced. "Must you be so vulgar?"

"Never mind. I'll ask the doctor." I let her off the hook, then asked, "So if Mom's not here, why are you?"

"I came to get her nightgowns and a few other things," she explained. Then she ordered, "Help me find her Bible."

"Did she ask for her Bible?"

"No, but if she'd been reading it more often, she wouldn't be in this predicament."

"You mean if she had read her Bible more she wouldn't have cancer?"

"Exactly. Now are you going to help me or not? Maybe God will still heal her if she repents."

Repents for what? I thought. My mother was too scared and timid to engage in anything more debauched than watching soap operas.

Though she'd always been a sanctimonious snit, even as a child, my sister's callousness still shocked me. I halfheartedly rummaged through Mom's belongings in search of the sacred text. I looked around at the four bare walls and the sparse furnishings. My eyes landed on a brownish water stain on the ceiling where the roof had leaked. An overhead light was on, but it wasn't strong enough to cast out the darkness created by the warped chipboard paneling and the heavy blankets used for curtains.

As a kid living in abject poverty, I used to think money would be the answer to all our problems. If only my parents worked harder and made more money, then all the misery that surrounded us would dissipate. Now after working extensively with poor families, I understood that poverty is not merely a financial status that needs altered, nor is it a moral failure of the individual. It is a plague, a contagious strain of hopelessness and despair that cripples entire communities for generations. To paraphrase Gandhi, the way we collectively respond to the cries of the poor reveals the true heart of our nation. Poverty is an unsanitary scalpel that tears away the aesthetic flesh of society and leaves the gritty, gutty, grimy innards exposed.

"Why does she stay here?" I pondered aloud. I'd told her repeatedly that I would get a place big enough for both of us if only she would leave this low-rent mausoleum.

"Because she can still feel Daddy's presence in this house," Janice answered the rhetorical question.

"Yeah. Me too," I sighed as I sat down on my mother's hard, lumpy bed. A spring poked out of the mattress and into my flesh.

I felt my father's presence as tangibly as if he had never worked himself up into a senseless rage that caused a hemorrhagic stroke, a ruptured aneurysm that left him incapacitated for two years before his death. I still heard that booming voice reverberating through the tiny shack. I still saw his fists, hands that to my frightened mind seemed the size of tennis rackets, doubled into two fiery balls of steel. I even sensed the gluttony, the way he devoured every morsel of food at the table with all the satiety of a necrophile left alone in a morgue.

"Why do you hate him?" Janice, the least empathetic person I knew, somehow sensed my current emotion.

I thought a better question was, *Why* don't *you hate him?*

"I don't hate him, Jan," I lied. I caught a glimpse of the missing Bible sticking out from under a pillow.

"Here it is." I held the book up for Janice to see, glad to have a distraction.

"You can ride to the hospital with me," she said, as though I had no choice in the matter.

"I'd really rather take my own car," I insisted, determined to get away from Janice and her self-righteous attitude. She started to argue. Then I thought of a perfectly logical explanation why taking separate vehicles made sense. Both my sister and I lived some distance from the old homeplace and in different directions. "I don't want to have to come all the way back here to get my car, and I'm sure you don't want to drive me back to get it, either."

For once, she conceded that I was right. I could not fathom being alone with that woman in a moving vehicle. Jumping out at the nearest overpass would have been an attractive option. I climbed into my SUV and struggled getting the key in the ignition with my vision clouded by tears. How had I not known my mother had a serious illness? I tried to recall how long it had been since the last time I spoke with her. She called me often, but when she didn't initiate the contact, I rarely ever made the first move.

I sat on the parking lot at the hospital until I saw Janice's midnight blue sedan leaving the premises. Slowly, I made my way to the automatic doors. I tried to fake a smile, so my mother wouldn't know how upset and worried I was. How had she gotten so good at phony smiles? Maybe I would get her to teach me.

Janice had not prepared me for the seriousness of Mom's condition. I had falsely assumed my mother's cancer was in the beginning stages and there was still hope. I found her hooked up to a feeding tube and a morphine drip, with a metastatic tumor gnawing away at her internal organs.

"It is the fastest growing, most aggressive tumor I have ever seen," her primary physician told me when I demanded a meeting with him. He sat behind the desk in a cramped office, his hands folded in front of him.

"Doctor, isn't there anything we can do? Any hope at all?" I pleaded, trying to still the swivel chair that fought to move despite my best efforts to control it.

"It's too late for chemotherapy or surgery," he responded sympathetically, his eyes filled with compassion. "Anything we could do now would only prolong her suffering, and it wouldn't help at all. If only your mother would have done what I asked her to do. Ovarian cancer is hard to detect even in the best situations, and I am not a specialist. I begged your mother to see a gynecologist, but she simply wouldn't go. She wouldn't even let me give her a thorough examination."

And then I knew. I knew the name of the malignancy that was

killing my mother; it had been slowly killing her all her life. It was religion. A religion that made her so ashamed of her own body she would rather risk death than be examined by a highly trained, highly educated professional. It was the same religion that made her stay in an abusive marriage. Then when fate intervened and her nightmare should have ended, it was that same religion that guilted her into sitting at the bedside of her rapist, nursing and comforting the man who had brutalized and sodomized her for decades.

Trey was understanding when I called and told him I couldn't babysit for a while. I suggested my neighbor, Mrs. Whitten as a possible alternative. I spent the next few nights in Mom's hospital room, sleeping in a leather recliner, listening to the tentative bleeping of a heart monitor. She moaned in agony. The morphine was administered in small doses, as though giving her more would have altered the outcome in any way. Besides the piteous moaning, she was completely silent. When visitors came, she even pasted on a weak smile.

Growing up, I was a feisty ginger-haired tomboy who preferred football and Tonka trucks to ballet and Barbie dolls. Most of my playmates were boys. I viewed other girls as weak, pathetic, and easily victimized. Now I realized I had based that blanket judgment solely on my perception of my own mother.

Part of me wanted to scream, *Just say it! Just freaking say it! Say I'm scared! Say I'm mad! Say I got screwed! Say I was a good person, and I deserved better than this!*

But the churchgoers were filing in and out, and it wouldn't do to express any doubt or malcontent in their presence. After all, weren't they the ones who had the power to condemn the dying to hell? It certainly seemed that way sometimes.

The night before my mother's funeral, Bronte succumbed to old age and an undetected heart murmur. Otherwise, I don't think I could have mustered a solitary tear when we buried the matriarch of my dysfunctional family. In my view, she'd been dead for as long as I could remember, effectively murdered by her husband and her religion.

CHAPTER 6

*T*he funeral was mercifully short. The preacher kept clearing his throat and checking his watch, as though he had better things to do than bury a faithful member of his flock whose tithe wasn't big enough to be missed. He ended his short speech with an even shorter prayer, and the crowd dispersed. Janice stopped and chatted with a few of the church ladies, and I decided to make a run for it.

She intercepted me before I got to my car.

"You're being incredibly rude," the schoolmarm reprimanded her troublesome student. "These are Mom's friends. The least you could do is thank them for coming."

I knew they weren't really Mom's friends. Automatons are incapable of friendships, and this particular model was programmed only for fake smiles, petty gossip, and arranging potluck dinners for funerals.

"Look, Jan, I really have to go," I said as I got into my SUV and wrestled with the seatbelt.

"We're getting together at the church. The ladies have prepared a huge meal for us. You need to be there." She paused and then sarcastically added, "Unless, of course, you have something else you'd rather do."

There are a lot of things I'd rather do, I thought. *I'd rather scoop my eyeballs out with a hot spoon and shove them back in by way of my nostrils. I'd rather dance naked in a cactus field or get accused of adultery in Saudi Arabia.*

"Okay," I finally relented. "I'll meet you at the church."

A victorious smirk crossed her face, and she let go of my car door. I put the vehicle in gear and headed straight for home. There was no way in the nine circles of Dante's vision of hell I was going to waste another minute listening to a bunch of self-righteous religionists talk about my mother as though they really knew her—as though anyone really knew her. Even I never fully understood or appreciated her. To the rest of the world, she was an insignificant woman, a silver-haired granule of sand on an old lady beach. Her trait people most admired was her timidity, and they spoke about it as though quietness in a woman were a virtue and not a manifestation of abuse and oppression.

We buried Mama in her hometown, fifty miles from Ashford, so I braced myself for a long, lonely drive home. When I reached the next town, I stopped at a McDonald's for coffee and a small salad. I picked the order up at the drive-thru window and then pulled into a parking space to put sugar and cream in the coffee. I had barely gotten the lid off the cup when a pair of petite feminine hands tapped on my window. Startled, I jumped, and a portion of the steaming hot liquid trickled down my blouse, burning my skin.

Rose Detwiler stood before me, dressed in full McDonald's regalia, her hair pinned up high in a messy bun. The involuntary jerking and twitching had subsided, and I concluded that the rehab must have been successful.

"Hi Emily," she greeted me when I rolled the window down. "I thought I recognized your voice when I took your order."

"Hello, Rose," I returned the greeting. This time I mastered my mother's phony smile. "I see you got a job."

"Yep. I already got a promotion too." She pointed at the words

"Shift Manager" on her badge and beamed as proudly as though they had made her CEO.

"That's fantastic," I feigned cheerfulness when all I really wanted to do was get away from her as soon as possible and go home. I missed Andi, and to a lesser extent, Trey. Connie had graciously given me a leave of absence during my mother's illness, but I was anxious to get back to work.

"Guess what?" She didn't wait for my response before she continued. "Me and Luke got divorced. He didn't fight me on it or anything. I haven't even seen him since that day he got arrested for what he did to Thomas."

"How are the kids?" I asked, purposely changing the subject, but genuinely concerned.

"Oh, they're great," she gushed, like any proud mother would. "Growing like little weeds. I just had their pictures taken. First time I ever had their photographs done professionally. If I had your address, I'd send you copies."

"That's okay," I assured her. "Tell them I said hello."

"No, really. I want to send you pictures of them," she persisted. "You saved our lives. It would be our way of saying thank you."

"Honestly, Rose, it's okay. I really do have to go." God, how badly I wanted to get out of there and get this hellish day over with.

She produced a yellow notepad and a pin from the pocket of her uniform top and insisted, "Write down your address."

Physically exhausted and emotionally drained, I took her offerings and scribbled down: 907 North Woodland Drive, Apt. 52.

STUPID! Stupid! Stupid! I chastised myself on the drive home. *Boundaries! Boundaries! Boundaries!* All social workers are trained to practice and enforce healthy boundaries with their clients. Never get personally involved in their lives, never give them money, and for the love of God and all things holy, never, ever give out personal information to a client.

Panic set in—tiny ripples at first, then tsunami-strength waves—and I had to talk myself down. Technically, Rose wasn't my client anymore, and she said she hadn't seen Luke since she moved into the shelter. *Everything is going to be okay*, I told myself repeatedly, until I convinced myself I hadn't just made the worst mistake of my life.

CHAPTER 7

I felt them before I heard or saw them—hot, excited breathing on my face and neck. I scrambled for the switch on the bedside lamp. There were three of them. The Beast, Luke Detwiler, stood over me, his empty soulless eyes fixated on something in the bed beside me. He grinned maniacally, and even in the dimly lit room, I could see the nicotine stains on his crooked teeth. Next to him was The Mangy Dog, a fat man with patches of red whiskers scattered indiscriminately across his ruddy face. He looked as though no one ever taught him how to shave. Copper-colored curls sprung out of his head, but there were not enough of them to completely cover his pink scalp. Then there was The Coyote, a scrawny cartoonish looking derelict with crazy bloodshot eyes and greasy unkempt hair. He kept nervously giggling and fidgeting with the belt loops on his filthy blue jeans, like an idiotic teenager watching his first porn flick.

There was mace in my purse, if only I could get to it, but they already had me pinned to the bed. Cold steel clamped down on my wrists. Handcuffs. One of them handcuffed my hands above my head. I kicked wildly, but they quickly subdued me.

Arms. Legs. Hands. Feet. Sweaty, smelly bodies everywhere. Touching. Hitting. Punching. Poking. Prodding. Grabbing. Groping.

Where were my neighbors? Why hadn't someone called the police? It was an apartment complex, for God's sake! Surely someone could hear me screaming. Only I wasn't screaming. I had no voice. What had they done to my goddamned voice? Now I understood what Luke meant by his threat. "You take what's mine, and I'll take what's yours," he'd said. I took his family, and he took my dignity, my autonomy, and somehow even my voice.

Suddenly, it occurred to me that I was no longer on the bed, at least not the part of me that registered such things as fear, pain, and humiliation. That part of me floated away, detached from the body that was being so brutally assaulted. It was like a near death experience, sans bright lights and dead people. Body and soul torn apart, separated like monozygotic twins ripped from the bloody womb of a lunatic. I hovered above the crime scene, a disinterested third-party in my own struggle for survival.

On some level, I understood what was happening inside my head. I drifted back to an Introductory Psych lecture I sat through years ago. What were those words the professor used?

Depersonalization…

Derealization…

Dissociation…

Dissociation occurs when a traumatic event overwhelms the individual's ability to cope. Contrary to popular belief, it is not the process of losing one's mind, rather it is a remarkable testament of the human mind's extraordinary ability to protect and preserve itself, even when it cannot protect and preserve the body.

I never called that professor by his real name. I always called him Professor Pangloss in honor of his naively optimistic worldview. He was a demure little man with a British accent and an agglomeration of whimsical bowties as expansive and eclectic as Imelda Marcos' shoe collection. I stayed in contact with him for a while, until he wrote a book on Christian humanism and became the Salman Rushdie of the Bible Belt. One famed critic called my professor's writing "a proverbial finger-in-the face of the religious establishment." Another reviewer said the academician had "thrown down the gauntlet" and that the book was comparable to Martin Luther pinning *The Ninety-Five Theses* on the door at Wittenberg. Before he vanished from my life, Professor Pangloss gave me a signed copy of his controversial work. Inside the front cover, he scribbled out a quote from the father of the Protestant movement, "Sin boldly, but all the more boldly trust in Christ." The last I heard my teacher had sought asylum somewhere in the San Francisco Bay Area, but why was I thinking about that now, and why the hell wasn't I screaming?

The last thing I remembered was a dull thud, like the sound of the Sunday newspaper hitting the sidewalk.

I AWOKE in a private room at Mt. Olive. My throbbing temples and blurry vision made me feel like I had gone ten rounds in the ring with Mike Tyson. Connie hovered over me, fluffing my pillows and straightening the sheets around me.

"Oh, good. You're awake," she squealed with delight when my eyes fluttered open. She removed the lid from a covered plate on the bedside table, moved closer to me, and started spoon feeding me lime Jell-o. "Take a bite," she coaxed. "You've got to get your strength back."

"How did I get here?" I shoved the spoon away from my lips. I had been certain I was going to die alone, and no one would find me for days.

"One of your neighbors saw the men leaving your apartment and called 911."

Thank God for Mrs. Whitten's insomnia. I knew the elderly woman stayed up all night, playing neighborhood watch. Too bad she didn't see them going *into* my apartment.

I shifted my body and groaned in excruciating pain.

Connie winced. "You must feel like you got hit by a train, you poor thing."

"I'm just glad Trey had taken the night off and kept Andi home with him."

Confusion clouded Connie's azure eyes. "Andi wasn't with you?"

"No. Thank God."

Connie reached through the metal bedrails and patted my arm. "Well now, that is good news."

When word got around that I was fully conscious and alert, a police investigator stopped by to take my statement. Connie left the room, and the detective introduced herself as Nora Flynn. I told her as much as I could recall about The Beast, The Mangy Dog, and The Coyote. She nodded encouragingly and prodded me with questions while she wrote on a clipboard.

After I told her everything I remembered, she lowered the bedrail and sat next to me. She squeezed my hand, and said, "Miss Kirk, I know this is going to be difficult, but I have to ask you about the little girl."

"Little girl?" Now it was my turn to be confused. "Do you mean Andi? She wasn't there. Her father kept her that night."

How did she know about Andi?

The investigator opened her mouth to respond, but Connie peeked her head through the door and called Det. Flynn aside.

I was glad to be through with the initial interview. Alone in the silent room, my head pounding and the rest of my aching body slowly succumbing to the pain medication that mercifully dripped through the iv tube and into my veins, I drifted off to sleep, or maybe I blacked out. A few hours later, I jerked awake when I thought I heard the Sunday newspaper hitting the sidewalk.

CHAPTER 8

"I can't go back to that apartment," I told Connie after the doctor signed my release papers. I stood in front of the mirror in my hospital room, applying concealer to my bruised and swollen face and preparing to face the outside world for the first time since The Incident.

"Of course not," she agreed. "That's why I've arranged to have some of your things delivered to my house. You're going to stay with me awhile."

"That should be fun," I said sarcastically as I dabbed on a light pink lipstick. "Living with my boss."

She draped a light sweater—it must have been hers—over my shoulders, even though it was summertime in Texas, and I needed a sweater as much as a frog needs cowboy boots. I guess she wanted to feel like she was helping, when the truth was she couldn't help. Nobody could.

"Emily, there's something I've been meaning to tell you." We walked slowly toward the elevator. My body ached more with each step, and I began thinking the doctor had released me prematurely. "It's about that crack you made, you know, about living with your boss. The truth is I'm not going to be your boss for a while."

"Did you get another job?" Connie was a clinical psychologist. She could have made a lot more money in private practice, but for reasons all her own, she chose to supervise a ragtag team of social workers at Child Protective Services.

"No. I didn't get another job. That's not it." Her voice trailed off and for a moment, I worried about her health. "Emily, there's no way you are ready to go back to work. Not physically, and certainly not mentally. I've put you on an indefinite leave of absence."

The automatic doors worked their magic and I stepped outside into a record heatwave. I shrugged off Connie's superfluous sweater and handed it to her.

"I have to work," I protested. The sunlight exacerbated my headache and made me dizzy.

"No, you don't, sweetie. Not for now. You know my alimony check is big enough to cover both our expenses for a couple of months." She laughed, then added, "We'll piss my ex-husband off good when he finds out he's supporting two women he can't sleep with."

Money wasn't my only concern, although I was uncomfortable with letting Connie take care of my financial obligations. I felt certain Trey would not allow Andi to visit until Luke and his cronies were captured. Det. Flynn told me they had not found The Beast, and they still hadn't identified The Mangy Dog and The Coyote. Work was all I had to look forward to.

"Please let me go back to work," I begged. "I'm ready."

Connie abruptly changed the subject. "Where's Andi, Emily?"

"I already told you," I snapped, and instantly regretted my impatience. I softened my tone. "She's with her father."

Connie smiled sweetly, "Let's get you home," she said as she helped me get into her car. "You can go back to work when you've rested."

———

CONNIE LIVED in such a snooty neighborhood my mere presence probably lowered the property values by ten percent. Her house was one of those chic, ultra-modern monstrosities that seemed to have a voice of its own. A voice that boasted, "Look at me! I provide shelter for rich people!" Or, "Look at me! My designer won the pissing contest in architectural engineering school!" There were marble tile floors, vaulted ceilings, stainless steel appliances, granite countertops, and gold plaited doorknobs. Every time I took a step, I looked back to make sure I wasn't leaving a trail like a slug who slithered her way out of the sewer and into the Taj Mahal.

Of course, Connie had not bought such a lavish abode with her salary. She scored it in a divorce settlement when her husband, a plastic surgeon in Dallas, sculpted a new body for a formerly obese hairstylist, then in true Pygmalion fashion, fell in love with his own creation.

"Mommy's home!" she squeaked, and a legion of miniature poodles and chihuahuas pranced into the room. They had pink hair-bows and matching pedicures. In addition to the dogs, there were two iguanas, a tortoiseshell cat, and an aquarium full of exotic fish. Except for the marine life, Connie greeted each animal individually. She picked it up, called it by name, and kissed the top of its head.

She assigned me to a room with a queen size bed and a walk-in closet. My new domain was so spacious and comfortable, I would have been equally satisfied if the bed had been in the closet. An hour later, when I finally convinced my hostess I wouldn't spontaneously combust if left alone, I fell limply onto the unspeakably soft mattress. Ordinarily, the fresh scent of clean linen would have put me to sleep faster than Ambien, but my thoughts raced, and my mind refused to be quieted. Each time I closed my eyes I saw my The Mangy Dog and The Coyote standing over me. I felt their filthy hands on every inch of my body, and I heard their diabolical laughter as they violated me.

I retrieved my phone from the bottom of my purse and dialed Trey's number, hoping he would let me see Andi. Connie had a grand-daughter, Erica, who stayed with her sometimes. Erica was about Andi's age, and I wanted the two of them to become friends. Andi had difficulty connecting with her new classmates. Academically, she was lightyears ahead of them, and she'd had cultural experiences most of them would never have.

I listened as the phone on the other end rang seven times, and then I heard a recording. "Your call has been forwarded to an automated voice messaging service." I waited a few minutes and tried again. This time my call went directly to voicemail.

Was he rejecting my calls? Was I now so horribly and irreparably damaged in his eyes that he couldn't even pick up the phone and talk to me? My relationship with Trey had never been serious, but I thought we were at least friends. I considered myself a good judge of character. People rarely ever surprised or disappointed me. I generally knew precisely what I was getting when I dealt with people. Had I grossly misjudged this man? Was he the type of man who believed women instigated the violence perpetrated against them, and they got what they deserved?

I'd left the door open just wide enough for a cinnamon colored miniature poodle to squeeze through. She looked up at me with big chocolate eyes that begged for attention. I grinned, probably the first time I'd smiled since The Incident. I petted the furry little thing's head, and my touch triggered a frenzy of excited barking. I remembered Rose's story about the poor murdered dog, and I shivered. Unnerved, I chased the helpless creature out of the room, shut the door, and collapsed against the wall. Somehow, the doll Trey gave Andi for her birthday—the one that looked exactly like her— ended up with my things Connie had transported to her house. I grabbed the toy and cradled it in my arms. Ever since The Incident, my tears had been like the dripping of a leaky faucet, a droplet or spurt here and there. Now they gushed out in torrents, pouring down my cheeks and saturating the high collar of my pink blouse.

CHAPTER 9

ape. The Incident was rape. I was strong enough to say that now, but the doctors, lawyers, and detectives weren't there yet. They preferred the watered down legal jargon of "sexual assault," as though the addition of a few syllables in any way negated the vileness of the act. As if calling it a fuzzy kitten could change the *Chupacabra* into a house pet, or as though referring to a hurricane as a spring rain ameliorated its damaging effects.

When I was in high school, my classmates called me "Word Nerd" because I had an extensive vocabulary and I wasn't afraid to use it. I loved etymologies and definitions. I loved the way phonemes and morphemes could be linked together and manipulated to paint mental images as vivid and three-dimensional as Byzantine sculptures. I even liked the ugly words. In fact, I liked them best, because they conveyed more of the raw power, pain, and passion that constituted the human condition.

The proverbial "they"—those who determine what things shall be socially acceptable—don't like the ugly words, and rape is the ugliest word of all. So, they sanitized it; they aestheticized it. They bathed the ugly word in Evian water, soaked it in saline solution, sprayed it with perfume, and pressed and starched it neatly until it came out "sexual assault." Now the ugly word can only be uttered in hushed tones, but the violated woman still screams it.

She screams it when she scarfs down her third helping of her niece's birthday cake. She screams it when she avoids looking in reflective glass, because she is repulsed by the disgusting hag who mocks her. She screams it when she recoils from the most benign touch from the kindest, most loving man. She screams it when she sits in the bathtub, with the razor blade poised above the puffy, purple vein in her wrist, praying for the courage to press down a little deeper.

She screams the word, but nobody hears her. Somebody dropped the dictionary in a vat of bleach and whited out the ugly word. Now all anyone can hear is a whimper. A whisper. An echo of sexual assault.

"When you were assaulted—," the doctor began.

"When I was raped," I corrected.

"After you were assaulted—," the detective started.

"After I was raped," I countered.

I made them say it. I made them think it. I made them acknowledge it. I made them know that it exists, and it is rampant, and it is horrible, and it leaves a gaping, bleeding wound so deep inside it can't be stitched up and it can't be treated with antiseptic. I made them say the word. I made them say *rape*.

CONNIE INSISTED that I go through counseling at the local rape crisis center before she would even consider letting me go back to work. The first night of group therapy I expected to find a room full of Rose Detwilers—uneducated, unemployed victims who consistently put themselves in vulnerable situations. Instead, I encountered a group of women whose occupations and education levels were as diverse as their stories and their skin tones, and they were all at different stages of the healing process.

We met in the musty basement of an old church, cloaked in anonymity like alcoholics, or people who had something to be ashamed of. We were seated around an oblong folding table. An obsolete window air conditioning unit rattled noisily but worked sufficiently. The uncomfortable metal chair I sat in froze the backs of my legs, and I wished I hadn't worn shorts.

One by one, every survivor introduced herself—first names only, of course—and gave a brief synopsis of her history.

Anita was a seventy-two-year-old retired school teacher who was robbed and raped at gunpoint by her grandson's friends after she refused to buy them a pack of cigarettes.

Evangeline, twenty-six, was a Filipino woman who had answered an ad for a mail-order bride and became the unwitting prey of sex traffickers. She had a jagged scar around her neck where one of her captors tried to kill her.

Meg, our group leader, had been a twenty-three-year-old college grad student when she was assaulted by a former boyfriend. Her roommate, whom she considered her best friend, recorded the dreadful event and uploaded it to social media for the whole world to gawk at.

Rosalita was a housekeeper for a wealthy family. Her employer raped her repeatedly and threatened her with deportation if she told anyone. To this day, she hadn't spoken about it to anybody outside the group.

At age eleven, Gia was the youngest survivor. She'd already been raped twice, once by her mother's boyfriend, and once by a neighbor who offered her a popsicle if she came in his house and "kept him company for a while." Self-mutilation marks decorated her arms like tattoo sleeves.

Trisha was a thirty-seven-year-old stay-at-home mother who answered the door for a man claiming to be from the gas company. He even wore the uniform and said he was checking for leaks.

There was even a familiar face in the crowd. Annie was the ER doctor on duty the night I had visited Thomas there. She had been a young intern at an inner-city hospital. Exhausted after a thirty-six-hour shift, she let her guard down while rambling through the poorly lit parking lot, searching for her car. Five men accosted her. She was stabbed fifteen times and left in a shallow ravine to die. The temperature plummeted to below freezing that night, but two stray dogs curled up beside her and shielded her from the elements with their own malnourished bodies. Annie was rescued when animal control showed up to collect the canines.

When everyone else had spoken, Meg turned to me. "Emily, you are the newest member of our group. Is there anything you'd like to share?"

I looked around at their empathetic faces and blurted out, "It was my fault." I was wrecked with shame. I had allowed myself to be outwitted by a loathsome Neanderthal and his dimwitted wife.

They bombarded me with hugs, sympathy, and a resounding chorus of "No, it was not."

I told them how Rose duped me into giving her my address, even after I'd been threatened by her husband.

Anita reached across the table and cupped my face in her hands. She smelled like lavender soap and baby powder, and her skin was damp and velvety soft.

"Listen to me, dear." Her voice was stern but kind. I imagined she had been an excellent teacher. "In the entire history of the world, no woman has ever done anything stupid enough, or dressed provocatively enough, or gotten drunk enough, or in any other way done anything that justified her being raped. Do you understand me?"

It felt good hearing someone absolve me of the guilt I had carried around since that awful night. Still, I couldn't quite convince myself I wasn't to blame. I believed what Anita said as it pertained to other women, but in my case, it truly was my fault.

CHAPTER 10

*T*rey continued ignoring my calls. I hadn't seen him or Andi since I was attacked. I even tried calling him at the police station, but I was informed Officer Scoggins had taken time off for personal matters. I decided a face-to-face confrontation was the best way to resolve the issue.

Connie had a standing appointment with her manicurist every other Thursday. I waited for her departure, because even though she encouraged me to socialize with others, she strongly advised me to stay away from Trey. She'd known him longer than I had, so I assumed there must be some bad blood.

I soon deduced the reason for Trey's reticence. He reluctantly answered the door after I rang the bell several times. Sarah stepped out of the shadows. When she saw me, she gulped, covered her face with both hands, and ducked out of the room as though I had caught them in the middle of some deviant sex act.

"Now I get it," I said accusingly as Trey walked outside and shut the door behind himself, creating a barrier between my rival and me.

"No, Emily, you don't get it," he snapped angrily. "You don't get anything."

"It's okay," I assured him. We weren't a couple. We had made no commitments to each other. "I noticed the attraction between you two at Andi's birthday party. It's really good you're working things out. Andi must be thrilled to have her parents back together."

"What are you even doing here?" he demanded.

"Look, Trey. All I want is to see Andi. There is no reason I can't still be part of her life." I peered around him, trying to see if I could spot Andi through the opened blinds. He squared his body, blocking my view.

He threw both arms over his head in frustration and shifted restlessly on his feet. Obviously, something about my presence evoked his ire. Maybe he really did see me as horribly tainted now. I blamed myself for what happened. Why shouldn't he blame me too?

Dark stubble covered his normally clean-shaven face, and his military style haircut was a little longer than I was accustomed to seeing. His eyes were red and puffy, and I attributed that to lack of sleep. *Probably too thrilled having his family back together to worry about things like shaving, sleeping, or getting a haircut*, I thought.

"So, can I see her?" I persisted when he remained silent.

"No. No, you cannot see Andi. Get that through your head. You are never going to see her again."

Why was he so angry? I told him I wasn't mad about his reunion with Sarah. His vicious behavior was inexcusable.

"You let me get close to her," I sobbed. I'd always thought of Trey as a fair and just man. I couldn't understand this sudden cruel streak. "You let me love her. When it was convenient for you, when you needed a free babysitter. Now that her mother's here, I'm supposed to forget about her?"

"Why won't you leave us alone?"

"Why didn't you tell me you and Sarah were getting back together? Did you think I was too fragile to take the truth?" It infuriated me that people thought they had to treat me like a hyper-sensitive child because I had been raped. Nobody seemed honest and forthcoming with me anymore.

His eyes widened in disbelief as though I had stumbled upon some buried secret he thought I wasn't smart enough to figure out. "Yes,

Emily. That's exactly it. I think you are too goddamned fragile to take the truth."

With that one last sledgehammer blow to my heart, he opened the door and disappeared inside. Feeling dejected and demoralized, I dawdled down the sidewalk toward my car. Summers in Texas can be brutal, and we were in the middle of one of the worst in history. The oppressive heat rested on my pale skin and my unprotected areas reddened instantly. Mosquitos sucked at my neck like an army of pissed off vampires. Despite the miserable conditions, I lingered outside, hoping to catch a glimpse of Andi coming out to play or walk her dog. Eventually, I gave up.

Though Trey seemed undeterred by my visit, something I said must have gotten through to him. When I returned to Connie's house, Andi was there, standing at the aquarium, feeding the fish.

I dropped my purse and keychain on the nearest solid surface and ran to her. I threw my arms around her and pulled her close to me. It must have been longer than I thought since I'd seen her. She was a full two inches taller, and other things were different too. Even the texture of her hair had changed; I noticed when I caressed her head.

"I missed you so much!" Her body stiffened, and she pulled away from me.

"What's the matter, Andi?" I was hurt by her rejection.

Connie appeared from another room, and Andi rushed to her.

"She's scaring me!" The girl cried.

Andi hadn't been frightened of me since that first day when she was too shy to shake my hand. Nothing made any sense.

"It's okay," Connie consoled her. "Go to your room. I'll take care of it."

"Why is she scared of me? What's going on?" I darted after Andi, but Connie stepped in front of me.

"Emily, I need you to tell me where Andi is." Connie took both my wrists and led me to the sofa. We sat down side by side. "Where is Andi?

"She was just here. You saw her."

"No, Emily. That was Erica. That was my grandbaby. Where's Andi?"

"Then she must be with her father," I surmised. "He won't let me see her." My head spun violently as I tried desperately to make sense of it all. I had been certain it was Andi feeding the fish.

"No, Emily. Where's Andi?" Connie was persistent but gentle.

I felt dizzy and nauseated, tired and detached from the world. I wanted to sleep. I wanted to run away from all this confusion. I wanted to escape from my own brain and its powerful attempt to force me back into reality.

"Emily, honey, you know what's happening. You've had the classes. You've had the training. Now what's happening to you?"

Again, I was in that lecture hall, surrounded by apathetic teenagers, grappling with the professor's words.

Depersonalization…

Derealization…

Dissociation…

"Dissociation," I parroted my teacher. "Dissociation occurs when the traumatic event overwhelms the individual's ability to cope."

"That's right, sweetie," Connie prodded. "You dissociated from the situation, because you weren't strong enough to face reality. You are stronger now, and I need you to tell me where Andi is."

Truth—unavoidable, irrefutable, bitter, cruel, ugly truth—sliced through my heart with a serrated knife. A toxic soup of unmitigated sorrow and outrage boiled over, like lava from Mount Vesuvius. I heard a low guttural moan. It took a moment before I realized that horrible sound emanated from the depths of my soul. I opened my mouth, and Vesuvius erupted.

"*She's dead!*" I bellowed. "*Oh, dear God! She's dead!*"

I broke away from Connie and ran into my room. The Andi looka-like doll was on the bed. I jerked it up and hurled the useless hunk of plastic across the room. It hit the wall with a sickening thud and fell to the floor. The toy stared up at me with lifeless eyes, orbitals that chilled my spine. Then I remembered everything.

Andi was at my apartment that night. In fact, she'd had a nightmare and crawled in bed beside me. When I became aware of the intruders, I shoved her to the floor.

"Run!" I ordered. "Go to Mrs. Whitten's and call 911!"

It was too late. The Beast already had his grimy, murderous paws around her tiny fragile neck, choking the life out of her.

Leave her alone, I tried to scream, but The Mangy Dog lowered a boom on my forehead, and I was incapable of any further resistance.

When her body went limp and she stopped struggling, The Beast threw her against the wall like an inanimate object he'd grown weary of. It made a dull thud, like the Sunday newspaper hitting the sidewalk. The Beast had looked back at me and taunted, "*You took mine. I took yours.*"

Connie joined me on the foot of the bed. I collapsed my head against her stomach. I held her waist so tightly I thought our bodies might coalesce.

"Mommy! Mommy! Mommy!" I vomited out those two syllables as though I had been choking on the word while some invisible entity performed the Heimlich maneuver on me. I begged for the warmth of maternal connection I'd been so long deprived of, and Connie sweetly obliged. She enveloped me in the warmest embrace I had ever felt and rocked me gently. I pulled my knees up to my chin, and I became a fetus safely ensconced in a Chanel-scented womb.

CHAPTER 11

*I*n the beginning, it was easy for me to indulge in my fantasy world where Andi still lived, breathed, laughed, loved, learned, and played. I abstained from watching television or using the Internet because I didn't want to see snippets of my story being rehashed by total strangers. I supposed Connie carefully vetted my visitors and told them what topics were off limits. Even the detectives skirted around the issue at her request. But truth is a wanton exhibitionist. It reveals itself, and it wants to be seen. It demands to be acknowledged, and eventually it always gets its way.

Now I felt deflated, like a balloon carelessly discarded in a field of broken glass. Trey and I sat on the veranda at Connie's house; the giant parasol that shaded us ruffled slightly in the soft breeze. Puffy cumulus clouds dotted the sky and gave us a reprieve from the dangerously high temperatures. I poured iced tea from a tall plastic pitcher, and he started the conversation.

"I heard you had a breakthrough."

At least now I understood why he treated me with such hostility. It must have been so painful for him, listening to me carry on about his daughter as though she were still alive. I had even demanded to see her.

"Oh, Trey," I groaned as I offered him a packet of artificial sweetener. "Why didn't you just tell me she was gone?"

"Connie thought it was best if we let you come to that conclusion on your own. She thought it might do more damage if we blurted it out."

He looked away from me and my eyes followed his gaze. All four pupils landed on his hands, stretched out on the patio table. I'd felt those hands before. They were the calloused hands of a working man, strong enough to wrestle a knife or loaded gun away from a violent criminal, but tender enough to French braid a little girl's hair. Rough patches tantalized my contrastingly smooth skin whenever he touched me. God, how I needed to feel those hands now, but I had no right to ask. I was the reason he was grieving.

"I'm sorry I was such an asshole," he finally broke the silence.

"Please don't apologize. I understand why you hate me." I stirred my tea with a long spoon and listened to the ice cubes tinkling against the side of the glass.

"I don't hate you." He sounded sincere. "Why on earth would I hate you?"

"It was my fault," I said between the sobs that suddenly overtook me. "I gave Luke's wife ...my address. I practically...invited him into my apartment."

"You blame yourself for giving out your address. I blame myself for not keeping you both safe. Sarah blames herself for sending Andi to me."

"Poor Sarah." My heart broke all over again when I thought about the bereaved mother. "She sent Andi down here to keep her safe and look what happened."

"Trust me. She is aware of the irony. Anyway, I'm going to tell you and Sarah the same thing I tell the crime victims I work with every day. Let the guilty carry the shame. We have enough to deal with. Don't carry around the added weight of the guilt that is not yours to carry."

As I refilled our glasses, I forced myself to ask, "How's the investigation going? Nobody ever tells me anything. I guess they still think I'm too fragile."

"That's what I came here to talk to you about. They picked Luke up in a barfight in Oklahoma. He's being extradited back to Texas tomorrow for a preliminary hearing."

I sighed in relief. "Thank God they finally caught him."

"It's not all good news. He's claiming he spent that whole weekend in Oklahoma City with his wife."

"That's not possible," I protested, anger rising up in the pit of my stomach. "Rose lives in a battered women's shelter."

"We checked that out. Mrs. Detwiler left the shelter the day before everything happened. She left her kids with a friend; she quit her job, and nobody knew where she went to for a while." He paused, then added. "Emily, she's backing him up. She's giving him an alibi."

"She's lying!" I screeched hysterically, wildly gesturing with my hands and knocking my glass over. The cold liquid spread across the table and dripped into my lap. Trey hurriedly righted the glass, and I cleaned up the mess with a roll of paper towels I had brought outside.

When things calmed down, Trey concurred with my outburst. "I know she's lying, and it shouldn't be hard prove it. You will be a more credible witness."

I cringed at the terminology. I'd dealt with the courts enough to know that "more credible" often meant "more prestigious social standing." I didn't want to be believed because I was better educated and better connected socially than Rose. I wanted to be believed because I was the one telling the truth.

"What about DNA evidence or fingerprints?" *Dear lord,* I wondered. *How are we sitting here talking about this so rationally, like neither of us has any stake in the outcome of this investigation? How were my words coming out so sterile and perfunctory when my thoughts were a maelstrom of hostility and hatred?*

"Most of the DNA they collected came from the rape. Since Luke didn't participate in that, there might not be much physical evidence linking him to the scene." *He didn't participate because he was too busy murdering an innocent child,* I thought bitterly. "Apparently he wore gloves because none of the fingerprints matched his, either."

Trey sighed, and his eyes glossed over. "There was one tiny thing.

The forensics team got a little piece of skin from under one of Andi's fingernails. We're hoping we can trace that to Luke."

She fought back. She fought to live. I saw her kicking. Apparently, she clawed too.

"What about the other two guys?" I knew who the murderer was, but I didn't know who the rapists were. I had the sensation of needing to vomit when I mentioned the duo.

"We still haven't found them. Of course, Detwiler is claiming he doesn't know anything about it, so he's not pointing any fingers. The good news is those two buffoons left their DNA all over the place. It should be easy to convict them once we catch them. They're just not in any of the national databases yet. Do you think you could identify them if you saw them?"

I thought about Mangy Dog with his fat belly, semi-bald head, and poorly shaved face. Then I thought about The Coyote with his crazy bloodshot eyes and hyena laughter.

"There is not a doubt in my mind I could identify them both," I could never forget those disgusting faces. Identifying them would be easy.

"Hopefully, you will get that chance soon." Trey looked at his watch and stood to leave. He made some flimsy excuse about needing to check in at work, but I knew he was still on leave. He was going home to be with Sarah. I escorted him through the house and to the front door.

Before he left, he placed both his hands on my sides. I felt the rough callouses through my thin blouse. I felt those hands that had disarmed psychopaths and braided a little girl's dark brown hair, maybe even on the same day. If I were capable of loving a man, then Officer Trey Scoggins would certainly be the one. Sadly, that part of my life had been robbed from me long before Luke Detwiler and his minions took everything else that mattered. The knowledge that I would never experience the uniquely human joy of romantic love exacerbated the pain and emptiness I felt inside.

"Go home to Sarah, Trey." I stopped him from kissing me.

PART II
PHILIA

"...there is a friend who stays closer than a brother." — Proverbs 18:14

CHAPTER 12

$\mathcal{C}$onnie and I settled into a comfortable routine, like roommates, or spouses who'd been married too long for such trivial things as sexual attraction or romantic feelings. She stopped hovering and even allowed me to cook occasionally. I was making strawberry daiquiris to go with our steak fajitas when the poodles and chihuahuas sounded off. At first I thought it was the noise from the blender that agitated them, but they continued yapping and pacing, even when I hit the "off" switch.

I was in the kitchen, and Connie sat in an adjoining alcove, reading the newspaper.

"What's wrong with the dogs?" I asked anxiously. Ever since the attack, I had been hypervigilant about my surroundings. Two of the assailants were still at large and that heightened my sense of vulnerability.

"Probably nothing. I noticed it looked stormy before dark. Maybe they hear thunder we can't hear yet. Their little ears are sensitive that way, you know?"

She knew her animals better than I did. If she wasn't concerned, I shouldn't be either. I relaxed my guard, but the dogs kept going to a sliding glass door, spinning in circles and barking furiously. Their toenails clicked rhythmically on the marble tile.

"Are you sure nothing is out there?" I started getting a little freaked out. Instinctively, I tightened my grip on the knife I was using to cut the steak.

"Don't worry, Em," she soothed me. "This place is fully equipped with a state-of-the-art security system. Nobody is getting in here without every law enforcement agency in three counties knowing about it."

She almost had me convinced there was nothing to worry about when a giant rock smashed through the glass door and a hairy arm reached through the resulting hole and turned the lock. The alarm screamed shrilly, and the whole menagerie went crazy. The intruder fled faster than he would have been physically capable of if not motivated by the flight end of the fight-or-flight response. But I'd seen him. I'd seen his fat belly hanging below his dingy T-shirt, and I'd seen the patches of red whiskers scattered across the ruddy face.

Connie reached into a coat closet and produced a shotgun I didn't know she had. I heard the menacing sound of the safety being released, and my mentor aimed her weapon as confidently as a trained markswoman as she exited through the compromised door.

My fingers trembled as they dialed 911, and it seemed like an eternity before I heard the emergency operator's voice. Outside, the gun exploded violently, and Mangy Dog yelped in pain. I was still sputtering out the story when Connie returned, grinning triumphantly like an American soldier on V-day. She took the phone from my hand and spoke calmly into the receiver. "Tell them to look for a big red mangy dog with an ass full of buckshot."

Less than ten minutes later, lights flashed, sirens wailed, and a cacophony of radio transmissions penetrated the late evening calm of Ashford's most affluent neighborhood. Soon it seemed every law enforcement officer in three counties, as Connie put it, descended on the front lawn. Trey was there, in street clothes and his own personal vehicle since he wasn't part of the official investigation.

The manhunt ended abruptly when a neighbor called police and reported finding a stranger hunkered down in her garage, bleeding profusely and crying hysterically. Alone and frightened, she thought she'd overreacted when she clobbered the wounded man with a shovel and knocked him unconscious. All in all, it was not a pleasant evening for Tony Detwiler, Luke's kid brother.

We watched as Mangy Dog was loaded into an ambulance and carted away like a stray animal nobody wanted.

One by one, the black and white patrol cars left the scene, no lights and no sirens. Trey stayed behind and followed me inside. He surveyed the damaged door and scoffed, "What kind of braindead idiot breaks into a house that looks like Mar-a-Lago and doesn't expect there to be any alarms?"

"Would you like something to drink?" I offered. "I made daiquiris." I never knew human beings could feel as many emotions at one time as I felt at that moment. The sadness and outrage were still there, and so was the terror, but there were stirrings of more pleasant feelings, too.

"No, thanks. I need to get home."

Any momentary pleasantness I experienced quickly dissolved into petty jealousy.

"Right. Sarah must be worried," I said in an accusing tone. I kept telling myself I should be happy for him. At least he and Sarah could help each other through this horrible ordeal. But how could I be happy for him when there was no one to comfort me?

"You jump to too many conclusions, Emily," he scolded. "Sarah flew home this morning. She only came down so we could mourn the loss of our daughter together. We never discussed reuniting as a couple. Never even thought about it."

He looked hurt, and I felt terrible knowing that I had caused him even more pain. He started to walk away, but I tugged at his shirt sleeve and said three words I had never spoken to a man before.

I said, "Please don't go."

We never went to bed. He fell asleep in a recliner, with me sitting on his lap. I rested my head on his masculine shoulder, as though I could absorb his strength. As though somehow, through osmosis, I could take in the love I desperately needed but was afraid to feel.

For the first time in weeks, I didn't dream about beasts or mangy dogs or coyotes. I didn't wake up clawing at the covers and gasping for air. I dreamed Trey and I were strolling through a beautiful, peaceful garden in a time before the rape.

CHAPTER 13

a man fitting The Coyote's description showed up at Tony's hospital room, drunk and belligerent. They arrested him for public intoxication. The lead investigator on the case called and asked me to come to the police station. He wanted me to pick the rapist out of a lineup.

Connie accompanied me to the precinct downtown. When we arrived, two plain clothes detectives met us in the foyer. One was Nora Flynn, the first to interview me at Mt. Olive. The other was the lead investigator on the case, an African-American named Ron Tyler. Karen Tobias, the assistant district attorney charged with prosecuting my assailants, hurried through another entrance, balancing an arm full of folders and loose papers in her arms. I knew Karen well because she also prosecuted crimes against children. Plump, pleasant-faced, and fiftyish, she had unnaturally coal black hair with silver streaks.

TREY HAD RETURNED to work and sat behind a desk, filling out paper-work. He glanced up at me and smiled warmly. I had forgotten how handsome he looked in his uniform.

"Are we ready to do this?" Ron asked, meaning *Are* you *ready?*

"Let's get this over with," I responded anxiously. I remembered The Coyote giggling idiotically when he looked down at my frightened and helpless body. If this guy was him, I wanted him to suffer. I didn't want justice. I wanted revenge.

"You all go ahead. I'll wait out here," Connie said, sounding as sweet as a Georgia peach. I knew she'd be discreetly psychoanalyzing the prisoners as they were escorted in and out.

Trey, the two detectives, and the ADA led me out of the room and into a hallway. We walked down the corridor until we came to an unassuming glass partition. There we stopped and waited while five men in orange jumpsuits were lined up against a gray wall. Trey stood close beside me, gently touching that place in the small of my back that sends oxytocin shooting through my central nervous system like hollow point bullets on a trajectory straight for the heart. All the suspects were approximately the same height, skinny, with gaunt faces and shaggy brown hair, but I instantly recognized The Coyote. He nervously fidgeted with the mid-section of his prison attire.

"Don't worry," Karen assured me. "They can't see or hear you."

"Do you recognize the man you call The Coyote?" Detective Tyler prodded.

"Number three," I announced without hesitation. I would recognize those bloodshot eyes anywhere. Next to Luke's eyes, they were the emptiest I had ever seen.

Ron looked surprised that I answered so quickly. "Are you sure you don't need more time? You need to be certain."

"It's number three," I reiterated. Part of me wished there wasn't a bulletproof wall of glass between us, and we weren't surrounded by law enforcement. I believed I was angry enough to have killed that slimy monster with my bare hands.

The three officers gave each other knowing looks and nodded in unison.

"His name is Leonard Horton," Det. Tyler informed me. "Drifted up here from Dallas about a year ago. He has a few priors for possession and petty theft, things of that nature. Nothing like this, though."

"I'll get a court order to test his DNA against the bodily fluids left at the scene." Karen sounded excited to finally be getting the ball rolling on the prosecution.

The criminals were taken away, and I followed my entourage back into the foyer. I scanned the room searching for Connie. Instead, I came face to face with Andi's murderer. Luke was dressed in iconic prison stripes, his hands bound behind his back. A stout looking uniformed policeman guided him by the elbow. The killer spotted me, and I looked into those empty, soulless eyes. He smiled that demonic grin, showing all his crooked nicotine-stained teeth.

"Well, hello, sweetheart. I haven't seen you in a while." He greeted me as though we were old friends at a high school reunion.

Angry and fearful, I tried to verbalize my shock and disdain, but my throat constricted into a tight fist at the center of my neck. A thousand words fought to escape the narrow hatch in my closed larynx. All that came out was a tiny whimper. My mind screamed *Somebody get me out of here!* My heart screamed for Connie to appear so that we could leave. My mouth remained silent though. Again, I had no voice. No speech. No words. Nothing. I felt like I would faint. Somebody shoved a chair behind me, so when I collapsed, I landed in the seat. I gasped for air as if I was drowning in a sea of fear and intimidation.

Noticing my distress, and probably experiencing his own, Trey addressed the officer guarding Luke. "Get him out of here!" he ordered.

Connie appeared from out of nowhere. Now she fussed over me as if I was one of her poodles and someone had mistreated me.

With Luke out of sight, my voice returned. "Take me home," I begged anyone who would listen.

LEONARD HORTON DIDN'T MAKE it through his first night in jail. There was a mix up in the paperwork, Trey told me, and the alleged sex offender was released into the general population. After dinner, the inmates were taken to a recreation room where they watched television. A local news bulletin came on, and they talked about Andi's death. Horton was identified as a suspect. Some of the prisoners became agitated, believing a child killer was in their midst. A brief riot ensued and a rookie guard was overpowered and relieved of his firearm. The Coyote was gunned down like the predatory nuisance he was. When I heard the news, I felt a sense of morbid satisfaction. I silently prayed his killer would find mercy in the courts and in the eyes of God.

INITIALLY, Tony Detwiler claimed he only broke into Connie's house because he heard a woman lived alone in that mansion and he intended to rob her. He denied knowing anything about what had happened to Andi or me. When confronted with the DNA evidence against him, he confessed to the rape, but he blamed the murder on Leonard Horton, a dead man who could not contradict the false allegation. He admitted the attack was retribution for my having interfered with Luke's family but claimed his brother knew nothing about the diabolical deed. Even when offered a plea deal in exchange for his testimony against Luke, Tony chose taking his chances with the notoriously brutal Texas correctional system rather than risk incurring the wrath of his older sibling.

Rose stuck by her story that Luke was with her that night, one hundred miles away from the crime scene. Luke's lawyer successfully argued against having his client's DNA tested as a possible match for the skin found under Andi's nail, claiming the police mishandled the situation when collecting the sample. After all, the victim was a cop's kid. Wasn't the entire department ganging up on the poor innocent man because they desperately needed a scapegoat? Mrs. Whitten reported seeing three men leaving my apartment, but it was too dark for her to identify any of them. My accusation, Karen Tobias told me, was the only thing that linked Luke to those two violent acts. My testimony, she said, was crucial.

CHAPTER 14

Sometimes I thought I was crazy. Not Hannibal Lechter eat your kidneys with a fine chianti crazy. More like Sylvia Plath head stuck in the bell jar— can't breathe— oh my God— somebody shatter this glass and get me out of here crazy. Ever since I was raped and Andi was murdered, I struggled with depression. Now it was so severe, I caught myself googling things like "most painless ways to kill yourself."

Connie said I was in a state of "disequilibrium." She wanted me to seek counseling beyond what I was getting at the rape crisis center. Because we were friends and co-workers, professional ethics restrained her from acting as my therapist, and I wasn't prepared to spill my guts to a stranger. My sister reminded me there was another option.

A few days after Tony and Leonard were arrested, and The Coyote was gunned down, Janice stopped by for a visit. She claimed she had been looking for me this whole time, and didn't I know how worried she'd been when I just disappeared like that? She only found me now because she kept calling my workplace until someone violated my privacy and told her my whereabouts.

Her eyes darted around Connie's immaculate living room and I knew she wanted to view the rest of the house, so I took her on a tour.

We went from room to room, and she gawked at the elegant décor and fine furnishings. She didn't mention anything about the rape, and I supposed it was possible she didn't know about it. My name was never mentioned on the local news, and I had never told Janice about my relationship with Andi. I was glad she didn't know. She was the type of person who believed only loose, amoral women ever got raped. We went out to the veranda and sat at the same patio table where Trey and I had discussed the investigation.

"What's the matter with you, Emily?" my sister asked. "Why did you leave your job, and why are you staying here?" She made it sound like she wasn't envious of my current living situation.

"I plan on going back to work soon." I honestly intended to. "Social workers have a high rate of burnout. I guess I just needed a break." I fought back an onslaught of tears. Any sign of weakness gave the she-bear an opportunity to strike.

"Oh sweetie. I understand." She sounded genuinely empathetic, and I wondered when she had acquired that gift.

"You do?"

"Yes. Of course. We all go through things like this. We all have times when we're not sure about the directions our lives have taken, and we just need a little time to compose ourselves and figure things out."

"Yeah. Exactly." I was still suspicious of her motives, but I wanted to believe she truly understood.

"Emily, you know what you need." She spoke as if speaking to a wayward child who wouldn't take her medicine. "You need to come to church. We're having a deliverance service this Sunday, and God will deliver you from whatever is troubling you."

I hadn't always been scornful of religion. In fact, I remembered a time when church was my sanctuary in every sense of the word. My father was nicer there, and my mother was happier. Even Janice wasn't as mean when we were at church.

Practically everyone I knew believed in divine healing. Over the years, I had heard stories of people being miraculously healed of everything from typhus to toe fungus, so why not depression?

"Maybe you're right," I reluctantly conceded. Even if I didn't get healed of my depression, I reasoned, Janice was all the family I had left. It might be nice to connect with her on a deeper level.

I convinced Connie she should go with me. The plan was to get there after the service began, then we could sneak out before the closing prayer ended so we wouldn't have to talk to anybody. We missed the mark. The vestibule was packed with people, wearing so many different fragrances the amalgamation of smells sent my olfactory glands into overdrive, and I sneezed, loudly heralding our arrival.

"Emily, you're here!" Janice lunged at me with open arms and for a second, I wasn't sure if she was going to hug me or tackle me. "Everybody, I want you to meet my little sister, Emily, and her friend, Connie," she addressed the other congregants. Then she added, "Connie lives in the Bentley Hills subdivision in one of those gorgeous homes." I wondered if Connie lived in the River's Edge Mobile Home Park, would Janice have been so quick to reveal my friend's place of residence?

In Pentecostal churches, new people often get love bombed. That's when the congregation bombards the visitors with ridiculously hyperbolic gestures of what they think love and kindness are supposed to look like. After Connie and I had been sufficiently love bombed, Janice showed us into the main sanctuary. It looked like a Pepto-Bismol factory had exploded. Everything was a shade of pink, from the plush pew cushions to the Kleenex boxes on the altars. All the women wore the poofy hairstyles and gaudy makeup reminiscent of the nineteen-eighties. Their Xanax and double-shot espresso-induced smiles made them appear happy, but each one carried a hodgepodge of miseries wrapped in a Gucci bow. As we selected our seats, Connie leaned in close to my ear and whispered giddily, "Oh, my Lord! I have died and gone to Tammy Fay Bakker's house."

"I've got to introduce you to Pastor Steve," Janice announced excitedly, as if we were at a Rolling Stones concert and she was personal friends with Mick Jagger. She stepped across our feet and flagged down a man who'd already passed by us.

Pastor Steve turned out to be a man in his mid-forties with balding reddish-brown hair and a thin mustache. In lieu of a suit, he wore a nice buttoned-down shirt and heavily starched blue jeans. The thing that caught my attention was his belt buckle. It was so huge it looked like he might have won it in a professional wrestling match. Apparently, while I was gawking at his buckle, Pastor Steve said something to me, because I heard Connie say, "You have to excuse her. She's going through a lot, and she's experiencing some anxiety."

The preacher condescended. "Well, if she had more Jesus in her heart, she wouldn't have room in there for that old anxiety, would she?" He chuckled as if he had just told a hilarious joke.

"Except," Connie explained, "her anxiety is not in her heart. It's in the hypothalamus region of her brain and her pituitary and adrenal glands." She obfuscated him with her knowledge. The minister stared blankly, so now it was Connie's turn to condescend. "But I guess that's mere details to you, isn't it?"

She really wasn't making fun of him. One drawback of being highly intelligent is you sometimes forget everyone isn't on your level.

The crowd hushed, and Pastor Steve took his place behind the pulpit. Music started playing—a few low, repetitive chords. As if on cue, people started speaking in tongues and falling on the floor, "slain in the spirit."

Pastor Steve spoke in an ominous voice. "The Holy Spirit is in this place. If you need healing, now is the time. If you need deliverance, now is the time."

People started making their way toward the altars, some shouting, some crying, some gyrating wildly. Connie poked my side. "What are they doing?" she asked.

"They're going down to the altars so they can be delivered from demonic oppression. Don't they ever do that at your church?"

She smiled sweetly and quipped, "Honey, you know I'm a Methodist. We don't go around casting demons out. They're too fun to drink with."

Pastor Steve shot us a disapproving look, as though our whispers could be heard above all the music, weeping, and glossolalia. "Today is the day of your deliverance. If you don't come down to this altar today, don't blame God when you walk out those doors and go right back to the filthy gutter you came out of. God wants to heal you today."

A woman fell down at the altar, and the entire congregation descended on her as if she were the one being summoned directly by God, through Pastor Steve. She raised her arms, and they shouted victoriously.

"This is ridiculous," I muttered, wondering how I ever let my sister talk me into this. "Let's go."

"No," Connie protested. "I want to see what happens. This is like *The Beverly Hillbillies* meet *The Exorcist*."

The woman being prayed for looked a lot like Rose Detwiler, except a little plumper and a few years older. Pastor Steve had her head between his hands, shaking it frantically. "Come out of her, you devil!" he screamed in her face.

"Forgive me, Lord!" the allegedly possessed woman cried out.

"How will we know when the devil comes out?' Connie asked, obviously enjoying the bizarre ritual. "Will we see him? What's he look like?"

I stifled a laugh and implored her again, "Let's just leave."

We gathered our purses and Bibles and headed for the door. Then Pastor Steve spoke again. "The Lord will forgive you, sister. If you truly repent and turn from your wicked ways, the Lord will forgive you and deliver you from that devil of schizophrenia."

Connie stopped dead in her tracks, and her face darkened with concern. "Hold up the train, Jesse James." She used a catchphrase she often utilized when somebody said something so morally egregious, she wasn't sure she heard correctly.

"Let's go. Let's go. Right now, let's go." I resorted to begging and pulling at the sleeve of her silk blouse.

She ignored me, turned around, and started toward the altars. To my chagrin, she made her way onto the stage and accosted a microphone off its pole. "Preacher," she spoke in her syrupiest, sweetest voice. "Are you telling me this woman is a diagnosed schizophrenic?"

"That's what the doctors say," he admitted, and the crowd grew silent. "But we know God is going to deliver her from the demon of mental illness."

"Well, preacher, I think you need to be delivered from the demon of dumbassery."

The entire congregation gasped in unison and took a step back from Connie, as though avoiding the inevitable bolt of lightning that would soon strike her. I pretended I was slain in the spirit, so I would have an excuse to fall on the floor, slide under a pew, and hide from the debacle that unfolded onstage.

I peeked out from under the seat, and I saw Pastor Steve approach Connie, like a political candidate trying to intimidate his opponent in a debate. "Are you telling me you don't think this woman needs to be healed and delivered?"

"I'm telling you, if she's schizophrenic, she needs medication and therapy."

I pitied Connie. She thought her adversary was merely ignorant and he could be persuaded with reason and logic. But I knew he was something far more sinister and dangerous than simply ignorant. He was zealous, and Connie was fighting a losing battle. Ten tons of logic never outweighed a single ounce of earnest zeal. In the Pentecostal world of quick fixes and easy solutions, there were no schizophrenics. They all got healed one night at a Benny Hinn crusade, along with all the paralytics and homosexuals.

"Look, lady. The Bible says…"

"Well, now. There's your problem. You've got the wrong religious icon stuck in the wrong anatomical part. If you'd get that Bible out of your ass and get some Jesus in your heart, you might get somewhere."

Pastor Steve was angry now. How dare this interloper encroach on his territory and attempt to enlighten his sheep? "This woman is suffering because of her sin. She needs deliverance."

Connie remained steadfast and defiant. "Preacher, if God gave us mental illnesses as the punishment for our sins, there would be no one left to fasten the straightjackets."

Janice found me. She stuck her head under the pew, and she resurrected the schoolmarm. "Get her out of here!" she ordered.

I slid out of my hiding place and rushed on the stage, mortified, but also a little proud of my boss. I took Connie by the arm and started guiding her toward the nearest exit. She resisted, and I was surprised at her physical strength when motivated by moral indignation. The poor schizophrenic woman bawled so loudly, I thought it might do permanent damage to her vocal chords.

Connie stopped in front of her and spoke softly. "Sweetheart, are you taking your meds? Do you have a good therapist?" My determined friend reached into her purse and pulled out a business card. "If you ever need me, any time of the day or night, give me a call. You're a beautiful person." Then she started throwing business cards indiscriminately around the room. "All of you call me. You all need help. You people are disturbed."

The crowd resumed praying and tongue talking, but the atmosphere had shifted. They were fearful now, and their terror was palpable. The schizophrenic woman just had a lowly demon, but Connie had brought Satan himself into the sanctuary.

Back at *Chateau* Parsons, I started lunch. Connie continued ranting about the mistreatment of the mentally ill in evangelical churches. Ordinarily, she seemed indefatigable; she epitomized emotional strength and stability. I'd never seen her so irate, and I wanted to calm her.

"Aren't you forgetting something?" I prompted while I chopped the lettuce for our sandwiches. "Cultural awareness?" I pulled those two words straight out of the American Psychological Association's Code of Ethics. She knew I was reminding her that an effective therapist must be respectful of a troubled person's cultural background, including her religious preference.

"I guess my little tirade wasn't too professional, was it?"

"Not really," I concurred. I found a package of salami in the bottom of the refrigerator and tore open the reusable seal. "But everybody is allowed an off day now and then. I'd say you were about due one."

It was true. She had been a pillar of strength for so many, for so long, it was time for someone to be strong for her.

After we ate, I sank down on a chaise lounge and started reading.

Connie disappeared into her bedroom and reemerged with a hairbrush, which she handed to me. "Sometimes I like somebody to do it for me," she explained as she glided down gracefully on an ottoman in front of me. Though she was fast approaching sixty, she had not caved into the social edict that dictates older women must wear shorter coiffures. Soft white curls tumbled midway down her back.

She slid off her high-heeled pumps and massaged her arches, as though it were her feet that hurt and not her heart.

As I brushed her hair, Connie asked, "Emily, did I ever tell you about my mama?" Her voice was low and distant. I strained my ears to hear her.

"Mmm-hmm. I don't think so."

"Mama was bipolar. Of course, we didn't know what to call it back then. We just said she was moody or unpredictable, but she'd spend three straight days in bed, weeping like she'd just lost a child. Then she'd be up for a week, painting the house in all these bright, neon colors. She used these broad, sweeping strokes that left spots and streaks everywhere. Or she'd drag us out of bed in the dead of winter to go gather wild berries and honeysuckle. Of course, there wasn't any, so we'd ramble around all night in our pajamas listening to her tell us how she was going to be a famous singer and we would all be rich. Mama couldn't carry a tune in a tin can with the lid sealed.

"When she was depressed, Daddy would tell us 'stay away from your mama. She's having an episode.' When she was manic, he wouldn't allow her out in public because she embarrassed him. I used to come home from school and she'd be praying, crying out to God to forgive her for whatever she'd done that He was punishing her for. One day, she just got tired of all the highs and lows and ups and downs. She went out to Daddy's truck and got his old hunting rifle. We found her body down at the creek, in the same spot where she taught me how to swim."

"I'm so sorry," I consoled her, but the story wasn't over.

"At her funeral, the preacher stood up and said it was too bad Mama didn't get her heart right with God, and she went to hell, because she really was a good person. But he told us kids not to worry about it, because we wouldn't miss her when we got to heaven. We wouldn't even notice she wasn't there. Daddy just sat there nodding like he agreed with every word of that nonsense. What kind of vile, despicable, subhuman garbage tells a kid something like that?"

"Some people are just shitty," I bluntly opined, pulling the brush through a difficult knot in the baby fine tresses. "And they use their shitty religion for an excuse to be even shittier."

"I hate those people, Em. I know in our profession we're supposed to practice 'unconditional positive regard' for everyone, but I hate those people. The ones who form a self-serving opinions about the most misread, misused, mistranslated, misinterpreted, and misunderstood book in history, and then they think they have all the answers for life's most complicated problems."

"Maybe they're just ignorant." That's what I always told myself about my own family. It was easier than admitting they purposely used religion as a means of devaluing people they didn't understand.

"The difference between evil and ignorance is evil knows better and does it anyway. Some people are just ignorant, I'll grant you that, but that preacher who told me my mama was burning in hell was evil. Pure evil."

"Do you think that woman was really schizophrenic?" I asked, changing the subject back to the events at the church. In social work, we learned to detect when a person needed a break from talking about their personal trauma, and Connie was ready for a break.

"I don't know. It's a long and arduous process making a diagnosis of that magnitude, and I've never spoken with her. I'll tell you one thing for certain, though. She damn sure wasn't mentally healthy." Her voice trailed off, and she laughed in a self-deprecating tone. "I can't believe I acted like such an idiot today."

Wanting to lighten the mood, I snickered. "Demon of dumbassery? Did you learn about that at the University of Texas Graduate School of Behavioral Sciences?"

"It's a new clinical diagnosis," she joked.

She grew silent, and I soon realized she had fallen asleep with her head on my lap. I continued brushing her hair until my arm grew weary and I dropped the brush. Then I lightly kissed her cheek and tasted the powdery rouge that darkened her otherwise ghostly white face.

I didn't get healed from depression that day, and I didn't form a closer bond with my sister, but I received something even more precious. I gained a deeper understanding of my dearest and truest friend.

CHAPTER 15

$\mathcal{O}$n the day of Luke's preliminary hearing, I had breakfast with the prosecutor at a small café near the courthouse. At Karen's request, the waiter seated us in a corner, away from the establishment's other patrons. As we drank weak coffee and ate runny omelets, the ADA prepped me for the barrage of questions I'd likely face from the defense attorney. How dark was it in that room with only the lamplight to see by? How could I be sure the third man in my apartment was indeed the defendant? How could I even be sure there was a third man, since I had clearly stated that I was only raped by two? Was it true I'd had some sort of psychotic break? Was it possible I was still delusional? Why would a man I knew and could easily identify break into my apartment and commit such a heinous crime without even attempting to disguise himself?

I had answers for all those questions. Yes, the light was dim, but I could see three human forms. I knew it was Luke because I looked into those empty, soulless eyes. Nobody else has eyes like that. No, I'd not had a psychotic break. I temporarily dissociated from the trauma, because the pain was unbearable. No, I was not now, nor had I ever been delusional. No, Luke did not rape me, but he did murder Andi. He didn't go incognito because his goons were supposed to kill me so I couldn't testify, but they bungled the job. That's the same reason his brother broke into Connie's house—to finish the job and silence me permanently. And that was the truth, the whole truth, and nothing but the truth. All I had to do was get the words out.

Karen looked at her phone. "Almost ten-thirty," she announced. "We'd better get over there. This judge is a real stickler for punctuality."

From the outside, the courthouse looked like a stately Old South manor, with a domed roof. Reporters jostled each other on the front steps, hoping to get a glimpse of the heretofore anonymous "sexual assault" victim they'd reported on. Karen led me to a side entrance, and we avoided the cameras and microphones. Inside, the first two floors looked like a modern office building with suites divided into cubicles. We made our way through a maze of hallways and staircases until we came to the rotunda.

"All you have to do is tell the truth," Karen reminded me before she opened the door to the courtroom. *As if I have any reason to lie*, I thought. Nobody wanted this homicidal creep put away more than I did, and if my testimony could make that happen, then of course I was going to tell the truth.

Rose was already there, sitting behind the area reserved for Luke and the defense team. They had her dolled up like a prim housewife from a fifties' sitcom. She wore a long, straight cream-colored skirt and matching jacket. I was sure she hadn't chosen the ensemble. Her hair was pinned back in a tight bun on the nape of her neck. I also knew she hadn't chosen the hairstyle.

On the other side of the room, Trey was there with Sarah. I wasn't jealous this time. I knew she needed to be there, and I knew he needed her there. An older woman I didn't recognize sat with them. Nora Flynn and Ron Tyler also sat on our side along with a few media representatives and curious onlookers.

I sat next to Karen, but this case was not about the rape. That matter took care of itself with Leonard's murder and Tony's guilty plea. This hearing was about the cold-blooded killing of an innocent child.

For a while, I felt like I was living a *Law & Order* episode. Everything was somber and ceremonial. The bailiff stood stiff and serious in front of the judge's bench. "All rise!" he barked out, and everybody complied. The judge made his entrance, wearing the black robe that clearly identified him as the magistrate. His silver mustache and goatee along with the bifocals balanced precariously on the edge of his crooked nose gave him a grandfatherly appearance that belied the serious nature of his job. After the judge took his place behind the oaken judge's bench, tall enough it obscured his entire body except for his thick neck and round face, the crowd was told to be seated. Luke was escorted in by his lawyer and a court officer. Even in shackles and prison clothes, he still looked smug and unconcerned. I was the first witness called. I was nervous but confident, confident that the truth would be believed, good would defeat evil, and justice would prevail.

As I made my way to the witness stand, I didn't have butterflies in my stomach. I had a flock of angry crows methodically pecking at my intestines. But all I had to do was tell the truth. I just had to open my mouth and tell the truth. That's what Karen said. That's what the bailiff asked of me when he extended a white Bible in front of me. Did I swear to tell the truth, the whole truth, and nothing but the truth, so help me God?

I did. I swore to tell the truth because I had no reason not to. I desperately wanted to tell the truth, but I made one fatal error. Before I answered the bailiff's question, I looked at the defendant, and I saw those empty, soulless eyes. I felt the fist forming in my neck again, restricting my airway and stifling my speech. *I do*, my heart replied. *I do swear to tell the truth*, my soul echoed, but no words came out of my mouth. Complete silence filled the room. A little annoyed, the bailiff repeated the question. I heard gasping. Was that me? Was I hyperventilating? The court officer took a third stab at it, then Karen intervened.

"Your honor," the prosecutor implored. "Obviously, the state's witness is not well. May I have a moment to speak with her?"

"Make it fast, counselor," the judge replied. Then to me, "You may step down."

My hands trembling and my whole body shaking, I opened the tiny gate and stepped down from the elevated platform. Karen and I went into a conference room and sat at opposite ends of a long table. Feeling embarrassed and annoyed at myself, I ducked my head and stared at the steel table. "What happened to you in there?" Her voice was laced with both concern and frustration.

The closed fist in my throat opened and I muttered sheepishly, "I can't talk when I see him."

"See who?"

"Luke," I answered. My lower lip quivered uncontrollably. "The defendant. It happens every time I see him. It happened the day I took his kids, and he was screaming and threatening me. It happened that night he was in my apartment, and it happened that day I saw him at the police station, when I identified Leonard Horton."

"Are you saying the defendant makes you speechless?" The prosecutor sounded confused.

"Not speechless," I corrected. Nothing frustrated me more than incorrect words, words that didn't convey the full impact of a situation. "Voiceless. Speechless means you don't know what to say. I know exactly what to say. I just don't have the physical ability to say it."

"Have you spoken to your therapist friend about this?"

"I didn't realize it was going to happen every single time." I didn't want to look at the prosecutor. I had the feeling I'd disappointed her. I concentrated my focus on the grooves in the table. I stared at the narrow lines until my vision blurred and I grew dizzy.

The judge sent the bailiff into the conference room with a message. It was time for court to resume. Karen argued for a continuance, but it was denied. I didn't stick around to hear Rose perjure herself. I ran outside and gulped in the fresh air. Even though it was officially autumn now, the drought and subsequent heatwave lingered obstinately, drenching me in sweat the instant I exited the courtroom.

I remembered the path Karen showed me to escape the reporters, and I made my way back to the café where we'd had breakfast. I locked myself in the bathroom and cried. Andi would never have justice, and it was my fault. It was because of my weakness, the weakness I inherited from my mother.

Half an hour later someone tapped urgently on the bathroom door. I heard a familiar voice call out, "Hurry up in there! I gotta go bad." I hurriedly splashed cold water on my face and composed myself. I threw the door open, and there she was. Rose stood before me, still dressed in her June Cleaver garb. Her hands were on her hips, and she twisted her legs from side to side.

She must have seen the anger flashing in my eyes, because she quickly forgot her bodily functions and ran away from me faster than a shoplifter leaving Walmart. I wasn't about to let her get away. I chased after her.

"Get back here, you mindless little twit!" I shouted as we darted across the state highway. Both of us narrowly missed being hit by a semi.

I chased her through a field of Texas bluebonnets and up a steep incline. At the apex of the hill, I caught her. I grabbed her by the hair, pulling the bun loose. I spun her around and made her face me.

"What do you want from me?" she cried.

"I want you to tell the damn truth, you stupid lying useless twit" I smacked her face, and her cheek instantly reddened in the shape of my hand. All the rage I had been suppressing now overflowed, and I ran my sharp nails down the bridge of her nose, pulling away flesh and leaving a bloody trail.

"You ain't supposed to be talking to me," she whimpered. "I'm pretty sure there's a rule against that."

"I'm pretty sure there is also a rule against lying under oath," I reminded her, my tone low and venomous. "If you don't mind violating that one, what makes you think I give a flying fuck about your rule?"

"I didn't lie," she insisted. "I said Luke was with me in Oklahoma City that weekend, and that's the truth. I heard you went crazy after it happened. Maybe you just imagined Luke being there."

I shook my head in disgust. "I used to think you had real potential. I thought with Luke out of the picture and with the right support system, you could really do something with your life. I guess I was

81

wrong. You're just another useless meth head who'd sell her own grandmother for a chance to get high."

She looked wounded, like the small half-frozen kitten I found in the garbage two days after Christmas, whining and mewing for its mother who was too sick and too starved to produce milk or offer anything more maternal than the occasional growl of a reprimand. I couldn't save Rose like I saved the cat. There was no formula I could buy at the pet store that would substitute for what she was lacking. "Don't talk about me like that, Emily," she pleaded.

"Screw you, bitch." I slapped her again, this time even harder. Then, both literally and figuratively, I turned my back on her.

Everyone close to the prosecution met at Connie's house to discuss my predicament. It turned out the ligature marks on Andi's neck were a perfect fit for Luke's right hand, and that miniscule piece of flesh found under her nail was a partial match for Tony Detwiler's genetic profile, meaning that the infinitesimal shred of human skin belonged to a close relative of The Mangy Dog. Those two incriminatory facts were enough for an indictment. They would not be enough for a conviction, Karen warned. The relevance of my testimony escalated from crucial to vital.

"What do you make of this, Connie?" Trey asked the psychologist in reference to my peculiar problem. It turned out there was no bad blood between the two of them. Connie had just wanted to protect both Trey and me when I thought Andi was still alive.

She shrugged. "It's hard to say. It seems like it may be an extreme manifestation of post-traumatic stress disorder. We do occasionally see trauma-induced mutism—most generally in children—but those people usually go completely silent, or at least they become mute in all uncomfortable social situations. Emily's mutism seems to be triggered by a very specific stimulus named Luke Detwiler."

"She's got to pull herself together," Karen stated emphatically. Funny how when you lose voice, you also seem to lose your corporeality. They talked about me as though I wasn't physically present. "I must have that testimony, or this creep is going to walk."

"Maybe we could get the judge to let her sign a sworn affidavit giving her testimony," Trey suggested. "Or let her have her testimony recorded when Luke's not in the room."

"Emily knows sign language!" Connie chimed in. "We could call in a sign language interpreter!"

Karen shook her head. "Recorded testimonies and affidavits are sometimes used in the cases of traumatized children, but I don't think this judge will go for it in the case of a healthy, fully functioning adult. Too many Sixth Amendment issues. The accused has the right to be confronted by his accuser. The sign language interpreter would work if she was really mute, but I'm afraid not in this situation. There's simply no way around it. Emily has to testify. She has to do it verbally, and she has to do it in front of the defendant."

"Well, the trial date isn't for a couple of months," Connie pointed out. "I'm sure I can have her ready by then."

I tuned out the rest of the conversation and fixed my eyes on Sarah. She was staring wistfully out the now repaired glass door Tony had broken into. Unlike most people, grief hadn't soured her countenance. She wore her sadness like a tasteful accessory, a barely noticeable trinket that only made her more appealing. I liked the way she wore her hair, shoulder length and curled under at the ends, like a Hollywood starlet from the *noir* era. In many ways, she was the same beautiful and elegant woman I had met at Andi's birthday party, but something was different too. Something in her eyes. Something vaguely familiar, haunting and frightening. A dark flicker I often saw when looking in the mirror. When I saw it in my own eyes, I hadn't recognized it, but now I realized what it was and why it frightened me so much. It was a flicker of hatred, not hate directed toward an individual but hate for a world of injustice, cruelty, and abject human suffering. Ironically, that kind of hatred only proliferates the very things that ignited it in the first place, and that's what makes it so terrifying. That kind of hate metastasizes, like cancer. It corrodes the human spirit until all that is left is an abyss of violent anger and a pair of empty soulless eyes. I hoped Sarah dealt with her hatred before it consumed her.

CHAPTER 16

*C*onnie's idea of getting me ready for the trial included introducing me to a slew of her psychotherapist friends and letting them poke and prod at my psyche. Eventually, the shrinks came to a consensus on a cocktail of psychotropic medications they thought would calm me enough that I could testify. I had to start taking the meds immediately, so they would be in my system by the time the trial started. The most noticeable side-effect was grogginess. I always felt numb and sleepy.

That was how I felt the morning Connie came into my room and announced she was leaving for a while. "I've got to go to the bank, Em," she said, sounding a bit irritated. "There has been some sort of mix up with my alimony check again. Do you need anything while I'm out, Sugar?"

"Mmm…no, thank you." I answered, stretching my arms and yawning noisily. After she left, I turned on the television, hoping it would keep me from falling asleep again. It didn't. I was in that weird stage between sleep and wakefulness where chunks and pieces of reality seep into the dreams. I could hear the news anchor talking, but just a random word here and there registered in my mind.

"Hostage situation… Southside Bank…Ashford…one confirmed fatality…"

I started dreaming that Andi and I were visiting the zoo and playing with a baby elephant, but the reporter's words kept invading the peaceful realm of my unconsciousness.

Hostage situation…Southside Bank…Ashford…one confirmed fatality…

I jerked awake. "No!" I cried out audibly, though no one was there to hear me. I found the remote control on my nightstand and started frantically pushing buttons, trying to find more local news. Nothing. I scoured the Internet for anything about a bank robbery in North Texas. It was still too soon. All I found was a couple of ambiguous Facebook posts alluding to "something major going down in Ashford."

Maybe it was all part of the dream. One of the shrinks told me that some of the meds could cause disturbing nightmares. *Oh, God*, I prayed silently. *Please let it be a dream. I cannot lose anybody else.*

The day dragged on, and Connie did not return. Finally, the news came on again, and the anchor revealed there had indeed been a hostage situation at the Southside Bank in Ashford, and there was one confirmed fatality.

Okay, I calmed myself. *Just because there was a fatality doesn't mean it was Connie. Maybe she just hasn't come home because she is counseling people traumatized by the crisis situation. Of course, that is it. She is making sure everyone else is okay. That's how she operates.*

I heard a car pull up in the driveway, and I flew outside, hoping to see Connie's black Mercedes. My heart sank when I saw Trey, still dressed in tactical gear, head hung low and broad shoulders drooping.

"No! No! No!" I started screaming before he ever reached me, and I flung myself in his arms as soon as he was close enough to catch me. When I was calm enough to hear his voice, he relayed the story to me.

"She was our liaison inside the bank. Somehow she convinced him to let her talk to us by phone. All she kept telling us was 'don't shoot him. He's having hallucinations. I can handle this.' She said he told her the voices were making him do it, and if he didn't obey them, they would make his head implode. She was so sure she could handle the situation, and I think she could have except one of our younger guys got antsy and got a little too close."

He paused for a moment, then continued, "Emily, I have been a cop most of my adult life, and I have served alongside some of the finest men and women you could ever hope to meet, but what your friend did today was extraordinary. I have never seen anyone braver, more filled with genuine compassion, more committed to justice. At one point, a couple of us had infiltrated the building, and she thought we were getting ready to shoot him. They were both sitting on the floor. She wrapped her body around his in such a way there wasn't an angle we could get at that we didn't risk hitting her, and this whole time he had a gun aimed straight at her head. She was truly more concerned for that man's safety than for her own. Even after he shot her, and she must have known she was dying, she kept telling him, 'Don't be afraid. Everything is going to be okay now. They're going to get you the help you need.' The last words she spoke were words of comfort for her killer."

CONNIE'S SON wasted no time taking possession of his mother's house. I hadn't worked in months, so getting a place of my own was out of the question. With Andi and Connie both gone, I had only two significant people left in my life: a sister I couldn't stand and a man I couldn't fully love. I chose the man.

There was a storage shed on Connie's property, hidden tastefully behind a hedge of hydrangea bushes. When Erica's father called to tell me he was moving his family into his mother's mansion, and would I please vacate the premises as quickly as possible, he offered me anything I wanted out of the shed as a consolation prize. All I wanted was boxes, so I could pack my belongings.

Most of the stuff in that building had no value to anyone but the original owner. There were plastic containers filled with costume jewelry, a few faded photo albums, and stacks of love letters from old beaus. One thing caught my attention. It was a painting propped against the wall. Not just any painting. It was the portrait of Eve I'd seen at the art exhibit the first day I met Andi.

I stared at it in disbelief. My philanthropic friend probably just bought the masterpiece to help a struggling artist and support the local art community. She couldn't possibly have known how much the woman depicted in that painting spoke to me. Something in her sad, frightened eyes beckoned me. She wanted me to free her from her chains. She wanted me to rescue her. I placed the frame in one of the boxes I took with me. That stunning, lifelike work of art was the only thing I kept of Connie's.

TREY'S HOUSE was a sharp contrast to the mansion I'd been living in. Its designer won no pissing contests, and if it spoke at all, it just said, "Look at me. I'm a house." It was a plain wooden structure, painted white and trimmed in black. The interior was equally unimpressive. A few tasteless wall hangings and mismatched furniture were indicative of a single man's existence. Most of the rooms were done in dull neutral colors, but the one Trey said was mine was awash in pastels. It had been Andi's room. The walls were painted with a herd of unicorns galloping gaily across a pale blue background and leaping over minia-ture rainbows; their purple manes flowed down the lengths of their snowy white bodies. The middle of the room was occupied by a bed with a purple canopy, covered with a ruffled lavender comforter, both the comforter and canopy were dotted with little white hearts. Along-side one wall was a bookcase. I scanned the titles and saw all my old favorites: *Little Women, Anne of Green Gables, The Chronicles of Narnia,* and several books by Charles Dickens. The top shelf was reserved for her collection of ballerina figurines, little porcelain dancers in frilly pink tutus perched on wooden pedastals. Gingerly, I removed one of the statuettes and held it close to my heart. I hadn't felt Andi's presence this strongly since her death. She had loved this room, and I had the feeling her father hadn't touched a single thing in it since he lost her.

"Are you going to be okay in here?" Trey stood behind me in the doorway.

"Yeah," I didn't know if I would be okay in that room or not. I just knew I didn't have anywhere else to go.

It was getting late, and Trey had an early shift the next morning. "If you need anything, I'm right down the hall."

"I'll be okay," I assured him again, still uncertain if it was true. He put his hand on my back. "Good night, Trey," I said, sounding more forceful than I intended. He reluctantly turned away, and I shut the door, but I didn't lock it. Sinking down on her bed reminded me of that last embrace. Like her skin, the covers were soft, warm, and sweet smelling. I hadn't noticed Andi's dog, a scrappy working-class version of one of Connie's canines, was trapped inside the room until he curled up beside me. I placed my hand on his side. His faint heartbeat and shallow breathing comforted me.

I stayed awake for hours, thinking about all I'd lost over the past few months. I felt like my heart had been compressed in a grist mill until all that remained was a pile of mealy crumbs. I wondered if I would ever feel love or happiness again. He'd said I could come to him if I needed anything. When other people said stuff like that, I dismissed it as rhetorical social protocol, but I felt certain Trey really meant it. If I needed anything, I could come to him. If I needed to talk, if I needed comforted, even if I needed to be loved, he was right down the hall.

The light in my room was still on and I stared at the closed door. It was just an ordinary door with a silver knob, easily opened and easily exited, but it might as well have been a massive boulder standing between Trey and me. I didn't have the strength to push it aside and go to him. I couldn't trust him, I told myself, but that was a lie. I could trust him. I did trust him. I'd seen his goodness in the way he treated his daughter, and I'd seen his loyalty in the way he respected his former wife. The problem wasn't that I didn't trust him. It was that I didn't deserve him. I was responsible for the death of his child. How could he ever truly forgive me for that?

I heard him shuffling about in the kitchen, so I assumed he couldn't sleep, either. His footsteps stopped, and I could see the tips of his bare toes under the crack at the bottom of the door. I saw the knob turn ever-so-slightly, but not enough to open.

It's not locked. I'm awake. Please come in. But he wasn't the type of man to enter a woman's bedroom without an invitation, and I simply didn't have the strength to open the door or even to call out to him. Finally, I fell asleep to the persistent whirring of a low hanging ceiling fan.

PART III
PHILAUTIA

"…love yourself…"—Mark 12:31

CHAPTER 17

The next morning, I made breakfast for Trey. Not because he asked me to or because I felt obligated to, but because I liked cooking and I had no one else left to do it for. We ate at a square wooden table. A passerby peeping in the big bay window might have mistaken us for a married couple enjoying a routine start to the day after a night of connubial bliss.

After Trey left for work, I busied myself unpacking my things in Andi's room. I hung the portrait of Eve above the dresser. It looked out of place amid the rest of the cheery décor, but I wanted her somewhere I could look at her. I wanted to understand exactly what she was asking of me. I stared at the masterpiece until I realized I was not looking at an artist's depiction of a mythical character. This woman really existed, and not in some bygone era. She existed in the here and now. I knew her. I had spoken to her. I had slapped her, clawed her face, and turned my back on her. The hair was darker and the skin was flawless, unmarred by the physical manifestations of addiction and emotional trauma, but it was Rose who begged me to free her from her chains.

Intrigued, I placed my hand in the center of the frame. For a brief moment, I felt the tiniest flutter of a heartbeat. Startled, I jumped back.

It was just my overactive imagination, I told myself. I needed to find something to occupy my mind. I thought about cleaning, but Trey's house was always immaculate. That alone set him apart from every other man I had ever known. I tried reading, but my mind raced and concentration was impossible. I thought about calling the new supervisor at CPS and talking to her about getting my job back, but I couldn't imagine working there without Connie. Besides, it seemed dishonorable to Andi's memory for me to keep protecting other children when I couldn't protect the one child I loved more than life itself. I knew I would have to find a new job soon. I couldn't stay with Trey indefinitely, at least not without contributing to the household income. When a man financially invests in a woman, he starts expecting returns on his dividends.

I didn't even know where to start job hunting, so I went walking instead. The homes in Trey's neighborhood were all like his, well-kept but not extravagant. The lawns were freshly mown and the few neighbors who dawdled about outside all smiled warm greetings as I walked by. I stumbled upon a little park tucked away behind a row of evergreens. Like the rest of the neighborhood, it was pleasant and modest: just some playground equipment, two dark green benches, and a small pond.

The meds started making me feel groggy again, and I plopped down on one of the benches. A soft breeze rustled through the pines and made the temperature more bearable. Mallard ducks swam gaily in the murky pond, then came ashore and pecked the ground for food. I wondered who was taking care of Connie's menagerie. I didn't know the rest of her family, but I thought Erica was too spoiled and self-centered to invest much time in other living creatures.

Then I thought about the house I had been effectively evicted from. Though I hated to admit it, I missed the house as much as I missed the owner. It sounded strange, and I knew it was impossible, but I always felt like that mansion had been designed specifically for me. Every nook and cranny was laid out exactly the way I would have wanted it if the architect had requested my input.

Soon, I found myself drifting back to the night before. It had been a long, uncomfortable evening alone with Trey in his home. In the dangerously seductive stillness of night, I stood like Sidney Carton at the guillotine, about to lose my head for love. In the cold hard light of day, I was glad I had resisted. Though Trey seemed different than any other man I'd ever known, I couldn't take a chance on love right now. I had already lost too much. One more loss, one more heartbreak, one more disappointment, and I would go spiraling headfirst into the shadowy depths of a canyon of despair, and I might never be able to crawl out.

I must have dozed off on the park bench, because when I opened my eyes I noticed black clouds had darkened the sky and rain had begun falling. The oppressive heatwave ended in what we Texans call a gullywasher, a sudden downpour so necessary and so revitalizing, it cleanses all of creation. I ran home, temporarily forgetting my misery and reveling in the refreshing rainfall. When I got there, Trey's patrol car was parked in the driveway. Inside, I heard the shower running. I quickly found a towel in the other bathroom, dried off, and cleaned up the pool I left on the floor. When I glanced up, I noticed Trey's bedroom door was open. I saw something shiny on the dresser. It must have been a rough day, because when Andi lived there he always locked it up as soon as he got home.

I tiptoed into his room. Slowly, like a kid sneaking a cookie off the cooling tray, I removed the gun from its holster. It was heavier than I imagined, and colder. Much colder. And the power. I'd never held so much power, the incredible God-like power of life and death. My hand trembled as I raised the weapon to my temple. It was a nine-millimeter. I don't remember where I learned, but I knew how to shoot it. Release the safety, pull the slide to chamber a round, and then pull the trigger. Three simple steps, and it could all be over.

Release the safety.

Click.

Pull the slide.

Clack.

Pull the trigger.

Boom!

I was thirteen when I first heard The Whispers. They weren't really voices that I heard audibly. They were more like nudges that I felt in my spirit, something telling me I always had a choice. It was sort of an ironic way I soothed myself when things got too stressful. No matter how bad my life was or how badly I screwed up, there was always Plan B, and Plan B was suicide. Standing there with the icy tip of Trey's service revolver touching my temple was the closest I ever came to obeying The Whispers. But what would happen after I obeyed?

Click.

Clack.

Boom!

Heaven.

My mother is standing there, beautiful and whole. She has been waiting for me on the shore of a river where the water is so clear, I can see all the way to the bottom, and the river flows over a bed of precious jewels: diamonds, pearls, and amethysts. Mother wants to show me around, but first we must make it across the river, and I am afraid. I am not a strong swimmer.

"Don't be afraid. We don't have to swim. We will walk across," Mama says, and we do; we glide across the stream like two swans. On the other side, every where we step, flowers bloom in our wake: roses, lilies, and marigolds. Music emanates all around us, but it is unlike anything I have ever heard, so beautiful and serene. We walk up a golden pathway to a mansion that looks like Connie's house, except it is made of pure gold.

"This is where they live, and it is where you will live also."

"Where who lives, Mama?" Then Trey, Andi, and Connie appear, like a single entity, cloaked in radiance and reaching out for me. But Trey is not dead, how could he be here?

Click.

Clack.

Boom!

Hell.

I am falling down a deep hole. My father is at the bottom of the pit, and he's angry, like he always was. He blames me for his death. He knows I killed him with my mind. If I hadn't been such a rebellious child, he would never have grown so full of hate and anger that God banished him to hell. There is no lake of fire, consuming the souls of the damned, and no pitchfork-wielding devil tormenting his subjects. It's just a lot of angry, unforgiving people roasting over the flames of their own hatred.

CLICK.

Clack

Boom!

Oblivion.

How does a human being who has only ever known time, space, and matter even comprehend nothingness? Never knowing anything again. Never feeling anything again. Never loving anyone again. Perhaps that is the truest hell.

ENGROSSED IN MY INNER-DIALOGUE, either trying to talk myself into or out of suicide, I hadn't heard the shower stop running. I never heard the bare feet walking softly but swiftly across the carpeted floor. I snapped out of my reverie when a strong masculine arm reached around me and immobilized my upper-body. With his free hand, Trey wrestled the gun out of my grasp. Still restraining me with one arm, he somehow removed the magazine from the weapon. Then he tossed both the ammunition and the instrument of death to the floor and kicked them out of reach. With both of our safety ensured, he relaxed the restraint into an embrace. I leaned my head against his bare chest, still cool and damp from the shower.

"I'm so tired," I sobbed miserably. "I'm just so damned tired."

I knew what he would do—what he had to do. Like social workers, police officers are morally, ethically, and legally mandated to intervene when someone is thought to be a danger to herself.

CHAPTER 18

Sunnyvale was a charming facility on a vast expanse of lush green lawn overlooking beautiful Lake Sutton. At least, that was how it was described in the brochures Connie used to leave lying around when she was trying to convince me to check myself in voluntarily. It wasn't the type of place where people usually ended up when sent away for a psychiatric evaluation by way of an emergency order of detention, but Connie had connections here. It turned out she told Trey this was where I must be sent should the time ever arise. You know your friends think you're crazy when they make a standing reservation for you at a state-of-the-art mental hospital.

Not much happened my first night at Sunnyvale. I stayed in my room. Being in that room was like being trapped inside a box, a stuffy windowless enclosure with four beige walls. A nurse came in and administered my meds to make sure I was taking them. She told me the therapist would be in to see me soon. Within moments, I fell asleep.

I awakened the next morning to the sound of someone moaning. The pitiful crying was so loud and clear, I thought there was someone in my room. I looked around and saw no one. There was nothing in the tiny space to obscure my view, and the bed was too low for anyone to be hiding under it. Still, the weeping was so near. I wondered for a moment if I was the one making that noise.

After breakfast, the therapist arrived. She couldn't have been more than a year beyond grad school. She wore her blonde hair in a stylish bob and she was dressed in a navy blue pant suit. Her body was adorned with matching silver earrings, necklace, and bracelets. I always wondered why psychologists and counselors found it necessary to dress like bankers and stockbrokers. As a social worker, I learned the importance of dressing down. Clean and modest apparel was suffi-cient. "Helping professionals" who looked a little too well-put-together intimidated their clients, who often struggled just to brush their teeth.

For all her attempts to appear professional, she blew it by smacking on gum that she habitually popped in the corner of her mouth. She twirled her pen as if she was practicing her baton routine for the talent portion of the Miss I'm-Better-Than-You Pageant.

"So, are you feeling better today?" Smack. Smack.

"Yes. I feel fine."

"I hear you have been through a lot lately." Smack. Smack. Pop. Pop.

"I guess you could say that."

"What made you want to kill yourself last night?" Smack. Pop. Smack. Pop.

"I didn't want to kill myself. I just wanted to imagine what it might be like."

Dear God, what an annoying little twit. If I hadn't been suicidal before, I certainly would be after a few sessions with this charlatan. Then again, maybe I judged her too harshly. Maybe Connie set the bar too high, and I assumed all psychologists would be as authentic and empathic as she had been.

The moaning started up again. Though no words were uttered, I could tell it was a feminine voice. The crying woman grieved so loudly and so continuously, it seemed as though she carried all the sadness in the world within the cramped spaces of her atria and ventricles. I inter-rupted the therapist mid-smack and demanded, "Who is making that God-awful noise?"

The psychologist raised a sculpted eyebrow. "What noise?"

I assumed the perpetrator of the racket must have been a long time resident of Sunnyvale and the staff was so accustomed to the moaning, they tuned it out. I didn't pursue the issue further.

We weren't locked up in padded cells. None of us were that kind of crazy. After the therapist left, I wandered up and down the halls, exploring my new surroundings. I had to escape the moaning of the invisible woman, and the hallways were surprisingly quiet. Occasionally, I heard the clanging of the cue ball hitting its targets on the pool table in the recreation room. They served us lunch in the cafeteria—dry meatloaf and lumpy mashed potatoes. Then I returned to my stuffy chamber.

I found the culprit of the incessant noise sitting in the middle of my bed. She was probably about my age, but it was hard to tell. Her face was horribly disfigured. Her flesh was covered in pink, gray, and white scars that looked like hieroglyphics telling the tale of an ancient battle. She seemed unaware of my presence, but I wanted to read that history written on her distorted face. I sat across from her on the bed, both of us cross legged.

"What is your name?" I asked. She just kept weeping and moaning, but she touched my forehead with a mangled forefinger and started moving it slowly and methodically on my skin. She did it a couple of times before I realized she was spelling out her name. I closed my eyes and deciphered the letters. L-O-L-A. Her name was Lola.

Then I remembered her. A few years back, her story dominated the local news when her former boyfriend caught her pumping gas at a convenience store. He doused her with gasoline and set her on fire.

"Does it hurt?" I gently touched her face with my palms, and she shook her head.

She took my hand and placed it on her heart. I didn't see her lips move, and the moaning never stopped, but I clearly heard her say, "It hurts here."

The nurse came in and administered my meds. She didn't say anything about Lola being in my room. In fact, I don't think she even noticed my visitor. I soon became groggy and fell back on the bed.

Lola curled up beside me. I cradled her in my arms, like a mother soothing a colicky infant. I lowered my mouth to her ear and sang the only lullaby I remembered from childhood.

Jesus loves me this I know, for the Bible tells me so... For a while, the pitiful weeping stopped.

I COULDN'T WAIT to get rid of the therapist when she showed up for our next session. I wanted to be alone with Lola. Bonding with my mournful new friend was the most therapeutic thing I'd ever done. I decided the best way to handle the psychologist was to play along. I knew how to convince somebody I wasn't crazy. A social work degree is very nearly the same as a psychology degree, and I was much more seasoned than the young professional. She went strictly by the text-book, so I knew exactly the key phrases, actions, and body language she was looking for. When my seventy-two hours was up, I would have no trouble being released. I just needed to dispense of the phony shrink so I could spend the brief time I had left at Sunnyvale with Lola.

When the psychologist left, Lola and I resumed our positions in the middle of the bed, cross-legged and facing each other. She handed me a tube of salve, and I deduced she wanted me to put the balm on her scars. *So they do still hurt*, I thought. I squeezed a little of the medicine on the tips of my first two fingers, then I cautiously ran my fingertips across the ruddy peaks and valleys of her scarred face.

As I suspected, the scars told a history, but it wasn't Lola's history. It was my own. Each scar told a story about me. Stories I kept hidden in the dank and dusty attic of my hippocampus, buried deep beneath warm, pleasant memories that I was more apt to drag out and share with others. The first wound took me back to six-years-old. There was a visitor at the old converted barn. I called him The Round Man, because he was as wide as he was tall, and the striped T-shirt he always wore made him look like a beach ball. For some odd reason, he always smelled like a sickening mix of sweat, motor oil, and wet dog. He was my father's friend, and he visited us often. I liked him because he always requested to see me and never Janice. He always brought my favorite candy, and he made me fish it out of his pocket. To this day, the thought of green apple Jolly Ranchers makes me nauseous.

He also brought his guitar, and he sat on a tree stump. He strummed out all the most popular country and western songs and sang along to his own accompaniment. Now I knew both the instrument and the singer were woefully out of tune, but back then, I loved to hear him play, because it was the only time music was allowed near our home. My father usually sat outside with us, but on this day, he went inside "to see what was taking the old lady so long with the sandwiches."

Nobody ever told me about "good touching" versus "bad touching," but I knew instinctively the way The Round Man touched me was wrong. That night I told my mother what happened. A look of horror crossed her face, and she grabbed my shoulders. "We mustn't talk about such things," she gasped. "It's naughty, and God doesn't like naughty little girls."

That's when I learned molestation was a sin, but it wasn't his sin for doing it to me. It was my sin for talking about it. So I never spoke about the abuse again. As I grew older, The Round Man visited more frequently and took greater liberties with my developing body. After one particularly painful and embarrassing encounter with The Round Man, I developed severe abdominal pains, and my parents rushed me to the hospital.

For years, I was told I had appendicitis, and God miraculously healed me, so I never had surgery. As an adult, I accessed my medical records and learned I had been treated for salpingitis, or inflammation of the fallopian tubes, a classic symptom of chlamydia. I wondered how many adults had been privy to that information and did absolutely nothing.

In recalling my own abuse, I realized what had really drawn me to the social work profession. It wasn't the noble, selfless career everybody thought it was. In fact, it was the most selfish and despicable thing I'd ever done. I wasn't interested in saving other children. Why should I rescue them? Nobody came for me. Nobody saved me. The only child I was really trying to save was myself.

CHAPTER 19

I continued traveling down the bumpy roads of charred flesh, and each sanguine avenue led to a significant event in my past. One scar transported me back to the age of eight. My best friend was a boy named Jeremiah. When I looked back on those days, I fondly thought of us as the Patroclus and Achilles of the playground, sharing dreams and adventures. My parents warned me to stay away from him because they said his family was trash. My mother was so psychologically damaged she couldn't contribute anything to society, and my father's uncontrollable rage prevented him from keeping any job longer than just a few months. Jeremiah's mother was a licensed professional counselor and his father was the local leader of the NAACP, but my parents had the nerve, the audacity, the sheer unmitigated gall to call my friend's family "trash" because they were black.

On Fridays, an ice cream truck stopped by our school at recess time. I never had any money, so Jeremiah always gave me fifty cents. Both Jeremiah and I like the orange sherbet Push-up. One Friday, we heard the tinkling bell summoning us, and we raced to the edge of the road. It seemed every kid in school beat us there. We stood in line, holding our quarters and smiling in anticipation. When we got to the front of the line, we could see there was only one Push-up left. The vendor knew what we both wanted; we got the same thing every week. He reached into his cooler, pulled out the coveted treat, reached around my friend and handed the sherbet to me. Then he turned to my friend and said, "Sorry, kid. Fresh out."

Still in the throes of childhood egocentrism, I devoured the frozen sweetness right in front of Jeremiah, never noticing the pleading look in his eyes or the rivulet of saliva flowing from the corner of his mouth. Over the years, I wondered why that vendor deemed me worthier of his last orange sherbet Push-up than the boy who gave me the money to buy it. There wasn't a solitary answer I could conjure that didn't involve skin pigmentation.

WHEN I WAS TWELVE, we attended one of those old-fashioned hellfire and brimstone southern Pentecostal churches, where God seemed scarier than Satan. Everything was a sin, and God sat on His throne, annihilating people at the first sign of human weakness. Every news-worthy event pointed to the ever-approaching Apocalypse, and every person who attained the slightest amount of political power was poten-tially the Anti-Christ. Any unfortunate occurrence or negative emotion was evidence of demonic activity in that person's life and proof that the struggling person was spiritually inferior and derelict in his Chris-tian duties of prayer and scripture reading. By the time I reached adolescence, I was trapped in a prison of fear and self-condemnation. No matter how much I prayed, I remained utterly convinced that I was destined for hell for some ambiguous sin I committed for which I could never be forgiven.

My father didn't beat me for punishment. He did that for stress relief. He had another, much more effective form of discipline. Any time I got out of line, all he had to do was remind me that I was a loathsome sinner, bound for hell, and I would meekly acquiesce and do his bidding. Until something happened and I decided if my fate was already sealed and there was nothing I could do to escape eternal damnation, then a little youthful rebellion couldn't hurt anything.

My grandparents moved to California. They sent one-way bus tickets for my mother, Janice, and me. We were leaving. My father wasn't going to hurt us anymore. Even Janice was excited about the move. I never saw her more joyful and animated. My father took a temporary job with a moving company, which required him to be gone for days at a time. Mama, Janice, and I packed our belongings and prepared to flee. Before we left, my mother made a fatal error in judgment. She called the pastor's wife to take us to the bus station.

Sister Marcy, as she was known to the congregation, barged into our house without knocking. She was accompanied by her husband, a tall, skinny, pompous, pious pontificator. I could tell right away there was going to be trouble. The preacher's wife had a haughty look on her wrinkled face and a Bible tucked beneath one of her flabby arms. I watched as Mama's joyous expression faded. I think it might have been the last time I saw a sincere smile cross my mother's lips.

"Now Sister Kirk," the righteous woman began. "What's this nonsense I hear about you wanting to leave your husband?"

The preacher stood behind his wife, blocking the doorway. He glared at Mama like she was his disobedient child and he was about to drag her to the woodshed.

Mama tried to explain her husband's abusive behavior, how he beat her mercilessly and starved her for days because he thought she was too fat. Sister Marcy thought that was no excuse for breaking the sacred marriage covenant. In fact, she was convinced any marital discord stemmed from Mama's ungodly behavior. Mama should dress better, despite the fact that her clothing budget afforded her little more than a pair of thrift store tennis shoes every year. Mama should do something with her hair, even though the only thing she had to wash it with was a bar of homemade lye soap. Mama should cook decent meals once in occasionally, as if she could magically turn a few drops of water and a quarter cup of flour into veal cutlets and tiramisu. If only Mama were a better, more submissive wife, like the Bible instructed her to be, then her husband wouldn't be so violent. It was all Mama's fault.

That was the first time I experienced seething hatred. It felt like someone dragged a flaming torch through my insides, burning a path from my stomach, through my heart, and into my brain. I hoped the stories they told me were true. I hoped there was a literal hell, where the wicked were eternally tormented in the fiery depths thereof, and I hoped it was full of heartless, merciless, smarmy jackass preachers and their stupid, haughty, fat cow wives.

After they ostensibly condemned my mother to death, Sister Marcy bent down to kiss my forehead; her Listerine breath burned my nasal passages. "I will see you in Sunday School, Emily."

I don't know where the words came from. I don't remember consciously forming them in my mind. They just fell out of my mouth, as though my body was expelling toxins. I stared up at the preacher's wife, and I said plainly and calmly, "I hate you, you fat bitch."

She gasped in horror, stumbled back a few steps, and looked like she might faint. Her husband charged at me and grabbed my arm. "How dare you speak to your elders that way!"

"Fuck you, you dumb fuck," I muttered venomously. I had never known expressing anger could feel so good.

When my father returned from his job, the kind, merciful Christians couldn't wait to tell him about my insolence. He was so infuriated by my having disgraced him in front of the church hierarchy that he soon forgot it was my mother's actions that precipitated the day's events. He focused all his fury on me, and I was glad.

He violently threw me over the arm of a raggedy old sofa. I dug my nails deep into the floral pattern of the upholstery and gritted my teeth in preparation for the assault. With each thunderous whack of the thick leather belt, I strengthened my resolve. Mentally, I closed the dam to my tear ducts and willed myself not to cry.

Thwack!

"You will apologize to the pastor and his wife!"

"I will not!"

Thwack!

"You will repent for your wickedness!"

"I will not!"

Thwack!

"I will beat that rebellious spirit out of you!"

"No. You will not."

My mother believed that all rebellion against authority was sinful, but I disagreed. I believed when the rebellion was against an immoral status quo, then the rebellious act became the quintessence of morality.

After my father fell asleep, exhausted from the physical exertion it took to beat someone less than a quarter of his size, I laid on my belly, and my mother tended my wounds with a damp washcloth. Finally, I cried, but not from pain, or even anger. My tears stemmed from sheer joy. I knew now I was strong enough to survive. I would not become meek and submissive like Janice or my mother. I would not lose myself to a father I despised and a religion I didn't understand. I faced down the only real demons I knew, and my rebellious spirit emerged victorious.

NEXT, I was transported back to two weeks after my high school graduation. I was eighteen, with no plans and no hope for a better future. I couldn't even look for a job, because my family only had one car and it had a busted radiator. "Don't worry," Mama said. "God will send you a husband soon." But I didn't want a husband. I wanted a life. I wanted a career. I wanted an education. I wanted to travel. I wanted a future. I wanted more than this miserable, God-forsaken existence I had been living.

My church's way of dealing with the atrocity of pre-marital sex was marrying their young people off as soon as their hormones kicked in. By the time I graduated high school, I was the only member of my youth group who wasn't at least engaged. Janice was already married and expecting baby number two, and she took it upon herself to find a suitable mate for me. She came to visit us one day and announced she had found my Prince Charming. He attended her mother-in-law's church and he was perfect for me. He would be picking me up the following evening around six.

Prince Charming didn't ride up on a big white stallion. He sputtered to a stop in a Ford Pinto. He drove us to some greasy hamburger joint where the noise and flashing lights that emanated from the Arcade games made my head hurt. The only word that accurately described my date was "thick." Not fat. Thick. Everything about him was thick, from his thick, hairy arms to his thick, bushy eyebrows. I ordered a salad. He ordered a bacon double cheeseburger. While we ate, he regaled me with stories about his stellar academic achievements. He graduated with a B average. I didn't tell him I never made a grade below an A. I didn't want him to feel inferior to a lowly woman. Besides, all the hard work I put into school seemed pointless now. It certainly wasn't getting me out of my parents' house any faster.

When he finished boasting about his intelligence, he started telling me about his future plans. He was going to work a couple of years at the local tire plant and save money for college. Then he was going to study dentistry. It was a lucrative field. After he made his fortune as a dentist, he was going to start his own film production company and make Christian movies. This sinful world needed a wholesome alternative to Hollywood's filth and smut, and God gifted him with a brilliantly creative mind. He talked incessantly while he devoured his meal. I could see him grinding the burger between his thick teeth while he told me what a good son he was and how any wife of his would have to accept his devotion to his mother. He slowly moved his thick jaws up and down and never completely closed his mouth. I thought if livestock had their own version of hell, then this surely must be it— churning in the putrid acids of a gluttonous man's digestive tract.

Mesmerized by my date's uncanny ability to boast shamelessly while exhibiting the table manners of an uncivilized jungle boy, I forgot I had a fork full of food in my own mouth. I let the utensil slide so far back in my in my throat that it triggered my gag reflex. I spat chunks of romaine lettuce and feta cheese all over Prince Charming's thick facial hair. He simply wiped the regurgitation away with his shirt sleeve and continued bragging about how he was the best husband any woman could hope for. Suddenly, I envisioned my future, and it involved a lot of cats.

109

THE OLD SHACK sat at the edge of a graveled country road that ended with a stop sign just beyond our property. For the last two weeks, every afternoon around four, a motorcycle pulled up to the corner and stayed longer than was necessary. I thought the idling engine sounded like a voice beckoning me. It called out, *Come on. Come on. Come on. Come on. Come on. Come on.* That's how I devised a plan. I had no idea who the mysterious biker was, where he came from or where he was going, but I knew the time had come. I had to take a chance.

I crammed a couple of changes of clothes and a toothbrush into a giant handbag and hid it behind the worn and tattered faded yellow love seat in the living room. That morning passed by slowly. The second hand on the clock dragged its way around the dial as languidly as a glacier making its way across Antarctica. I helped my mother with the chores, then sat down on the love seat and pretended to read. I stared out the dusty, cracked window pane, wondering what kind of life awaited me once I fled from the relative safety of the only home I'd ever known. My mother sat across from me; I could see her reflection in the glass, working the crossword puzzle in *The Dallas Morning News*. She was intelligent. Once, while digging through her things looking for a hairbrush, I found a college diploma. She had a degree in secondary education, with an emphasis in mathematics. *Summa cum laude*. Chi Omega Honor Society. She never even told me about it. Now newspaper puzzles were the only intellectual stimulation she could find, and all that knowledge she accrued was just a jumbled mess in the cobwebbed recesses of her atrophied mind.

Finally, it was almost four o'clock. I inhaled deeply and stood up. I could hear the distant humming of the motorcycle, making its way down the winding road. I reached behind the love seat and grabbed the bag. "Mama?" I said hesitantly.

"Hmmm?" She barely even looked up.

The bike screeched to a stop, and I heard it calling me. *Come on. Come on. Come on. Come on. Come on. Come on.*

"I love you. Mama," I said as I threw open the door. I didn't hear her say anything, and I didn't look back to see her reaction, but sometimes I imagined that she walked over to the window and watched me leaving. Maybe she even smiled a little. Maybe that night when she said her obligatory prayers she prayed for my safety. Maybe somewhere deep down inside, in a place the religionists hadn't yet killed, maybe she was proud of me.

CHAPTER 20

J ran like a prisoner fleeing from a brutal warden and his stupidly loyal German shepherd. My escape was as terrifying as it was exhilarating, as dangerous as it was liberating. The biker started to pull away from the stop sign. The sun glinted off the silver handlebars and illuminated his tan face when he turned toward me.

"Wait!" I screamed desperately as I straddled the back of the machine. I clung to the sides of his brown leather jacket, made warm to the touch by the unrelenting sun, as though I were drowning and he was the only solid object within reach. It never occurred to me that he might throw me off and refuse to take me with him. He didn't.

He shouted above the noisy engine, "Where do you want to go?"

I shouted my reply, "Everywhere!"

He turned the bike toward the west, and my life began. Trees and grass raced past my peripheral vision at a dizzying speed. The stranger rounded the sharp corners faster than was prudent for his skill level and a couple of times our knees almost touched pavement. The wind, intensified by the motion of the motorcycle, slapped fingers of warm air against my bare arms and I understood why my companion wore a jacket despite the heat. We rode through the night, stopping only once for gas. I fell asleep with my head pressed against his back and my arms wound tightly around his stomach. My muscles relaxed, and I lost my grip on the driver. I jerked awake when he hit a pothole and I nearly flew off the motorcycle. The sun nudged its way into the horizon as the flatlands merged with the foothills of the Rockies. *New Mexico?* I wondered

We finally stopped at an abandoned church that had been built on so unstable a foundation, the structure had settled and the steeple now leaned slightly to the left. Chipped white paint covered the four walls and broken stained glass windows exposed the interior.

The stranger and I dismounted the motorcycle and he removed his helmet. I saw him clearly for the first time. He was barely taller than me, as thin as Prince Charming was thick. He wore his dark hair short in the back and long in the front. A thin mustache covered his upper lip, and he sported a yin yang tattoo on his right forearm. I sighed in relief. He didn't look like a serial killer, but then again, most serial killers don't.

He peered into one of the broken windows. "I guess this will do,"

"Where are we?"

"Hell, I don't know. If you were going to be that picky about where we ended up, maybe you should have been more specific when I asked where you wanted to go."

He removed a backpack from the handlebars. "Whatcha got in there?" I tried to sound unconcerned but I kept thinking about all the stories I had heard on the news about female hitchhikers and the murderous men who gave them rides.

"Knife, rope, handcuffs, and duct tape," he answered caustically.

So, he was an asshole, but not in the same vein as my father. There's a world of difference between a violent asshole and a sarcastic one.

"I'm not afraid of you," I announced, sounding bolder than I felt.

He looked at me from under a fringe of long bangs and broke out in uproarious laughter. "If you weren't afraid of me, you probably wouldn't feel the need to tell me you weren't afraid."

We made our way inside the dilapidated building. Pews were

toppled over on top of each other and hymnals were strewn across the floor. A layer of dust blanketed the sanctuary. The room smelled musty, like an old root cellar. I thought about how orderly Sister Marcy kept everything at our church. This place would send her into full-on cardiac arrest. Maybe that's why I liked it.

If he told me his name, I don't remember. I often dehumanize men by giving them monikers based on some personality quirk or salient physical trait, rather than committing their names to memory. I told him my name was Desdemona. For some reason, I always related to Othello's ill-fated wife. Exhausted from our overnight journey, we slept most of the day. At dusk, he pulled a battery operated lamp out of his backpack, placed it in the center of the room, and turned it on.

He threw an open bag of Doritos at me and growled, "You hungry?" Then he produced a bottle of hard liquor and a plastic baggy full of what I presumed was marijuana.

"So tell me, Desdemona," he emphasized the name, letting me know he knew it was fake. "You ever been high before?"

"Sure. Lots of times," I lied. My parents had always kept me under such close surveillance it was impossible for me to partake in the usual rites of passage most teenagers experience.

He twisted the lid off the Wild Turkey and gulped it like it was Gatorade and he'd just run a marathon. Then he offered it to me. I hesitated. Drinking alcohol was right up there with sex on the list of things that were sure to get a person banished to hell. My biker friend didn't let my hesitancy dissuade him. He shoved the bottle closer to my lips and I tilted my head back. The amber liquid burned my insides as if I'd swallowed a lit firecracker that exploded in my esophagus

He looked my age, but he must have been older. He told me he was a graduate student at some trendy liberal arts college in New Jersey, studying philosophy. I asked him what he was doing in Texas and he explained that he had a childhood dream of working on a real ranch. That's when I knew he was really from New Jersey. Only a true city boy would waste countless hours of his fleeting youth dreaming about working ten-hour days in the brutal sun, knee-deep in cow shit.

There was a ranch a couple of miles down the road from the old shack. My neighbors had made The Philosopher's dream come true by giving him a temporary job. The cowboy life was not what he expected and he was on his way out of Texas the afternoon I hopped on his motorcycle. Otherwise, we would have ended up at a Motel 6 in Ashford. That's where he had been staying.

We downed most of the whiskey and then he took out a thin white sheet of paper out of the pocket of his jeans. He put some of the marijuana on it, rolled the paper, and lit the end on fire. The Philosopher wasn't really attractive, at least not by Texas standards. He was too small and too urbanized, but something about the way he held the joint appealed to me. So deliciously deviant, so beautifully blasé. I thought even if a band of nuns barged in on us, accompanied by every drug enforcement agent in America, he would have remained unfazed. With his defiant attitude and dark shaggy hair that obscured much of his face, he almost looked like James Dean had spawned a kid with Cousin It from *The Addams Family*.

I loved the smell of burning weed. It lingered in the atmosphere, like the aftermath of a fireworks show on Independence Day. My companion puffed on the joint and seductively blew the smoke in my face. Then he offered it to me. Unlike Bill Clinton, I inhaled, and my lungs screamed in protest. I coughed wildly.

The Philosopher laughed. "I thought you said you'd done this before."

"Yeah. I think I might have lied about that," I choked out between coughs.

When the joint grew so short there was no place to hold it without getting burned, he snuffed it out, reached into the backpack, and pulled out another little baggy; this one contained a white powdery substance. I thought it might be cocaine. It wasn't. I later found out it was crystal meth, a much more potent substance than coke or pot. He then produced what appeared to be a malformed halogen lightbulb. It had a small hole in the top and the metal end was gone. He poured the powder into the opening, flicked a cigarette lighter and held it under the glass. The substance liquified and then took on a crystallized form. He put the hollow end of the bulb to his mouth and breathed in deeply.

Smoke escaped from the tiny hole. I watched the evanescent trail expand and fill the room.

When he finished, he offered the bizarre looking pipe to me. I repeated his actions. Immediately, dopamine raced through my body, relieving me of every inhibition that ever stifled me. My usually troubled mind floated on a tranquil river of inner-peace and self-assuredness.

The Philosopher stared lustily at me. Although my parents sheltered me from the ways of the world, I wasn't one of those naïve girls who confused sex with love. I knew he didn't love me, nor did I love him. But he was exactly what I needed at that moment—someone my parents and the church leaders wouldn't approve of. And I was exactly what he needed. I was there.

He pushed me back on the only pew that looked sturdy enough to hold both our bodies. It didn't hurt like it did when The Round Man molested me, probably because I knew what was happening this time and I was prepared. Or more likely, because I was so high, getting impaled on the pointed steeple outside wouldn't have hurt much.

WE FOUND an elderly couple living on a nearby farm, where the daffodils were as copious as sunflowers in Kansas. They told us they needed help with their household chores but said they couldn't afford to pay us. We both agreed to do it in exchange for a daily bath and a few sandwiches. I assisted the old lady, who smelled like horse liniment and looked like the matronly aunt from a wholesome family television show, with the vacuuming and laundry while The Philosopher helped her husband mow the lawn and mend fences.

The clothesline was a venerable opponent for an old woman with gnarled hands and a scrawny teenager with a rapidly developing drug habit. It took both of us to subdue one wayward sheet after it ensnared me in a suffocating embrace. The linen smelled like generic detergent and a little like cat piss, because only Tide gets that out and she couldn't buy laundry soap with food stamps. Afterwards, we went indoors and she offered me a glass of unsweet tea. She asked me if The Philosopher was my husband, and I told her I wasn't even sure what his name was. She smiled and winked knowingly, and then she told me a story about a boyfriend she had once that her daddy didn't like, but she kissed him anyway, at dusk, behind the barn. She recounted her act of sedition with such surreptitious glee, one might have thought she snuck off to Woodstock and knocked Roman sandals with a hundred hippies. I guess every woman celebrates freedom and autonomy in her own way.

Every day I listened as the old lady recapitulated her not-so wayward youth while we beat rugs on the sidewalk or drank lemonade on the front porch. Every night my Nietzschean lover spewed existentialist bullshit until my frontal lobes ached beneath the weight of self-awareness. Pulled into the watery abyss by the rubbery tentacles of an octopus, I drowned in the Sea of Introspection. We discussed the Greek philosophers, read the great transcendentalist writers like Emerson and Thoreau, and we even argued semantics with Des Cartes. (I hurt therefore I am.) He taught me about Nietzsche and Kierkegaard, Maslow and Rogers, and he explained the importance of an internal locus of control.

Once, I told him that the two of us being alone in that abandoned church, so far from civilization and eagerly learning about life, reminded me of Adam and Eve. We'd smoked up all his dope and read all his books, so there was nothing else to do after sex besides talk. He scoffed, "You still believe that old myth?"

I had that defensive, knee-jerk reaction religious people get when their beliefs are questioned, and they don't have a logical rebuttal. "It is not a myth," I protested but I wasn't sure why his words had offended me.

"It is absolutely a myth in that there is not one credible shred of historical or scientific evidence that supports it."

"Are you an atheist?" I wasn't going to be angry with him if he answered in the affirmative. I had never met an atheist before, at least not anyone who admitted it. I was curious, the same way I would be if I met my first Hindu or my first liberal.

He shrugged, "Do you believe only atheists question the validity of that ridiculous creation story?"

"What's so ridiculous about it? Is it the talking serpent?" I read somewhere that was the hardest part for people to swallow.

"Well, no. That's not really my problem with it. Practically every culture studied by anthropologists has some legend to explain the origins of life. Anthropomorphized animals abound in those creation stories, and one of them is about as strange as the next. Over the centuries, most of those myths have become rotting debris on the junk heap of history. Nobody takes them seriously anymore, but people cling to Adam and Eve like they were eyewitnesses to the Garden of Eden. I think the part I find ridiculous is the enormous price humanity, especially women, have had to pay for that fable."

"What do you mean?" I no longer felt defensive. I was truly interested in what he had to say.

"The centuries of subjugation women have endured, at least in Western culture, can be traced right back to the Hebrew creation myth. Eve brought sin into the world, and every woman since then has been accursed. That, to me, is utterly ridiculous."

He paused, and we sat in silence while I pondered everything I'd ever been taught or believed to be true.

"Aren't you going to defend your faith?" he prodded me. He wanted me to argue, but I had no argument to proffer. He made infinitely more sense than the preachers and Sunday School teachers.

He went on. "Seriously, I've seen women get screwed by the universe so many times, it gave them three little universes and an STD. Still, they just brace themselves for the next assault, because they think they're still being punished for Eve's alleged transgressions."

Even though he chose a rather crude way of expressing it, I never knew a man more sympathetic with the plight of women, and I wondered briefly if I might be falling in love with him. I was afraid he would challenge me further, and I certainly wasn't prepared to debate someone as educated and worldly as he was. Thankfully, he moved on. After another extended silence, he finally said, "You know what I think it's like here? I think it's like Plato's cave. It's like we've been chained up in here our whole lives. You see those shadows over there?" The battery operated lamp cast a ghastly glow over the dark wall. "Those shadows have been our only reality. When we ventured out and met those old people, we started realizing that was what was real. But we get scared of that reality, because it required something of us, so we come running back here every night, back to the shadows. Back to a world where reality happens around us, but we don't participate."

WE STAYED at the church another month. The nights started getting bitterly cold. With all the windows shattered, we had no way to protect ourselves from the elements. I knew my time with The Philosopher was coming to an end. I slept late one morning, because the old lady was going to visit her grandchildren. I heard him zip up his backpack and walk towards me. I closed my eyes tightly, unsure of how he might leave me. I never fully trusted him. I thought he might kiss me good-bye. Or slit my throat. He did neither. Instead, he whispered in my ear, "We're gonna make it, Des." A moment later, the motorcycle roared to life, and he was gone.

And my season of self-discovery and personal growth ended as abruptly as it began. For that one tiny blip on the spacetime continuum, I was free, unencumbered by the shackles of self-doubt and self-loathing. But just like the way his face faded from my memory, and just as surely as the narcotics worked their way out of my bloodstream, all that equanimity soon vanished from my schema.

He left me his copy of *Walden*, opened to a certain page, with a passage highlighted in neon yellow:

"…I had not lived. I did not wish to live what was not life, living is so dear; nor did I want to practice resignation, unless it became quite necessary. I wanted to live deep and suck all the marrow out of life…"

In the margin beside the selected text, he left a printed acronym, one I didn't recognize. FAFSA. He underlined the letters twice, and I didn't know if he meant it as a cryptic message to me, or if it was a mnemonic of some sort that he used himself.

There was a town a few miles back. I remembered passing through it on our way to the church, and the elderly couple sent us there a few times for supplies. The hamlet looked big enough for a bus station. I ran track in high school, so I felt confident I could walk the distance from the church to town, and I still had some money people had given me for graduation. Enough for a bus ticket back to Ashford. I bade farewell to Plato's cave and stepped into a frightening reality, one that demanded my full participation.

I couldn't return to my parents' home. Even though I was eighteen and legally an adult, I knew my father would beat me. And this time I thought I deserved it. I was no longer the falsely accused Desdemona. I was now the condemned and branded Hester Prynne.

My Aunt Lil always told me I was welcome at her house anytime. She fought for custody of me when I was younger, until she came home one day and found both of her beautiful Siberian Huskies dead in the driveway. Still, she often reiterated her invitation for me to stay with her when I reached legal age.

Aunt Lil never married and lived with a woman I called Aunt Sophie. The latter of the two was a gifted architect and they resided in a split-level ranch house she had designed for them. They answered the door together.

"Emily!" Aunt Lil burst out gleefully.

I asked her if the invitation still stood. She hugged me tightly and responded, "Oh, sweet girl! You don't even have to ask. You already know the answer."

Those first days with my aunts all ended with the same phony routine. We finished dinner, and each one of us selected a different book from their expansive private library. Then we would go into the cozy den and read for an hour, until they looked longingly at each other, said good night, and retired to separate quarters. Over the years, I'd had my fill of hypocritical charades, so I decided I would break through their façade. The next evening when the wistful gazing started, I blurted out, "I know you two love each other."

Deafening silence infiltrated the room. Aunt Lil cautiously raised an eyebrow. "How does that make you feel, Emily?" she asked hesitantly.

"My parents believe you go to hell for being gay," I explained. "But I believe hell will be so full of religious folks there won't be any room for all the atheists, liberals, and homosexuals."

They both sighed in relief and then erupted in glorious laughter. Then they exited the den arm in arm and disappeared into their room. For the first time in my life, I had a healthy example of what romantic love should look like.

MY AUNTS LIVED LESS than five miles from the old shack, but I never visited my parents. In fact, I avoided them at all costs. If I saw them at the supermarket, I quickly darted down another aisle. I stayed off the street where their church was located. That was the only other place in town I worried I might see them. I never worried about them showing up at Aunt Lil's, because she had a permanent restraining order against my father.

I got a job cleaning rooms at a shabby motel. My parents had refused to sign the waiver allowing me to take a sex education class in ninth grade, so I was completely ignorant of how human gestation worked. For six months, I spent a sizable percentage of my earnings on home pregnancy tests, and I took one every week. To this day, if they excavated a certain spot on my aunts' property, they would find the rusty corpses of two dozen negative E.P.T.s.

Soon, I became comfortable in my new life but still yearned for more. I remembered the acronym The Philosopher wrote in the book he gave me. The Internet had not yet woven its way into the fabric of Americana, so I couldn't simply google it. Aunt Lil had an exquisite set of leather-bound encyclopedias. I found the one labeled E-G and searched for the mysterious letters. There it was in bold type. FAFSA: Free Application for Federal Student Aid. I learned how poor kids like me could get grants and scholarships for college, money that never had to be paid back. Then I understood The Philosopher's cryptic message.

He was telling me that I had just as good a chance as anyone of finding and following my dreams. Somebody believed in me; somebody saw I had potential, and it altered the trajectory of my life.

DURING THE TIME I spent with her, Aunt Lil showered me with attention and lavish gifts, but the greatest gift she gave me was a sense of heritage. My parents never told me much about my ancestors. The past was too shameful for them to talk about, but my aunt recited family history as succinctly as a Hindu priest reciting from *The Vedas*. My favorite story was one about my great-grandmother, Ruth. It showed me the women in my family hadn't always been week, pathetic, and easily victimized.

Before the Bolsheviks revolted, Grandma Ruth obtained a contraband copy of *The Communist Manifesto* that she kept hidden under her bed along with a tin of pipe tobacco and a handful of suffragette posters. She spouted out Marxist ideology in that same cheery, sing-song voice other women used when planning a wedding or announcing a pregnancy. Then she heard about the slaughter of the Romanovs, and especially poor Anastasia. Sad and disillusioned that her noble cause had led to such carnage, she burned her subversive literature. Soon after, she got married and started having babies.

Aunt Lil also told me about my spiritual heritage. I was Pentecostal on my father's side and Baptist on my mother's. In the American heartland, we wore those labels as though church affiliation was indelibly written in the genetic code, like hair color, or the chance of getting breast cancer. As though the odds of being Methodist or Lutheran could be calculated on a Punnett square. My mother identified everyone by his or her religious preference. "That Catholic lady who works at Piggly Wiggly" or "that nice Jehovah's Witness family down the road." Now I realized no matter what tag they wore, they were all still bound to a myth, a ridiculous myth that made them ashamed of their own humanity.

THERE WAS one more scar I hadn't explored, and I didn't want to touch it, because I knew what it would reveal. I dropped my hand away from Lola's face, but she picked it up and placed my fingertips on the deepest wound. The ugliest scar led me back to the darkest place in my life's journey, a place where I discovered the depravity of my own soul, the night my father died.

It was the week of my mother's birthday, and I made chocolate mousse, her favorite dessert. I hadn't been back to the old shack since I graduated high school, but I mustered the courage to deliver the treat in person. My father's stroke had paralyzed his left side and reduced his speech to a few guttural grunts and groans. I arranged for his admission into a nursing home, but Janice and the church hierarchy thought that was too cruel a fate for such a good man, so they shamed my mother into keeping him at home. Other than a hospice nurse who visited twice a week, she provided all her husband's care.

When I arrived at my childhood home, the door was open, and I let myself in. Instantly, a putrid stench knocked me back a few steps. I found my mother cleaning dried excrement off the old man's half-naked body. *Oh, Mama,* I cried silently. *What have they done to you?*

She looked embarrassed when she saw me, but she pasted on that crazy crescent-moon smile, the one that made me want to rip her head off but also made me want to hold her in my arms and weep with her.

I left her alone to finish cleaning up while I shoved the dessert in the refrigerator. Then we went outside and sat on the wooden swing. After I was properly chastised for not visiting more often, Mama told me her church was holding a revival the next evening and she would like to go, but there was no one to stay with my father.

"Can't you leave him by himself for a couple of hours?" I suggested, digging my heels into the ground to slow the motion of the swing.

"He's like a baby, Emily. If I leave him alone, anything could happen. The last time I left him alone just long enough to walk to the end of the road and check the mail he tried to get himself out of bed and ended up on the floor with three broken toes."

"Why can't Janice stay with him?"

"She's going to the revival."

"Of course she is," I snapped bitterly. "What about the hospice nurse?" I was growing more desperate, knowing where the conversation was headed.

"She doesn't work evenings."

"Okay, Mama," I relented before she even asked the question. "Just promise me it'll only be for two hours."

I hadn't touched illicit drugs since my summer with The Philosopher, but I remembered how they eased my anxiety and soothed my troubled mind. I needed something to get me through an evening alone with that crazy old bastard. I worked with some kids whose step-father was a known drug dealer. As an enticement, I waved a wad of twenties in his face, but he said he wasn't interested in my money. In exchange for a dime bag of marijuana and a few puffs on a meth pipe, I gave him what he *was* interested in.

When I returned to the converted barn, Janice and Mama were already gone. Slowly, deliberately, I forced my way to the psychopath's bedside.

"Jannie," he called me by my sister's nickname. It was the first coherent word I heard him utter since the stroke. Janice and I were close enough in age, appearance, and physical stature that, in his discombobulated state of mind, our father easily confused us. "Jannie," he said again and reached for my chest.

Repulsed by the incestuous gesture, I slapped his hand away and hurled myself against the wall, sickened by a disturbing truth I had overlooked my whole life. I despised Janice, but I also envied her. She shared a bond with our dad that I never experienced. He spent time with her and bought her things that he never did for me. He took her places I never got to go. Now I realized the special attention he showed her was no different than the affection The Round Man showered on me. In social work, we called it "grooming."

Realizing he'd groped the wrong daughter, the sick man cackled menacingly, mocking my repulsion.

My heart went ice cold, turning my veins to bloody popsicles. "Die," I ordered callously, and he grunted incoherently. "Die," I repeated, and he doubled his good fist and flung it at me, but I remained plastered against the wall, safely out of his reach.

"I can kill you," I told him as he writhed angrily in his bed. "I can kill you right here and right now, and nobody will ever know. I will use your own rage as a weapon against you, just like you used my innocent childlike faith to control me."

The more I spoke, the louder he grunted and groaned, and the more he flailed his fist at me. "Die, you sick fuck," I commanded.

"Aaaaaaahhhhh!" he responded furiously, wildly flinging his arm in my direction.

"Die, you heartless coward. Die, you useless piece of shit. Die and let my mother have some peace. Die and let us all have some peace."

I vomited out raw human emotion like a dry-heaving drunk, and my father responded with the only emotion he was capable of—unmitigated fury. He flopped around, trying to throw himself out of bed. He looked like a cockroach trapped on its back, drowning in pesticide and trying desperately to right itself before dying. I continued my macabre monologue until it reached a crescendo pitch of a single repeated word. "Die! Die! Die! Die! Die! Die! Die!"

Officially, they listed his cause of death as a brain aneurysm. Only I knew I murdered him. I never brandished a weapon and I never got closer than five-feet away from him, but I killed him as surely as if I had suffocated him with his own saliva stained pillow. I killed him with the sheer force of my will, and I never lost one minute of sleep because of it.

CHAPTER 21

I finished navigating Lola's face. The loud crying dropped a few octaves, and I assumed the medicine was working. Now that I had revisited my own horrific scars, I thought I understood the cause of her profound grief. "Are you ashamed of your wounds?" I asked empathetically.

She shook her head no.

"Then why are you so sad?"

She touched my forehead with the mangled finger. I closed my eyes and sensed the letters she formed on my skin. N-O-L-O-V-E. No love. I understood exactly how she felt. Except for the brief time I'd had with Andi, and then Connie, I never truly felt loved. My aunts were good to me, but they didn't really love me. They loved what I represented to them—a daughter. A daughter society and biology prevented them from having. By the time my summer with The Philosopher ended, I was confused about my feelings for him; I thought that might have been love, but I was sure he never loved me. Otherwise, he wouldn't have left me alone in that abandoned church, not knowing if I would ever make it back to civilization.

I thought love was one of the most overused words in the English language. We used the same word to express affection for our children that we used when describing our affinity for tacos. The ancient Greeks had multiple words to express all the varied forms of love. Suddenly, I had an idea. The therapist had given me a notebook and told me to keep a journal of my thoughts and feelings. I grabbed the notebook off the nightstand and fished a pen out of my purse.

"Lola, have you ever heard of Abraham Maslow?" I asked her excitedly. She nodded.

"Then you know about Maslow's hierarchy of needs?" Another nod. "Well, what if there is a hierarchy of love needs, and until you have your base love needs met, you can't possibly hope to reach the higher levels of love?"

She looked confused.

"Let me show you," I offered. I drew a triangle on a sheet of notebook paper and made five parallel lines going through it. On the bottom space, I wrote, *storge* (parent/child bond). Above that, I put *philia* (affection between friends). Next came *philautia* (self-love, not to be confused with selfishness). The penultimate stage of love was *eros*, or romantic love. The highest rung on the pyramid belonged to *agape*, or the pure, unconditional, unmerited love of God. This love is extended to everybody, and everybody experiences it in his or her own way. To some people, it is merely inner-peace. To others, it is a sense of spiritual fulfillment, or an intellectual awakening, or maybe a feeling of connectedness with the universe around them. Many Western philosophers called this state transcendence. Some theologians called it grace. Like Maslow's concept of self-actualization, few people ever walk in true agape, because their more basic love needs are not adequately met.

I examined the pyramid I'd drawn. I had not known *storge* love as a child, but I did experience it with Andi. Even though she had another mother she would have chosen over me if we had forced her to choose, I knew the bond I shared with her was what maternal love felt like. I had true friends, or *philia*, in elementary school, mostly boys. When we got older and they became interested in things besides football and Tonka trucks, and I became interested in art and literature, I ended those friendships and spent most of my high school years in the library, pretending I didn't need anybody.

As an adult, I wasn't a recluse. I socialized, mostly with co-workers and former college classmates. One doesn't get a master's degree in social work without understanding the importance of inter-personal relationships. Still, until I moved into Connie's house, there was no one I considered a best friend.

"I'm probably boring you with this nonsense," I said to Lola, and she shook her head, her crying now just a whimper. I looked at her, and I thought we must have had the same hairstylist, because her color was exactly the same as mine, even the caramel highlights.

"I love you, Lola," I declared, and she smiled a little through the pain. Then I did the most impulsive thing I'd done since I cursed at Sister Marcy and the preacher. I kissed the grieving woman. I ran my tongue along the folds and creases of her hideously beautiful scars. I drank her salty tears, and I tasted the healing balm. When I reached her mouth, her lips parted, and I deposited the ointment inside her.

Exhausted, I collapsed on the bed beside her and soon fell asleep. When I awoke, Sunnyvale was eerily silent, and Lola was gone.

My seventy-two hours expired. The therapist, who spent as much time with me as a billionaire playboy spends with his illegitimate prog-eny, deemed me no more suicidal than anyone else who endured what I'd been through. She signed my release papers under the condition that I continued taking the medication and seek further counseling. I called Trey to come get me. While I waited for him, I roamed the halls, peeking around corners and through opened doors.

"What are you looking for?" A grumpy nurse demanded from behind the nurse's station.

"I'm looking for my friend, Lola," I replied, taken a little aback by the nurse's gruff demeanor.

"There's nobody here by that name."

"Sure there is. She's the woman with all the scars."

"Hmmm…nope. Nobody like that here."

"She has been with me this entire time."

"Still don't know who you're talking about."

Somebody takes HIPAA a little too seriously, I thought as I resumed my search. Most of the doors were closed and I didn't dare breech the other patients' privacy by looking into their rooms. I kept wandering aimlessly down the sea green-tiled hallways, stopping to look at the still life paintings on the sterile white walls.

I felt a hand on my shoulder, and I heard Trey's voice. "Are you ready to go?"

"In a minute. I have to find Lola. I have to say good-bye."

"Who's Lola? Your therapist?"

"No. She's the woman who was on the news a few years ago. Her boyfriend poured gasoline on her and tried to burn her alive."

"That happened here? In Ashford? In recent years?" Trey sounded concern.

"Yes," I insisted.

"Emily, I have been a cop in this town for the better part of two decades. During that time, I have worked every violent crime that's been committed here. Nothing like that ever happened. I would remember."

Lola was my friend, my confidant, my healer. Had I imagined her? Had she really never existed? Following a severe trauma, in its gallant effort to regain homeostasis, the human mind often uses tricky and deceptive maneuvering. Lola, I reasoned, materialized from my brain's determination to heal itself and restore balance to my life. I never mentioned her name again. Sunnyvale wasn't as terrible as I imagined, but I had no desire to take up permanent residency.

Whether she was real or not, Lola rescued me. She saved me in a way no minister or psychologist ever could. Thanks to her, I wanted to live. I was ready to love.

PART IV
EROS

"…he who abides in love abides in God, and God in him…"— 1 John
4:16

CHAPTER 22

I climbed into the passenger seat of Trey's pickup. Feeling his presence an arm's length away from me, I remembered the awkwardness of being alone with him in his house. "I'm not ready to go home. I've been cooped up in that place for three days. Can we just stay out for a while?"

"Tell you what," he offered. "We're close to the lake. Why don't I take you and show you this great place where I used to take Andi fishing?"

"Andi fishing?" I smiled at the thought of the precocious little girl baiting a hook or handling a slimy, squirmy fish.

"Well," he corrected himself. "I fished. She sat there, telling me exactly where to stand and at what angle to cast the line for optimum fish catching potential."

"That sounds more like Andi."

I heard a sound I hadn't heard for a while. The sound of my own laughter reverberated in my ears. When we arrived at the lake, a battalion of oaks and pines greeted us with leafy waves. We got out of the vehicle and a sudden wind rushed across the Texas plain. Nature's symphony serenaded us. The treetops swayed rhythmically, and the waves pounded out the percussion while a flock of geese screeched out the discordant melody.

Trey climbed upon the hood of the truck and hoisted me up beside him. Then he laid back and stretched one sinewy arm across the length of the pickup. I rested my head on the rock-solid pectoral muscle. It was the first time I had actually laid beside him. I was astonished by the perfect symmetry of our bodies. It was like finding the missing piece of a jigsaw puzzle, not the one that completed the picture, but the one I needed to find, so the rest of the pieces would fit in place.

"Trey, do you think I'm crazy now?" I asked. For some reason, his opinion now seemed like the most important thing in the world to me.

"I could ask you the same thing. Do you think I'm crazy?"

"Of course not. You are probably the sanest person I know."

"Would you still feel that way if I told you I killed a man when I was twelve-years old?"

For a minute, I thought he must be joking. By this point, I'd so idealized Trey, I couldn't imagine him ever being violent, despite his chosen profession.

"It must have been some freak accident."

"Only if you call shooting somebody in the head at point blank range a freak accident."

Every muscle in my body stiffened, unsure of what he was confessing. He continued, "My daddy died when I was real young. There my mama was with a growing boy and a fifteen-hundred-acre ranch to take care of. She got scared and married the first guy who asked her, who just happened to be one of the meanest drunks in North Texas. He started laying down the law right away, telling me how he was the boss now, and I better listen to him. At first I just ignored him and did what I wanted, and took my ass whipping when he caught me. Then he started beating on my mama.

"It all came to a boil when I walked in and found him pounding her head against the refrigerator. I had this cousin who was getting married, and Mama had bought a new dress for the occasion. My step-father was irate about her spending his hard-earned money on something so frivolous. Every dime of money that came into that house came from me and Mama working my daddy's land. Mama's head was bleeding and she was crying. I tried to make him stop but he just pushed me away like I was nothing, like I didn't matter. When I woke up the next morning, he was sleeping on the couch. Back in those days, no self-respecting Texas boy would be caught dead without his own shotgun, and my daddy made sure I had mine before he died. I got it out of my closet and walked right up to that asshole. I nudged him in the side with the butt of the gun. I wanted him to see what I was doing. I wanted him to know it was me who killed him. He opened his eyes and reached for my gun. He didn't even make it to the end of the barrel."

"Oh my God!" I gasped. I was shocked, but not by Trey's act of violence. It was the horror that he had endured that evoked my response. "What happened? Were you convicted?"

"I only wish I had been. My mama came into the room just as I was pulling the trigger. She told me keep my mouth shut and let her handle it. I still remember her meticulously wiping my prints off the rifle and replacing them with her own. She even took the weapon out in the woods and fired it, in case they checked for residue. I don't even know how she knew to do that."

"So, what happened to your mother?" My heart ached for this man I now thought I might love.

"That was in the days before anybody knew much about battered-woman syndrome, or before anyone cared. Mama did fifteen years in prison for a crime I committed. At first, I was so scared I just did what she told me and kept my mouth shut. I was sent to live with relatives and she pled guilty so there wouldn't be a trial. After that, I went down to the police station every week and tried to tell them what really happened. Nobody would listen to me. That's how I became a cop; I spent so much time trying to get arrested I started looking up to some of those guys. Especially Ron Tyler. He was just a street cop then, like I am now. He took me to the side after I made my hundredth confession, and he said, 'Look, son. This is how she wants it. We've tried to get her to tell the truth. If you really want to honor her sacrifice, then make something of yourself. Do something good with your life.' That's when I knew I wanted to be a cop."

"You shouldn't feel guilty," I told him, knowing the weight he must have carried all these years. "You protected your mother, and then she protected you."

He sighed, "No, Emily, as much as I'd like to convince myself I was protecting my mother, it's just not true. I killed my step-father because I hated that son of a bitch."

He looked at me and saw the tears welling in my eyes. He gently brushed them away with his thumbs, and said, "Just a friendly reminder we're all a little screwed up."

At that moment, we passed the Rubicon. I'd heard his human story. Everybody has a story like that, a woeful tale they're a little ashamed of but probably shouldn't be. It's that excerpt everybody wants deleted from his biography, but without it, the book wouldn't be worth reading. It's that part of a person's life that makes him a little less perfect, a little less godlike, and far more human. It's impossible to truly know somebody until you've heard his human story, and until you know him, you can't possibly love him. I reciprocated Trey's transparency by telling him my own human story about how I ostensibly murdered my own father. And there we were, just two wounded people, bonding over patricide.

Never one to focus on the past too long, Trey changed the subject to my present state of mind. "Emily, are you okay? I mean, really okay? I know you were struggling. You've suffered some tremendous losses lately, not to mention a violent assault, but I had no idea it was so bad you wanted to die. I'm sorry I didn't see that."

"I never really wanted to die," I admitted. "I just…," I hesitated, searching for the right words, and then I borrowed the line from *Walden*. "…I did not wish to live what is not life…."

"Ah, yes. Good old Henry David Thoreau." It amazed me how easily he identified the quote.

"You've read *Walden*?" I instantly regretted the surprised tone in my voice.

"I am literate, you know?" He laughed softly, and I didn't know if

I'd hurt his feelings. I was relieved when he kept talking to me. "So, I guess if you do not wish to live what is *not* life, then you first must determine what *is* life? Have you come to any conclusions about that?"

"Well," I explained, staring up at a huge rabbit-shaped cloud that drifted across the darkening sky. "Thoreau thought life meant shunning modern conveniences and immersing himself in nature and simplicity. I think it is something even more basic and primal than that. I think it's love."

"I think you're right," he concurred, and I thought I felt him pull me a little closer.

That sparked a question I'd been afraid to ask, but now I desperately needed to know the answer. "Trey," I started. "Do you still love Sarah?"

"I don't think I have that switch."

"What an odd answer to a straightforward question." I thought he might be evading the uncomfortable topic.

"I mean, I don't have that switch other people seem to have where they can turn love on and off. Once I love you, it's forever. So, the answer to your question is, yes, I still love Sarah, but not the way you mean. It's changed. It's not as intense as it was back when we had Andi. It's more of a friendship now. It's certainly not the same way I love you."

He was so comfortable with the word I don't think he even realized he said it, but my heart heard it. And it rejoiced. It wasn't the first time a man told me he loved me, but it was the first time I accepted it without question.

"It's getting dark, and you're shivering," he observed. "Ready to go home now?"

Lighting streaked across the sky as we dove into his pickup and started home. When we got there, I allowed him to do something I never let a man do before. I let him love me, wholly and completely. And I loved him in return, unreservedly and unapologetically.

When he reached for me in the doorway of his bedroom, the first thing I noticed was his hands. So clean. Neatly trimmed nails and perfectly white cuticles sharply contrasted from the last men's hands that had touched me. Those hands, permanently stained with grease and filth, had dirty, crooked nails and unkempt cuticles. The spotless hands were only a symbol of how different this moment was from the rape. Everything was different. This was love. That was violence. This was my choice. That was my choice being taken from me. I willfully forced the painful memory out of my mind. My attackers had stolen all I would allow them to steal from me. I would not allow them to steal this moment. They would not steal my ability to love.

I undressed, slowly and methodically, and stood naked in front of Trey, every fault, flaw, and shortcoming exposed. I trembled in fear of his rejection, but he was not repulsed. Nor was he overwhelmed with lust. The only thing I saw in his eyes was pure, unadulterated, perfect love. He held his hand in the air, and I placed my palm in his. We intertwined our fingers, and he led me to the bed. With each jagged exhalation, he breathed life into my being. With each urgent touch of the calloused hands, he baptized me in fire. With each gentle, lingering kiss, he cleansed the farthest reaches of my soul. That first melding together of our bodies was not a union borne merely of physical desire, but one consecrated by spiritual destiny.

It saddened me thinking how much time I wasted, suffering alone, when I could have been comforted in his strong arms. I rested my head on his solid chest and the prickly hairs tickled my face.

"How long have you been waiting for me to turn to you?" I asked meekly.

"For all eternity," he breathed.

There in the dark, a full two hours after he said it first, my lips finally uttered what my heart had been saying for months. "I love you, Trey."

CHAPTER 23

*N*ow that we were officially a couple, Trey said we could squeak by on his income if I still wasn't ready to return to work, but I was more than ready. I needed to feel productive. I craved meaningful work the way an emphysema patient craves oxygen. Besides, I knew supporting another person meant Trey working more double shifts, and I selfishly wanted him with me as much as possible.

The rape crisis center where I had attended counseling had expanded and was now known as the North Texas Women's Crisis Recovery Network. In addition to rape survivors, they now provided services for women struggling through everything from job loss and unemployment to drug addiction, divorce, and domestic violence. I signed on as a counselor.

I still had a few days to kill while the agency performed a background check and ensured my professional credentials were up to date. Furthermore, because of my recent stay at Sunnyvale, they insisted I go through a battery of psychological testing with one of their therapists to determine my fitness for the job.

While Trey worked, I still struggled finding ways of keeping my mind occupied. I'd never seen Andi's gravesite. I was in the hospital when they buried her, and until now, I hadn't been strong enough to make the visit. So I stopped by a little florist shop and purchased a bouquet of lilies—her favorite. Then I drove to the cemetery. It wasn't hard locating her resting place. Trey sat on the ground, his head in his hands. I knelt beside him and put my arm around him.

Without looking up, he started explaining, "I spend my lunch hour with her every Wednesday."

"It's beautiful here," I remarked. "So serene."

Andi rested beneath a giant magnolia tree; a chip-winged cherub guarded the sacred spot.

"Sarah chose this exact location, because when the tree blooms in the spring, it makes a fluffy canopy, like a shade for a comfortable bed." He turned his head. I knew he didn't want me to see his tears, and I respected that, so I looked away.

I gazed up at the cloudless azure sky. I thought about the image I'd had of heaven when I contemplated suicide. "Where do you think she is?" I pondered.

"What do you mean?"

"I mean, do you believe there is a heaven? Do you believe in God?"

"Unequivocally. Yes, I believe in God. I just don't buy into this petty tyrant God some people like to push down our throats. This so-called loving and merciful God who condemns us to eternal damnation for the flaws and imperfections he allowed us to have."

"What about heaven? Do you believe in heaven?"

This time he hesitated before he responded, "Yeah, I guess I do. It may just be because I need to believe it, but yes, I believe she's still out there somewhere. Happy and at peace. Andi used to know this neat poem. Something about I've never seen the ocean. I've never seen heaven…"

I interrupted him and recited her favorite poem by her favorite poet.

"I never saw the moor.

I never saw the sea.

Yet know I how the heather looks

And what a wave must be.

I never spoke with God
Nor visited in heaven
Yet certain am I of that spot
As if the course were given."

Trey stared wistfully at the little cherub that had taken his place as Andi's protector. "I guess that sums up how I feel about heaven. I know it's out there somewhere." Then he asked me, "What about you, Emily? Do you believe in God and heaven?"

Other than when I held his gun to my head, I hadn't really given it much thought since my summer with The Philosopher, but now I realized I still believed. Not in the vengeful, angry God of my father, but in a God of love, grace, and mercy. I was a little astonished that my faith was still intact. Many people who grow up with religious abuse ultimately stop believing.

"I want to believe," I finally told Trey. "I just don't understand. If there is a God, then why did He drop us out on this planet? Why didn't He just keep us with Him, wherever He is, and protect us from all the cruelty and nastiness of this world?"

"Here's how I see it," Trey began. "Life is sort of like being a cop. It's eighty percent mundane and routine. Ten percent trauma and tragedy, but then you get these incredible moments. Moments that make the drudgery and the heartache seem meaningless. Like when a kid asks to feel my badge, or when a woman thanks me for saving her life. Like the first time Andi told me she loved me." He laughed softly at the memory.

"Tell me about that," I prodded, knowing it would be therapeutic for him to talk about her.

"By the time you met us, we'd already warmed up to each other, but it hadn't always been that way. Andi was about five the first time she came to stay with me. Sarah was on an extended honeymoon with the piano man. We'd been divorced for almost two years, and I'd only seen my daughter a handful of times since she and Sarah moved off to Boston. So when my little girl came to stay with me, she was mad as hell, and I was scared to death. At first, she wouldn't speak to me at all. She missed her friends, and she missed her mom. I tried everything to make her happy, but she said the only thing that would make her happy was if I bought her a pig. She said kids in Texas always had farm animals, and she wanted a cute, squealy pig. It's hard to outsmart a kid who's smarter than you, but I did. I told her we were going to the animal shelter to buy her a little piglet, knowing full well they wouldn't have one. It worked like a charm. She fell in love with the first dog she saw, and when I told her she could have him, she threw her tiny arms around me and screamed, 'I love you, Daddy!' My heart melted like butter in a hot pan. That's how I came to be the proud owner of an eight-pound rat terrier named Pig."

"That's a sweet memory."

"You see what I mean, Em? Even if that first 'I love you, Daddy' was the only good thing I had to hold onto of my daughter, and even knowing how it would end, I would do the whole nine years all over again just for that one fleeting moment. We have to cling to those happy memories. When life seems unbearable, we have to focus on things that are good and true and pure and wonderful. I think that's why God put us on this earth, so we could have those experiences. Maybe everything is so good in heaven, we wouldn't know how to appreciate little moments like that."

I had a feeling this conversation with Trey would become one of those things I would focus on whenever life seemed unbearable. With every passing second, I loved him more deeply. I cherished everything about the man—his bright smile, his warm laughter, his strong charac-ter, and his devotion to those he loved. I understood enough about neurotransmitters and the chemical processes of human emotions that I knew a time would come when his touch would no longer set my body and soul on fire, and that irresistible jackass grin wouldn't turn my brain to silly-putty. When that day came, it would be our long, intimate talks like this one that would sustain us. So, I cherished the sound of his voice most of all.

That night I started packing my things and moving them from Andi's room and into Trey's. He followed behind me, doing the heavy lifting. I stared at the brightly painted walls and the volumes of her beloved books, everything that made Andi who she was.

"Honey," I don't think I'd ever used that term of endearment before. "I don't want this room to always be a shrine to her. I don't think she'd want that."

He grinned teasingly. "I hoped someday we might convert it into a nursery."

His seemingly innocuous teasing triggered another dreaded but necessary conversation, like when I asked if he still loved Sarah. I was almost forty by the time my heart healed enough to let him in. Besides, with my family's history of gynecological cancers, my doctors were pushing for a full hysterectomy. Biological children seemed like a longshot.

"I don't know if I can," I murmured sadly. I don't know why I hadn't considered that Trey would want more kids. It would be unfair of me not to tell him the odds were against me ever conceiving. He deserved the right to find a younger, healthier partner who could give him the sacred gift of another baby.

"Can what?"

"Have children."

"Who says we have to have them? You and I have both been out in the real world enough to know there are plenty of kids who need us as much as we want them."

"I always thought about adopting," I confessed. Then I kissed him gingerly. "Let's talk about it later." For now, I was perfectly content having him all to myself.

I left Eve/Rose hanging on the wall in Andi's room. I still had access to her, but I didn't want Trey worried about my odd obsession with a painting, an obsession I couldn't explain.

CHAPTER 24

*B*efore Trey, I never dated a man long enough or seriously enough that it warranted an introduction to his mother, so I was nervous when we pulled up in front of a townhouse in a middle-class Fort Worth suburb. They had lost their ranch when she was incarcerated, but Trey said she'd adjusted well to city life. I was surprised he had his own key, and we let ourselves in.

Easels, canvases, and sundry other art supplies littered the living room. In the middle of all that beautiful chaos stood the older woman I'd seen at Luke's preliminary hearing. She wore a loose gray smock covered in paint splotches. Prison hadn't hardened her or changed her pleasant demeanor. She had her son's infectious smile and piercing blue eyes. Her face radiated with sheer love when she saw Trey. She dropped the paintbrush she was holding, and it left a bright red stain on the white carpet.

"My boy!" she squealed delightedly, and they embraced. I'd never seen a purer bond. It wasn't the unhealthy co-dependence some men have with their mothers. It was the kind of unity that could only be borne of sacrificial love. Suddenly, I understood why eros was so much easier for him than me. He'd experienced *storge*, both as a son and as a parent.

Trey took my hand and beamed proudly. He started with me. "Emily, I'd like you to meet my mother, Ms. Grace Scoggins." Then he turned to her. "Mama, I'd like you to meet my..." he searched for the right words. We were at that stage in our relationship when the juvenile terminology of "boyfriend/girlfriend" trivialized the intensity of our feelings, but "lover" was too crude, and "fiancé" too presumptuous. He finally found just the right words. "Well, Mama, this is my Emily." He laughed a little nervously.

"Well, now! How are ya, Trey's Emily?" She hugged me as warmly as if she had known me forever, and I had the strangest feeling she really had.

"It's nice to meet you, Mrs. Scoggins," I said when she released me.

"It's Grace," she corrected. "Just Grace."

I nodded my compliance. With the introductions completed, I walked around the living room admiring her exquisite artwork, dozens of portraits showing people engaged in various activities. Some picked fruit off trees, some star gazed at night, others danced in formalwear. All of them had the same rapturous expression on their faces, like they were doing the thing they enjoyed most in life.

"Grace, you have an amazing talent," I gushed, remembering the exhibit Andi and I attended. No wonder Andi loved art. Her mother had taken her to the finest museums and her grandmother was a talented artist.

"Not really. I just love to create. I think I was born to create," she explained modestly. Then she quickly changed the subject. "Mercy me!" she exclaimed. "Where are my manners? I haven't offered you two a thing to drink, and here it is almost noon. I better start cooking."

"No," I protested. "Let me cook. I love cooking. You stay in here and visit with your son."

"Well now, missy, if that's how you want it, you won't hear me complaining. Never was much of a cook myself. I prefer doing my creating on the canvas, not on the stove."

Grace's kitchen was in disarray, and I struggled to find cooking utensils and pots and pans. I eventually whipped up a decent broccoli and rice casserole that they both raved about. We visited until sunset, then I reminded Trey we had a long ride ahead of us. I'd finally gone back to work, and we both had early shifts the next day. We said our good-byes and headed for home.

"She's getting evicted," Trey told me when we were about a mile from her house.

"What? Why?" Judging from her cheerfulness, I wouldn't have thought the woman had a care in the world.

"When she first got out of prison, she couldn't get a job because of her criminal record. I used to send her money to help out, but after Andi came along, it just wasn't feasible. For a while she was able to sell enough of her artwork to get by, but that hasn't been going so well lately. Now her age is also working against her. She doesn't get much Social Security because she was unemployed all those years. She let herself get three months behind on rent before she even mentioned it to me."

"That settles it, then. She will just come live with us. We can decorate Andi's room however she likes."

"Of course, that's exactly what I told her, but she knows how small my house is. She's afraid there won't be room for all her art supplies. She's still hoping for a miracle. Right now, they're giving her ninety days to get out."

"Hoping for a miracle," I repeated. "I used to believe in those."

"Not anymore?"

"I think we make our own miracles by making good choices and working hard to achieve our goals."

He stretched his arm across the back of the seat and rested his hand on my shoulder. I felt that electric sensation that only his touch could trigger in me. "Whatever you do, don't tell my mother you don't believe in miracles, because she swears you are one. She thinks you're the answer to her prayers for me, and I can't say I disagree with her."

I basked in a feeling of warmth and acceptance, content in the knowledge that I'd won her approval.

LUKE'S TRIAL began in early summer, almost a full year after he took Andi from us. Sarah flew down for the legal proceedings. With Andi gone, she'd decided against moving back to Texas. When she discovered I now lived with Trey, she opted for a hotel room. Grace said she would wait until the sentencing phase. She was already working on her victim impact statement, but I wasn't nearly so optimistic. I only hoped there would be a sentencing phase.

I felt confident I'd be able to testify. Psychologically speaking, I was much healthier now than I had been at the preliminary hearing. I was still in therapy, but my therapist was weaning me off the meds. Love strengthened me and gave me more courage than I had ever known.

Trey, Sarah, and I rode to the courthouse together. We got there before the prosecutor. I took my place in the front of the room, determinedly focusing my gaze on my burgundy pumps. The defense team arrived. I heard them whispering loudly as they situated themselves across the aisle from me, but I refused to look up. The bailiff checked his watch and prepared to call court to order. Karen Tobias still wasn't there, and I grew a little panicky. Finally, she breezed in like a category one hurricane, folders and papers teetering in her arms.

"Brace yourself for a huge surprise," she whispered in my ear as the court officer commanded us to rise.

When the judge gave Karen permission to call her first witness, she stood, straightened her skirt, and cleared her throat dramatically.

"The state calls Rose Detwiler."

She could have called John F. Kennedy to the stand, and I wouldn't have been more stunned. I tugged at her arm. "What are you doing?" I screeched.

"We're about to blow his alibi wide open," she assured me.

Rose took her oath, the very one she had broken before, and Karen began the questioning.

"Ms. Detwiler, do you know what perjury is?"

"Yes, ma'am. I know what it is."

"Can you explain it to me?"

"It's when you lie after you already swore you'd tell the truth."

"And Ms. Detwiler, are you aware that it is a crime to commit perjury in a court of law?"

"Yes, ma'am. I know that."

Rose squirmed uncomfortably, and I felt a little sorry for her. She looked like a scared kid called into the principal's office for blowing spitballs at the teacher. Then Karen asked, "Ms. Detwiler, have you ever committed perjury?"

"Yes ma'am. I have."

"Can you tell me when that happened and the circumstances involved?"

"It was at Luke's hearing. I said he was with me the night that little girl got killed, but that was not true."

The prosecutor paused for dramatic effect, letting the jury reflect on Rose's confession. Then she went on. "So are you saying that the defendant, Luke Detwiler, *was not* with you at a motel in Oklahoma City on the night of July 10?"

"Yes, ma'am. That's what I'm saying. That was a Saturday. He was with me that Friday, and he was with me that Sunday, but he was gone all day Saturday, and all night. I don't know where he was, but he wasn't with me."

Karen reminded the jury that it was only a two-hour drive from Ashford to Oklahoma City. That meant the defendant had ample time to make the drive, commit the murder, and make it back to the motel early the next morning. In fact, he could have committed several more crimes within the timespan his whereabouts were unaccounted for.

The defense attorney cross-examined Rose, but she remained composed and insisted she was telling the truth this time. She only lied before, she explained, because she was still afraid of her husband, but now she realized justice for a murdered child was more important than anything he might do to her. I breathed a sigh of relief when the judge dismissed her from the stand. As she walked past me, she mouthed the words, "I'm sorry,"

Following Rose's testimony, the judge ordered a short recess. "How did you know she was going to change her story?" I demanded of Karen as she wrangled her stacks of paperwork.

"She called me a few days ago, out of the blue. She was bawling like a baby and said she wanted to tell the truth."

I watched the poor battered woman shrink fearfully past her shackled husband. He snarled at her like a rabid dog, but she kept going. Of all the complex personality types I'd ever encountered, Rose Detwiler was the most enigmatic person ever.

KAREN and I ate at the same café as before. With my blessing, Trey took Sarah to visit their daughter's grave. While we waited for our food, the attorney asked me, "How are you feeling?"

"I think I'm okay. I've come a long way these last few months." The waitress delivered our meals. I poked disappointedly at the thin BLT on my plate and I smothered my onion rings with ketchup.

"But will you be able to testify? Thanks to Rose's testimony, we now know where Luke wasn't that night, but we need you to say where he was. The defense attorney is going to put Tony Detwiler on the stand, and he's going to say he and Leonard Horton acted alone, and Horton committed the murder. Now the man you call Mangy Dog is a sniveling, cowardly cretin. If brains were bread crumbs, he wouldn't have enough to keep a single piss ant from starving. I will poke holes all through his story and have him begging for mercy in two seconds flat, but he's not going to roll over on his brother. He's too scared. Your testimony is still the only significant thing we have that links Luke to the crime. I ask you again, Emily, will you be able to testify?"

I answered as honestly as I could, "I hope so." The ravishing hunger pains I had felt gave way to rising anxiety and I pushed my food aside.

COURT RECONVENED, and as she predicted, Karen mentally slaughtered Tony Detwiler. By the time she finished her cross-examination, it was impossible to tell whose side benefitted most from his testimony. Then it was my turn. As I walked past the defendant on my way to the witness stand, I felt a foot lightly tap my ankle. Instinctively, I looked in the direction of the offending appendage, and I saw the empty soulless eyes. The Beast grinned demonically and whispered hoarsely, "Boo." I felt it this time. I felt my voice leaving my body as surely as if my larynx had been surgically removed. I looked back at Karen, and sadly shook my head.

The prosecutor successfully argued for a continuance based on my "ongoing health crisis." I refused to let Trey comfort me. I failed him. I failed Andi. And I felt as if I failed the entire human race.

CHAPTER 25

rey had his weekly lunch date with Andi, and I soon found my own way of honoring her. Each week, I'd buy a fresh bouquet of flowers and take them to her grave. I'd carefully place them beside the cherub, and then I'd sit on the soft grass and read poetry to her. Shortly after the latest courtroom fiasco, I drove out to the cemetery and parked about a hundred feet from the giant magnolia. Someone knelt in front of the little angel statue. At first, I thought it must be Trey, even though it wasn't Wednesday, but the human form was far too small for the strapping police officer. As I got closer, I realized it was Rose.

When she noticed me, she protectively threw both arms over her head and begged, "Please don't hit me."

"I'm not going to hit you, Rose," I assured her. Any desire I ever had for revenge was gone now. "What are you doing here?"

"I came here to tell her I was sorry. I am sorry for what Luke did to her. I am sorry I couldn't stop him. I am sorry I told him where you lived."

I cringed. In the back of my mind, I had suspected it since the beginning, but now Rose confirmed her betrayal.

"Why did you do it?" I had to know. "You knew he was after me.

You even told me he was going to hurt me. Why did you give him my address?'

She sniffled and wiped the tears away from her face with her shirt sleeve. "When I asked for your address, I really did just want to send you pictures of the kids. I hadn't seen or heard from Luke since you took us to the shelter, but right after I saw you, he showed up at my work. He waited for me to get off, and he made me get in the car with him." Her voice trailed off, and she picked up a stick, and started playing tic-tac-toe in the dirt.

"What did he do to you, Rose?" I prodded. "How did he make you tell him where I lived?"

She sobbed loudly, but kept playing her game, never looking at me. "He told me he knew where we could get some really stuff, but I had to go with him to get it. I'd been doing so good, Emily. I'd been doing so good."

"So, he took you to get the drugs? Then what happened?"

"I didn't know we was going all the way to Oklahoma City. I thought we was just gonna get it here like we always did. We got to the motel, and he had everything. The stuff. Pipes. Needles. Lighters. Luke liked the needles. I only smoked it."

"So he gave you drugs, and you gave him my personal information?" I grabbed the stick out of her hand and turned her chin toward me, forcing her to look at me.

"Not exactly. I had to give him the information first. He showed me what he had, and I reached for it, but he said no. I had to earn it. He said, 'You tell me where I can find that nosy goddamned social worker. You tell me where I can catch her alone at night.' I tried to tell him I didn't know, but he could always tell when I was lying."

She grew silent for a moment, then she reiterated, "God, Emily, I'd been doing so good." She erupted in a fit of violent sobs that shook her emaciated frame like a sapling fighting against a tornado.

I started mentally condemning her, cursing her for her weakness, but then I remembered how close I came to addiction that summer with The Philosopher, and I swallowed my judgment. I finally acknowledged something I hadn't allowed myself to think about before.

Ashford wasn't a booming metropolis, and there was no place to hide in a town this size. Not to mention a simple online people search would have revealed the same information. Once The Beast had me on his radar, he was going to find me. He only dragged his former wife into his evil scheme because he was a psychopath hellbent on destroying as many lives as possible. Rose was as a much his victim as Andi or me.

"None of this was your fault, Rose. The way I see it, our weaknesses only make us human. Using another person's weakness for our own gain makes us evil. He exploited your weakness for his own malicious purposes. That makes him evil. Not you."

"But I killed that baby. It is my fault she's dead."

"No," I contradicted her. "I was there that night. There was only one murderer, and it damn sure wasn't you."

Her violent sobbing ceased, and I handed her a tissue from my purse, because both her shirt sleeves were already saturated. The sun had worked its way into the middle of the sky, and I felt like a fast food burger, left too long under a heat lamp. I thought about leaving, but Rose started crying again.

"I lost the kids," she weakly confessed.

"Oh, Rose, no!" I sighed wearily. A deep well of compassion sprung up inside me, replacing the bitterness and contempt I'd felt for this poor beleaguered woman. "What happened?"

"I got so messed up I didn't know where I was for three days. I guess I must have left the kids alone that whole time, because Thomas said they got hungry and he wanted to make them a cake. He poked both his little arms in that oven without no protection. He got third-degree burns. Sweet little Harper called 911. They found me sleeping in a roadside ditch wearing nothing but my underwear."

I dropped to the ground beside her, and she crumpled herself on my lap. I smoothed her tangled hair with my fingers, and when I touched her back, I felt bones sticking out from under her blouse. "I'm so sorry," I groaned.

"Why are you sorry?" she asked innocently. "You didn't do anything."

"That's exactly why I'm sorry. I didn't do anything. You needed me. You were my responsibility, and I turned my back on you. I passed you off to complete strangers, like getting rid of clothes that don't fit anymore."

"I understand why you don't like me. We're just so different."

"Is that why you think I walked away from you? Because we're so different?" I continued caressing her hair and rubbing her back. "Rose, I rejected you because we are so incredibly alike, and it scared me; you reminded me of everything I loathed about myself."

She sniffled one last time and pulled herself up from my lap. Strangely, I'd never noticed her eyes before, how innocent and child-like they were, filled with both fear and wonder.

"Emily, did you really mean it when you said I had potential?"

I recalled how life-changing it was for me the first time someone believed I had potential. "Yes, sweetie. I really meant it. Without the drugs, and without an abusive husband weighing you down, I think you have incredible potential to achieve anything you set your mind to."

"Nobody ever told me that before."

"I know."

"I want to get my kids back. I stopped doing dope. I quit it cold turkey. This time for good. Now I have to figure out a way to make a living for us."

"Any thoughts about that?"

She giggled in a self-deprecating way, "I used to want to be a nurse."

"What's funny about that? It's a noble profession, and there is a nursing shortage all over the country right now."

"Yeah, but I ain't smart enough for that. I ain't even got a high school diploma."

"I know of an adult learning center where you can get a general equivalency diploma. After that, you can apply for grants at our local community college. From there, it's really up to you how far you want to go. You can also work and support your kids while you get your education. It won't be easy, but people do it all the time. Why don't you at least check into it?"

"Maybe later," she yawned, and I noticed her body still trembled, though she'd stopped crying again. "Right now, I'm so tired. I think I could sleep for days. And I'm so hungry. Plus, I keep getting this weird feeling that people are hiding in the trees, waiting to pounce on me."

I thought I recognized her symptoms. There was no tactful way to pose the question, so I blurted it out. "How long has it been since you've used meth?"

"About a week, I guess."

"You're having withdrawals. You need medical attention."

I tried pulling her up, but she resisted. "No, Emily. I need a friend."

Fortunately, I'd been around enough addicts I knew withdrawal from methamphetamine was not as severe and cruel as detoxing from alcohol or opioids. She'd probably sleep an extended period of time, and then she'd eat everything in sight, because the meth had suppressed her appetite to the point she'd literally been starving herself. The thing that concerned me most was the possibility of paranoia and delusions, but she refused hospitalization, and I simply couldn't turn my back on her a second time. I loaded her into her my car and took her home with me, not knowing what Trey's reaction might be, but I trusted in his goodness and his strong sense of empathy.

I put her in Andi's bed, and she begged me to stay, so I did. At first, she slept soundly while I sat beside her, reading. Trey called and said he'd be working late. He sounded stressed, so I elected not to tell him about my guest. I was about to doze off when she suddenly jerked awake. "He's here!" she screamed.

"No, sweetie. Nobody's here but us."

"He's here!" she reiterated, with sheer panic in her voice and a look of unmitigated terror on her face. "I saw him come through the back door."

It wasn't possible for her to see the back of the house from Andi's room, but she sounded so convinced, I almost believed her delusion. I armed myself with the mace from my purse and patrolled the house, checking every room. Then I returned to the brightly painted sanctum and reassured her that we were alone.

"No. He's here," she insisted. "Luke's here. He's come to kill me because I told the truth."

"Luke is in prison," I reminded her. "He can't hurt us."

"He's here. He's here. He's here," she chanted the creepy mantra, until I felt like I was trapped in a low-budget horror film. All I could do was hold her while she shrieked in terror. Well after midnight, she finally fell asleep again, and I followed suit in the bed beside her.

I awakened to the feel of Trey's gentle kiss on my forehead. I rolled out of bed and followed him to the kitchen.

"Honey, let me explain," I started as I rolled out of bed.

He smiled. "Explain what? That you are doing what you were made to do? What God put you on this earth to do?"

"She was detoxing, and she refused to go to the hospital. I couldn't very well just walk away from her and let her go through it by herself."

"Of course you couldn't, and I would never ask you to. Now will you please stop trying to justify and explain away all the wonderful things I love about you, and let's have some breakfast? I'm starving."

"So you're not mad that I brought her here without discussing it with you first?"

"Remember how my mother said she was born to create? Well, I think you were born for this, to nurture people and help them grow and overcome their circumstances. I could no more stop you from nurturing and helping people than I could stop my mother from painting. Why would I be mad at you for doing what you were designed to do? You never have to ask my permission to be yourself and do what comes naturally to you."

Despite my career choices, I never saw myself as a nurturer. Maybe I did years ago, back when I decided my college major, but life had hardened me. After a while, social work became just a job, just a way to pay the bills. Funny how the people who love you see the best in you, even when you can't see it in yourself.

As I suspected, after the paranoia and delusions subsided, Rose slept eighteen straight hours. When she awoke, she was ravenous. She wanted milk, and I poured her glass after glass until she polished off a half gallon. Then I made her steak and potatoes, with lemon meringue pie for dessert. Sometimes her hands shook so badly I had to hold the fork for her and feed her like an infant.

"You're not out of the woods yet," I told her as she devoured the first real meal she'd probably had in months. "You need to get back into rehab. There is a small in-patient treatment center here in Ashford. It's usually packed to capacity, with a long waiting list, but I'm friends with the director of the facility. I think I can get you in quickly if you agree to go."

She nodded vigorously as she jammed the last bite of steak into her mouth. When she finished eating, I loaded her back into my car and drove her to the clinic. My friend who ran the facility listened to her story and agreed that, because of the situation with her children, Rose's case was a priority. It just so happened that they had a bed opening up that day, and Rose was put at the top of the waiting list.

"I'm not abandoning you this time," I promised her. "I'll be back to check on your progress, and when you're done here, we'll continue our conversation about your future."

As I walked away, she called me back. "Emily." When I turned around to acknowledge her, she smiled weakly. "Thank you for being my friend."

I lightly kissed her cheek and replied, "Thank you for being mine."

CHAPTER 26

*E*ven in my dreams, she haunted me. She taunted me. She stalked me like a hungry lioness in pursuit of her prey. I ran through a field of withered vines and dry, cracked ground. I couldn't find Trey. It wasn't his physical being that I searched for. His spirit, his very essence, was gone. An impenetrable darkness engulfed the world around me, but I could still see. Eve/Rose chased after me, rolling around on the globe that encapsulated her feet. Every direction I turned, she ended up in front of me. Terrified, I screamed in the same pleading voice Rose once posed the same question to me, "What do you want from me?"

The apple remained secured in the woman's mouth, but somehow, she shouted her reply, "*Re-demp-tion!*"

I shot up in bed and Trey groggily pulled me closer to him. "I have to save her!" I whimpered.

"I know. You will." He comforted me with soft kisses all over my face. Though I never told him about my obsession with the painting and he never asked about the artwork I left hanging in his daughter's room, I had the feeling he knew more about my connection to Eve/Rose than I did.

RON TYLER WAS RETIRING and handing over the reins of lead detective on the case to Nora Flynn. Trey and several other officers who had the night off decided to give their friend and mentor a proper farewell. There was a bar on the outskirts of town called Rowdy's where the cops sometimes went to unwind after a stressful shift, and they decided it was as good a place as any for the salute to Detective Tyler. Ron's wife and I signed on as their designated drivers.

I hadn't been in a bar since college, and that was only to see a band I really liked. The dim lights gave me a headache and the smell of all that alcohol made me nauseous. The room was filled with loud, raucous men jostling each other and telling crude jokes, mostly involving female anatomical parts. I sat beside Trey, sipping on a Sprite, and prayed the time would go by quickly.

After a while, Mrs. Tyler tapped my elbow and uttered, "Uh-oh. Trouble."

I followed her gaze, and my eyes landed on a vicious looking character with red hair and a long, scraggly beard. He glared hostilely at Trey and his friends. I tried to get Trey's attention, but he was engrossed in listening to Ron's war stories.

"Fucking pigs," the derelict muttered as he moved his chair back from the table and stood up. None of the officers wore uniforms, so I suspected this was not Scraggly Beard's first encounter with the police.

The angry man removed a long silver blade from the top of his boot. I barely had time to scream the warning. "Trey, he's got a knife!" The sharp weapon stuck into Trey's neck, and a crimson rivulet flowed from the open wound. With lightning speed, my beloved turned the tables on his attacker. He grabbed the other man's wrist and twisted it mercilessly until the knife fell to the floor, and Ron scooped it up. Then, with the attacker disarmed and wholly incapable of causing more harm, Trey drew back a powerful arm, and he plowed his massive fist squarely into the criminal's face. Knuckles and septal cartilage colliding resulted in a loud *ka-pow*! Blood gushed from Scraggly Beard's nose.

"Damn! That sounded like a bomb," One of Trey's friends observed, and they all—including Trey—laughed.

"Police brutality!" Scraggly Beard screeched to anyone who would listen. "Y'all saw what he did to me!"

The police chief, who was also at the party, defended Trey's actions. "I tell you what I saw, boy," he said calmly. "I saw you come at one of my finest officers with a knife, without any provocation, and you got your ass handed to you. Now that's what I saw." He looked around at his subordinates. "What did you boys see?"

One by one, the men behind the thin blue line concurred with their superior.

"Yep."

"That's what I saw."

"That's what it looked like to me."

The man I loved, the man I thought I knew, then turned his attention to me. "Emily," he said, as proudly as if he were a hunter, and he'd just shot his first buck. "Meet Jack. Mama Detwiler's third son." He still held Jack's arm in the air, like a trophy. For the first time, I saw the man who, as a boy, killed someone because he hated him.

It was our first major disagreement as a couple. Trey couldn't understand my distaste for the way he handled the situation at Rowdy's. Trey was an avid weightlifter, in peak physical condition. There wasn't a scenario I could fathom where any of the three Detwiler brothers stood a chance against him in a fair fight. Therefore, I thought after the weapon was taken out of the equation, Trey should have backed down. I'd witnessed and perpetrated more than my share of violence. Now I wanted peace, and I wanted my significant other to want the same thing.

"Honey," he defended himself. "You saw him stab me." He pointed at his bandaged neck. "He had every intention of killing me. I had to do something."

"He dropped the knife, Trey," I asserted my position. "Ron had the weapon in his possession. The danger was over."

"People don't have to be armed to be dangerous," he lowered his voice to an angry scowl. "Luke wasn't armed when he killed my baby."

That, I thought, was a hit below the belt, and I abruptly ended the argument by leaving. I didn't go home after work that day. Something was drawing me back to the old shack. I stopped at a convenience store for gas on my way out of town. Ron Tyler was there filling up. He saw me and smiled and nodded his greeting.

"I'm sorry your retirement party was ruined," I told him.

"Yeah. I heard you were pretty upset about that." Tyler removed the nozzle from his gas tank and hooked it in its proper place.

"You understand, don't you?" I was desperate for someone to see my point of view.

"I don't know. I guess I see both sides." That was not good enough to satisfy my indignation.

"I just don't think he had to hit him like that. You had the weapon in your hand. And then, when it was all over, he laughed about the pain he'd inflicted on Jack Detwiler."

Ron sighed deeply. "There's something you have to understand, Emily. When a police officer's life is threatened, he has one-quarter of a second to decide how he will respond before it's too late for him to respond at all. I think Trey hit that scumbag because he hadn't had time to process the information and realize the danger had passed. The fact that he laughed—that we all laughed—I think can be attributed to the sheer release of adrenaline. We were just relieved things worked out the way they did and we didn't lose our brother."

"I still don't really get it," I confessed.

"Nelson Mandela was once considered a political terrorist by the United States government. He publicly admitted to organizing multiple terror campaigns throughout South Africa, yet without his bravery and heroic actions the rest of the world would have remained apathetic to the horrors of apartheid."

The retired detective's impromptu history lesson baffled me. "What does Mandela have to do with my current situation with Trey?"

"My point is, Emily, life is not a Marvel comic strip where we all cheer for the same person every time. In real life, sometimes the hero and the villain are under the same cape."

CHAPTER 27

*W*hen I saw Janice's car parked in front of the old shack, I almost turned around, but she'd already spotted me. She was carrying boxes out of the house. "Hello, Jan," I greeted her obligatorily.

"Thank goodness you're here." She jabbed a box into my stomach and released it before I had a firm grasp on the sides. It fell to the ground, and I heard dishes rattle and break.

"Oh, Emily. You're still such a klutz," my sister admonished me. Then she quickly apologized, something I'm not sure I'd ever heard her do. "I'm sorry, Em. I've been going through Mom's things and getting this place ready to sell. I guess it's stressing me out a little."

"Who'd buy it?" I wondered aloud.

"They'll probably tear the house down," she acknowledged. "But the land is valuable. In fact, I've already had a couple of offers on the land. Some of the neighboring farmers and ranchers are interested."

I stepped upon the sagging and lopsided wooden front porch, and it squeaked like a mouse beneath the heel of a merciless tyrant. I stared through the same dirty, cracked window pane I'd looked through that day twenty years ago when I waited for a stranger to ride by on his motorcycle. Only this time I was looking in, instead of out. The couch was the same one I had dug my nails into when I was being beaten. The love seat was the same one I sat on when I anxiously plotted my escape. I suddenly found myself nostalgic for a life I'd been ashamed of and people I thought I hated.

"It wasn't all bad, was it, Jan?"

"No," she answered. "It wasn't that bad. We were just poor. Lots of people are poor."

"I work with a lot of those poor people, Janice, and they don't do the things to their families that man did to us. What happened to us was abuse, plain and simple." I never told her I knew he molested her.

"Emily, I don't think he knew any better." He'd been dead and buried for more than a decade, and she still tried to justify his abhorrent behavior. "Besides, like you said it wasn't all bad. Remember how we used to plant green beans and watermelon seeds over there in that little patch of dirt every spring?" She pointed to the spot.

"And then we'd forget to water our little garden, and we'd blame each other because nothing we planted ever grew," I recalled with a smile.

"It wasn't my fault," she teased. "It was your job to do the watering."

I suddenly realized we were holding hands, but I didn't know who initiated the contact. It felt good to be standing close to her without fighting. Other than her two children, she was the only flesh and blood relative I had left. Because of the tension between their mother and me, I hadn't seen my nieces in years.

"How are the girls, Jan?" I asked.

That triggered an unexpected release of emotions from my usually stoic sister. She started crying, "Oh, Emily. I've lost Abby. I've lost her forever."

Abby was in her early twenties, so I knew Janice hadn't lost her in the same sense that Rose lost her kids, and I certainly hoped she hadn't lost her in the way Trey, Sarah, and I lost Andi.

"What do you mean you lost her?" I prodded.

"She got mixed up with some boy. Some unchurched, ungodly boy, and now she's... you know..."

"Pregnant?" I took pity on her and offered her the word she'd always struggled with.

"Yes!" she almost screamed it.

"Jan, it doesn't have to be the end of the world," I consoled her. "This is the twenty-first century."

"I don't care if it's the *thirty-first* century," she blubbered. "It's still sin in God's eyes."

"Does Abby know what she's going to do?"

"That's the worst part of all. She wants to have a...an...you know..."

"Abortion?" Again, I gave her the word.

"Yes! That's murder! That's infanticide! That's an abomination!"

"That's a personal choice," I corrected. "Abby is the only one who can make that decision. No matter what she decides, she is going to need you to stand by her."

"I can't. I just can't stand by her if she kills that baby. That makes me as guilty as her."

It saddened me that Janice had never been able to fully love her children. From the time they were born, she started programming them with religious dogma. She distanced herself from them every time they strayed from her strict teachings. Once, she found out Abby drank a glass of champagne to celebrate her twenty-first birthday, and she didn't speak to her for weeks. She worried so much about the eternity of her children's souls that she neglected their souls' present needs, such as unconditional acceptance and support.

Janice wasn't abusive like our father. She force fed religion to her family, because she sincerely believed they would perish without it. Our father used religion as a means of manipulation. Anything that annoyed him, which was almost everything, was sinful, and we didn't sin against God, we sinned against him, but God would send still send us to hell for it because we were supposed to honor our father. It is the highest and cruelest form of torture to instill faith in a child's heart, and then use that pure, innocent faith as a method of control. Of all that old man's many faults, and they were legion, that one was the most unforgivable.

My phone rang, and I knew it would be Trey, looking for me. I hurriedly explained to him that my sister and I were cleaning out our parents' house, and I might spend the night with her. He sounded hurt, but he said he loved me, and he would be waiting for me to come home.

I went home with Janice and slept in the pregnant and exiled Abby's room. When Eve/Rose chased me through the withered vines, there was no one there to comfort me when I awoke. The feeling in the dream, the feeling that Trey's spirit was gone, lingered, and the grief overwhelmed me.

My sister served breakfast on the patio: eggs and English muffins. I had barely finished eating when my phone rang. I assumed it would be Trey again, but I was wrong. When I glanced down and saw Connie's name and number flashing on the screen, I gasped in disbelief and dropped the fork I was holding.

"Hello?" My voice was almost a whisper. Janice gathered our dirty dishes and carried them inside. I was thankful for the privacy.

"Miss Kirk?" It was a male voice on the other line.

"Yes?" I answered hesitantly.

"It's Matthew. Matthew Parsons. Connie's son."

My heart returned to my chest from the place it had launched itself in my throat. "Oh, hello."

"Miss Kirk, I need to discuss some legal matters with you."

"Legal matters?"

"Yes, it's about my house. I mean, my mother's house. Actually, I guess I mean your house."

My house? Before I could verbalize the question, he continued, "You see, Miss Kirk, I jumped the gun in assuming my mother would want me to have her house. The truth is she and I hadn't been very close since she divorced my father. That was my fault; she tried many times to reach out to me. Anyway, there were some delays with the reading of the will, but we finally got it done yesterday. She wanted you, not me, to have her house."

Connie left her mansion to me? We had gotten close during the time I stayed with her, but I never dreamed she would will her most cherished material possession to me.

"Are you sure that's what she wanted?"

"It was right there in the will, plain as day."

As much as I wanted to live in that beautiful house again, I felt Matthew and his family had more right to it than I did, no matter what Connie put in some legal document. Besides, I was with Trey now, and even though we'd had our first dispute, I still had every intention of going home to him, even if meant living the rest of my life in his modest abode.

"Look, Matthew. If you want to keep the house, I'm not going to fight you for it."

He laughed heartily. "You know my mama would come back and haunt me until my dying day if I didn't follow her wishes on this. Besides, my wife and Erica miss the city life. They want to go back to Dallas."

"So it's really mine?" I wondered how Trey would feel about living in such luxury. He was quintessentially blue collar, and I certainly had no desire to live in that sprawling mansion alone.

"Sure is, but Miss Kirk, but there is one condition."

I braced myself for his stipulation. I thought Connie might have owed an exorbitant amount of back taxes. She tended to be a little careless with her ex-husband's money. "What is the condition?"

He chuckled jovially and said, "You've got to keep all those damn critters."

CHAPTER 28

*J*anice and I returned to the old shack to finish cleaning. We spent the morning dusting countertops, washing windows, and scrubbing walls and floors. I wondered why we were sterilizing a house that was soon to be demolished.

I didn't tell my sister about my inheritance. In fact, I never told her much about my life at all. I hadn't even told her about Trey. She had an extraordinary talent for exaggerating her own accomplishments and making my life events seem petty and insignificant.

We took a break for lunch and afterwards, we sat on the wooden swing that hung between two oak trees. That swing was the only decent thing my father ever gave my mother. He built it for her after he put her in the hospital with broken ribs, because he felt guilty. Janice and I languidly pushed ourselves back and forth with our feet. Again, we were holding hands, and again, I couldn't remember if I held hers first or if she grabbed mine.

I was about to ask her if she had given any more thought to the Abby situation, when she took in a deep breath and announced. "I know what happened to you, Emily, and I know about that little girl." I felt all my muscles stiffen.

"How did you find out about that?" I never wanted her to know about Andi or the rape.

"Oh, Em, you know how it is around here. People talk. You can't keep a secret in these small towns."

I stayed completely silent, hoping she would realize this was not a conversation I wanted to have with her, but Janice never was too perceptive. She went on, "You could have told me about it, you know?"

"And have you tell me how it was all my fault, and I should have been more careful?" Resentment bubbled up inside me, and I suddenly remembered why she and I had never been close.

She gasped indignantly, "I would have never said that!"

"I'm pretty sure you would have." I stared at the ground and made circles in dirt with the toes of my brown and pink Nikes.

"I don't think it was because you weren't careful enough. Something like this was bound to happen eventually, no matter how careful you were. You've been running from the Lord for years. You were out from under His protection. This tragedy happened so you would realize how much you need God in your life."

I turned my icy glare toward her in disbelief. I'd let life harden me, but I could never be as callous and uncompassionate as the woman sitting next to me.

"And what about Andi? An innocent little girl was murdered. Was that because she was running from the Lord?"

"Of course not!" If she'd stopped there, things would have gone very differently, but Janice never knew when to stop when she was on a moral tirade. She continued, "God was probably punishing her parents for their immoral lifestyle. The sins of the parents are visited upon the children."

"You don't even know her parents!" I was on the verge of hysteria. "They happen to be wonderful people. How can you pass judgment on people you don't even know?"

"I know the type of characters you hang out with. I swear, there's not a decent Christian in the lot of them. Take for instance, that deplorable Connie woman. The way she talked to my pastor was downright disgraceful."

I stifled my tongue and looked down at our interlocked fingers. For the life of me, I couldn't figure out who was holding onto whom. When I didn't respond, Janice sighed, "Oh, Emily, you poor dear lost soul. I do hope someday you find the Lord."

The epiphany hit me as forcefully as the wrecking ball would soon hit the house behind us. It wasn't nostalgia that drew me back to Janice and the old shack, and it damn sure wasn't love. It was fear. Like a traumatized toddler clinging to an abusive parent, I clung to the security of the familiar, never realizing it was the least secure place for me.

I reached deep down inside, and I channeled the imperturbable, indefatigable Connie Parsons. "Oh, Janice," I mocked her. "You poor dear stupid woman. I do hope someday you find some damn sense."

Then I released her and walked away. I walked away from her self-righteous judgment, and I walked away from my own self-condemnation. All my life, I'd been drawing from empty wells, trying to extract love from people who didn't have an ounce of genuine compassion to share with anybody, all because those wells were in my own backyard. Trey, Andi, and Connie taught me to drink in the pure, life-sustaining love that flowed from the geysers that sprung up in the most unexpected place. Because they taught me what love was, and more importantly, what it wasn't, I finally walked away from the last of the empty wells.

She followed me. "Emily," she called out. "Are you denouncing your faith?" She sounded terrified.

"No, Janice," I replied calmly. "In fact, I'm doing quite the opposite. I am denouncing my fear."

And that's exactly what I did. I denounced my fear of a literal, Dante-esque hell, and I denounced my fear of a demonic realm I'd often been warned about but saw no evidence of. I denounced my fear of a dead psychopath who used my innocent, childlike faith as a weapon against me. I denounced my fear of an eternity that might or might not await me on the other side of this life, and I denounced my fear of an imperfect world, where in the heat of battle, someone I loved might make a snap decision I didn't approve of. Perhaps most importantly, I denounced my fear of my own human frailty: my finite existence, my inherent flaws and weaknesses, and my hideously beautiful scars.

It was never the Christian faith that had stifled and restrained me; rather, it was the perversion, the corruption—the *rape*—of Christianity that instilled my heart with fear and my mind with self-doubt. In psychology, cognitive dissonance refers to the state of mental and emotional unrest that occurs when a person holds two diametrically opposing values. Faith and fear are mutually exclusive concepts; they are polar opposites. They cannot peacefully coexist within the confines of an individual's psyche. I could think of no greater cognitive dissonance than faith built on a foundation of fear.

As I released my fears, I reached the highest rung on the pyramid of love needs. I accepted *agape*, the pure, unconditional, and unmerited love of God. From the moment I was born, I was cast upon the Lord, and it was His unending and unfailing love that sustained me when no one else would look upon me. He was the one who guided me up the hierarchy, and it was He who provided the surrogates when I couldn't get the love I needed from the people I should have gotten it from. God wasn't some distant tyrant who wanted to destroy me. He was an ever-present entity who only wanted to love me. The forgiveness I had sought since early childhood had been extended to me before my sins were even committed.

Everyone experiences *agape* in his or her own way. For me, it was the casting out of a thousand crippling anxieties, the healing of a gaping bleeding wound, and the desire to share *agape* with others. Many Western philosophers called that state transcendence. I called it grace.

WHEN I WAS a safe distance away from the rubble of my past life, I pulled over to call Trey. I warbled out an apology I'm not sure he even heard. He was so overjoyed by the sound of my voice and my immanent return I thought he might slaughter a fatted calf. I told him about my inheritance and asked if he would be willing to live with me in my new home. He said he would live in the deepest, darkest blackhole in space as long as he could feel my presence near him.

In one of my life's greatest ironies, I lost my religion and found my salvation. Then I returned to my beloved in a mansion I believed was specifically designed for me.

PART V
AGAPE

"…and they overcame him through the blood of the lamb and by the word of their testimony…" – Revelation 14:11

CHAPTER 29

$\mathcal{T}$rey and I now had ample space to accommodate his mother and her art supplies. In fact, we decided she could have an entire wing to herself, and we'd still have plenty of room for all the children we eventually wanted to adopt. At first, Grace stubbornly resisted our offer, but she soon showed up on our doorstep with easels and canvases in tow. The working-class Pig quickly established his dominance among his pampered counterparts, and I hung Eve/Rose in a prominent area above the fireplace in the den. Neither Trey nor Grace ever asked about the odd painting, but occasionally I caught them looking at the masterpiece and then exchanging knowing glances. For the first time in my life, I had a real sense of family. I belonged somewhere. I wasn't just drifting through life anymore. I had a real home, but I knew someone who didn't.

The director of the rehab clinic called and told me Rose had done exceptionally well in the program and could be released if she had a safe place to go. I had an idea, but I needed Trey's approval. I waited until Grace had gone to bed and Trey and I were alone. He absently clicked buttons on the remote until I took the instrument from him and muted the television. Then I broached the subject.

"Sweetheart, we certainly have no need for two houses. Have you thought about what you're going to do with yours?" I snuggled up beside him, crowding him into the arm of the leather recliner, and I played with the collar of his shirt.

"I hadn't really thought about it," he admitted. "It's almost paid off. I guess we could fix it up and sell it. We could always use the extra cash."

"Do we really need the money that badly? Because I have something else in mind."

"What's your plan?"

"I thought we could turn it into a starter home for indigent women. Rose is getting out of rehab, and she needs a place to stay. Then when she gets a job and gets on her feet, another woman could move in until she gets established. What do you think?"

Trey squeezed my waist and kissed me gently. "I think I love you even more now than I did five minutes ago, and I didn't think that was even possible."

I ELECTED to surprise Rose with her new living quarters. I picked her up at the rehab and drove her to the place where I first allowed myself to love Trey.

"Why are you stopping at your house?" she demanded when I parked in the driveway. "I thought you were taking me home."

"I don't live here anymore," I announced, and then paused before adding, "Now you do."

Confusion clouded her face. "I can't afford a place like this."

"You don't understand. Nobody is asking you to pay anything. You will stay here until you get back on your feet and when you find a new place, another woman will move in."

"I get to live here?" Despite its small size and bland décor, I felt certain it was the nicest house Rose ever lived in.

"Let's go take a look inside," I suggested, excitedly pulling her by the arm. "So you can decide how you want to decorate it."

She walked through the humble shelter with a look of wonder on her face. I thought she looked a little like a kid at Disneyland. When we got to Andi's room, she hesitated at the door. The last time she was here she wasn't lucid enough to make the connection. Now her eyes clouded over. "This was her room, wasn't it?"

"Yes," I confirmed. We had put most of Andi's belongings in storage, but the unicorn covered walls made it obvious than the room had once belonged to young girl. "But it's okay. I can't explain it, but I know she'd want you here."

Rose decided she could convert the brightly painted bedroom into a boy's room so Thomas could have his privacy. Then she concluded that the master bedroom was big enough to be partitioned into a smaller area for Harper. She was certain she would get them back and her optimism was contagious. I started believing it, too.

Trey usually worked a few hours later than I did, and I spent that time with Rose, either painting walls and hanging window curtains, or picking out new furniture at Goodwill. Soon, we had her house arranged exactly the way she wanted it, so we moved on to our next project—finding a way for her to provide for herself and her children.

"Have you given any more thought to becoming a nurse?" I asked her as we filled out job applications at the kitchen table.

"It's like I told you," she responded sadly. "I ain't smart enough for that."

"What if you are? Remember how you didn't know you had potential until I told you that you did? Maybe you just don't think you're smart enough to be a nurse because nobody ever told you that you were."

The tiniest glimmer of hope crossed her face. "I really want to be a nurse," she admitted.

"Then I think you're smart enough to do it."

ROSE RECEIVED SEVERAL JOB OFFERS, but she chose one as a nurse's aide so she could get experience in the field. I helped her get enrolled at the adult learning center and whenever we had time off together, we studied for her general equivalency exam. We worked on polynomial equations and chemistry formulas until my head ached, but she was eager to learn and was a much better student than I expected her to be. She passed her exam the first try, and that was no easy feat, from what her instructor told me. The next step was getting her into community college, a springboard and lifeline for many women in Rose's situation.

The work I did with Rose was ostensibly the same thing as I did at my counseling job at the crisis center. I encouraged, uplifted, and advocated for my clients far more than I advised them. It was different working with these women than it had been working at CPS. I wasn't trying to save them the way I tried to rescue all the children. I merely hoped I could inspire a few of my adult clients to save themselves.

Because of our complicated history, I couldn't officially act in the capacity of Rose's counselor. Everything I did for her was because she was my friend, and it was what *agape* required of me. I started thinking Trey was right. I really was born to nurture other women—women, who like me, had been cheated out of their own mothers' love and nurturing. My favorite Sunday School story had always been the one about Jonah, the wayward prophet who refused to go where God sent him. I spent most of my adult life in the proverbial belly of the whale, obstinately refusing to reach out to the people God was sending me to. Jonah didn't want to go to a foreign land with a strange culture; he didn't want to minister to people who were different from him. My Nineveh was filled with women who were exactly like me. Hurting, struggling, emotionally scarred, and battle-weary women; women who, like Rose, reminded me of everything I once loathed about myself.

I KNEW the social worker assigned to Rose's case, and I didn't like her. Her name was Tessa, and she had little mercy on mothers she considered incompetent. I was trained that the ultimate goal of child social work was always family reunification, but with Tessa, punishing and shaming the mother took preeminence. She was one of those hard-nosed, by-the-book, inflexible bureaucrats who made all parents wary of Child Protective Services. With that in mind, I decided to run inter-ference on Rose's behalf.

I caught Tessa on the parking lot of CPS digging through an over-sized handbag, apparently looking for her keys. "Tessa," I started before she saw me approach her. "I'd like to talk to you about Rose Detwiler and her children."

She rolled her eyes when she realized who was talking. "That's my case now, Emily. You don't even work here anymore."

"That doesn't mean I don't still care about these families. Can we get a cup of coffee or something and talk about this?"

"Only if you drive. I seem to have misplaced my keys."

We ended up at a quaint little coffee shop where they had more flavors of java than Baskin-Robbins had of ice cream. A petite college-aged woman took our order and quickly served us. I saw no need for small talk, so I dove right in. "I know Rose has some pretty heavy issues going on right now, but I also know how much she loves those kids. Do you have any idea how hard she's working to get them back?"

"Oh, they all act like they're going to clean up, straighten up, and sober up until the second the kids get returned to them, and then it's right back to square one."

"I don't think that's going to happen with Rose. She's been through rehab and she's in a twelve-step program. She's going through domestic violence counseling. She's working and has her own place to live. She's even thinking about going to community college to get her nursing degree."

"And if she's doing all that, who's going to be taking care of her children?"

"Most of the time, they'll be in school. When they're not, we'll find child care services available for them. I even thought I could babysit occasionally if called upon." I blew at the steam rising from my decorative Styrofoam cup and watched a tiny whirlpool forming in the white chocolate-caramel cappuccino.

"I don't get you, Emily," Tessa looked at me skeptically over the rim of a red and black striped coffee mug. "Why are you so concerned about this family after what that monster did to you?"

I cringed at the thought of the man who orchestrated the rape and murdered Andi. "This is not about Luke. This is about Rose and her kids, and they shouldn't be punished for what he did."

"I'm not interested in Rose," Tessa stated callously. "My only interest is in helping those kids."

"If there is one thing I learned in all my years with CPS, it's that the best way—maybe the only way—to really help children is by helping their mothers."

"I'm not heartless, Emily," Tessa defended herself. "I know everybody thinks I am, but I just get so tired of seeing these poor kids suffer for their parents' selfishness."

"There is a difference between being selfish and being an addict," I corrected her.

"Not much," she cynically countered. Then she added, "I tell you what. Since you are so adamant about this, and I do trust your judgment, I will suggest to the judge that Rose be given supervised visits one weekend a month. We'll see how that goes for a few months, and then go from there. How does that sound?"

"We'll take it!" I exclaimed, feeling confident Rose would soon have her children back permanently.

"There's only one condition, Emily. You have to be the supervisor."

"I wouldn't have it any other way," I told her. Then Tessa remembered she had stuck her keys in the jacket pocket of her lime green pantsuit. I took her back to her car and we parted ways.

I enjoyed surprising Rose and seeing the look of childlike wonder on her face, so I didn't tell her she'd gotten supervised visits. I picked Thomas and Harper up at their foster home and took them to Rose's new place. They chatted giddily in the backseat, knowing they were going to see their mother. When we got there, I didn't take them directly to the front door. Instead, I

called her and asked her to come outside. She hesitantly stepped onto the porch, and I helped the kids unbuckle their safety belts. When she saw them, Rose collapsed on the ground in spasms of love and joy.

"My babies!" She cried jubilantly as she became entangled in four tiny arms.

CHAPTER 30

aren Tobias called and said the trial had been postponed again. Luke fired his public defender after Rose switched sides and the prosecutor eviscerated Mangy Dog's testimony. So the judge ordered another delay while Luke's new lawyer prepared his defense. I was both frustrated and relieved, frustrated because Luke was the only thing still binding me to the past, but relieved because I was worried I still wouldn't be able to testify. Every day, I grew a little stronger, so the more time that passed, the more likely I'd be able to aid the prosecution.

On the weekends Rose had visits with her kids and I had to be there to supervise, Trey volunteered for extra shifts. He said he didn't like being in that giant house without me. He amazed me with how supportive and understanding he was of my friendship with the ex-wife of his daughter's murderer.

I usually just sat back and let Rose enjoy mothering her children. She didn't really need a supervisor. Now that she was sober and didn't have an abusive husband draining the life out of her, she was an extraordinary parent. I made it a point to let her social worker know that.

"I've seen it, too," Tessa agreed. Rose was scheduled for a family court hearing, and as the court-ordered supervisor of her weekend visits, I was expected to be there.

This time I had no trouble testifying. I told the judge how I'd watched Rose interact with her children. She doted on them, but she did not hesitate to dole out firm discipline when it became necessary. I also told the court about Rose's enormous personal growth and her commitment to sobriety. After a few nerve-racking hours, the family court judge ordered that Rose's children be returned to her. Thomas and Harper were coming home permanently.

I wanted to throw a party for Rose to help her celebrate the reunification of her family, but I wanted to do it at the mansion. Trey hadn't really spoken to Rose since the day he arrested Luke. He was working most of the time when she detoxed at the little house, and when he saw her in the hallway, he only acknowledged her with a polite nod. In court, he viewed her with tacit skepticism. Even though he supported my friendship with her and allowed her to live in his old house, I feared her presence in our home for a celebratory occasion might trigger some painful emotions for him. He assured me it was safe to have the party at the mansion, but I still thought about having it at the park instead.

Grace and I tied balloons and streamers all over the house, along with a huge banner that read, "Happy Reunion, Rose, Thomas, and Harper!" I watched for Trey's reaction when the Detwiler family walked in. I'd been so concerned about Rose's impact on his emotional state that I hadn't even thought about how the kids would affect him. His eyes immediately fell on little Harper. He smiled sadly, nodded his acknowledgment to the family, and disappeared into another room.

"I get the feeling we shouldn't be here," Rose whimpered.

"It's okay," I assured her, patting her shoulder comfortingly. "He's still grieving, and sometimes it's hard for him to be around little girls."

"Probably even harder if that little girl's daddy is the one who took his little girl away."

Grace served the kids cake and ice cream while I took Rose on a tour of the house. When we returned to the kitchen, Grace and Thomas were still there, but Harper was gone.

"Where's my daughter?" Rose sounded a bit panicked.

"She wandered off. I guess she wanted to look around the house," Grace explained calmly, scooping a second helping of rocky road ice cream into Thomas's bowl.

"But this place is so huge, I'll never find her," Rose lamented.

I lightly touched the distraught mother's back. "Don't worry. I have a feeling I know where she is." I'd worked with kids enough to know they have an uncanny way of seeking out the person who needs them most. I went to the room where Trey disappeared when the family arrived. He sat there in his favorite chair with the missing girl on his lap, tenderly French braiding her long hair.

I motioned for Rose, and when she saw the heartrending scene, she gulped back a sob. When Trey became aware of our presence, he put Harper on the floor and explained to the child's mother, "I used to braid my daughter's hair like that."

"It looks really pretty that way," she complimented his handiwork. "I wish I was better at fixing her hair."

"It just takes practice," Trey encouraged her, his voice filled with grief.

Harper ran off to find her brother but Rose collapsed in a heap at Trey's feet. "I'm so, so, so sorry. Please forgive me."

"Rose," Trey started, his voice now filled with compassion. "I don't hold you responsible for anything that happened. I know you blame yourself because you told Luke where Emily lived, but I think we all know he would have eventually found her anyway, and chances are, Andi still would have been there when it happened."

"I think about her all the time," Rose sobbed. "Do you think she would forgive me?"

He sighed wistfully, "She was such a great kid, a wise old soul with this big, beautiful heart. I think she forgave you before you even asked." Then he offered Rose the advice Ron Tyler once gave him. "If you really want to honor her, then make something of yourself. Do something good with your life."

I noticed Trey struggling to keep his tears in check in front of us, so I quietly took Rose's arm and led her back to the kitchen.

Inspired by Trey's advice and emboldened by the absolution he gave her, Rose took the next step toward a better future. I helped her fill out the financial aid forms and she enrolled at North State Community College. She made an appointment with an academic adviser and asked me to go along for moral support. I waited in the lobby of the administrative office while she got her class schedule. I noticed a stack of flyers piled on the corner of a desk, and I absently picked one up.

Public lecture series continues Friday night, I read, Dr. Michael Peterson, PhD. Chairman of the Arts & Humanities Department discusses his new book on the life of Henry David Thoreau...

Several other speakers and topics were listed, but there was only one that interested me. And it wasn't the subject matter that caught my attention. It was the picture of the academician giving the lecture on Thoreau. My heart did a full-on somersault inside my chest when I saw that face. *Could it be possible? After all these years?* I asked myself. The dark hair was now streaked with silver, and the grey-blue eyes were clearly visible beneath a receding hairline, but it was him. I was almost certain of it. I circled the date of the lecture in my pocket calendar and shoved the flyer in my purse.

CHAPTER 31

$\mathcal{T}$rey worked the night of the public lecture, but I decided I should tell him about it anyway, so I showed him the flyer.

"Sounds interesting," he stated casually. "You've always been a big fan of Thoreau."

"Honey, that's not really the reason I'm going…"

He interrupted me with a kiss, and then said, "All I know is you feel like you need to be there, and that's good enough for me"

The auditorium was packed with college-aged kids, most of whom I assumed were getting extra credit for their attendance. Dr. Peterson's speech was the last one, so I listened to a psychology professor talk about nurture vs. nature, and I sat through a physics instructor's less-than-fascinating discussion on the wave and particle properties of light. Then the mystery man appeared on stage.

I leaned in closer, but I was too far away to see much more than a silhouette. I strained my ears to see if I heard something familiar in the voice. It wasn't a Texas accent, but that was all I could be certain of. The speaker didn't provide much information about his background, just that he had a PhD from Princeton and he thought he would never get acclimated to our crazy weather. Then he talked about his book and Thoreau's disdain for modernity, and he said if the famous essayist were alive today, he would be outraged by all our excesses and indulgences. Did any of us even know there was a life beyond social media and video games? And what was life anyway? Was it just a few squiggly lines on a heart monitor or some waves on an EEG? If that was life, then what was death but the ceasing of such utilitarian functions? If that were the case, then why was life preferred over death? The professor concluded that these were the questions Thoreau sought to answer, and Dr. Peterson asserted that the questions remained as valid and relevant today as they were at the height of the transcendentalist movement.

Following his speech, he offered to do a book signing. A small group of students stayed to get their books autographed. I assumed they were probably his students because they chatted with him familiarly and the line dwindled slowly. As I approached him, he rolled up the sleeves of his blue and white pin-striped dress shirt as if preparing for manual labor or a fist fight. I had to steady myself against the wall when I saw the yin-yang tattoo. I decided quickly not to tell him who I was if he didn't recognize me.

I didn't have a copy of the book he authored, but I handed him my copy—his copy—of *Walden*. He opened it to the page with the highlighted passage. Underneath the now faded acronym, he wrote, "I told you we would make it, Des."

CHAPTER 32

"I'm still a little mad at you," I told The Philosopher, who I now knew as Dr. Michael Peterson.

"For what?" he demanded as he walked me to my car. It was late evening, and the sky was opaque with streaks of mauve still adorning the western horizon. I leaned against my driver's side door, and he stood in front of me. I stared at his face, but his eyes were impossible to read. Like the symbol etched eternally on his forearm, his pupils conveyed a contradictory message of good and bad.

"For leaving me there alone. For all you knew, a band of gypsies could have kidnapped me and taken me off to Bucharest." I jabbed my book into his chest in mock anger.

"I think you would have been okay with that. I seem to recall a girl who was starving for adventure and knowledge. No better way to get that than world travel."

I tried to stifle a grin but failed. "Seriously, though. Why did you leave me? I would have gone anywhere with you."

"Oh, Des," he sucked in a deep breath and exhaled slowly. It reminded me of watching him smoke weed all those years ago. "You didn't need me. Back then, you had a better chance of making it without me. I was a pothead, a casual meth user, and a borderline alcoholic, and I had you on the verge of taking up all my bad habits. And I wasn't a grad student, either, like I told you I was. I had quit graduate school. I went back later, but then, I really thought I could drop out of society and live this idyllic Thoreauvian life. And then I met you, and all that stuff I was running from, you were running toward. Your parents locked you away from society and forced you to live the kind of life I thought I wanted. You were as miserable with all that simplicity as I was in a world of materialism."

"So that's why you left me there? You thought I was materialistic? We lived all those months without electricity, and we bathed at the neighbor's house, and I never once complained, but you thought I was materialistic?" I fetched my keys out of my purse and prepared to leave. If he really thought so little of me, then maybe that summer hadn't meant as much to him as it had to me.

"I guess materialism was the wrong word," he altered his thinking. "I never thought you were obsessed with money or possessions, but I knew you wanted more out of life than drifting from one abandoned building to the next, depending on the kindness of strangers to sustain us. I knew you desperately wanted an education, and you craved art and culture. You thirsted for things I carelessly threw away. Things you weren't going to find on the back of my motorcycle."

The wind picked up, and I shivered slightly, but it was enough for him to notice. He removed his jacket and draped it over my shoulders. I pulled the two sides together around my neck and held them there tightly, partly because of the unseasonably cool temperature, and partly because I was suddenly aware of my low cut blouse.

"I'm really not mad at you," I admitted. "I got over that as soon as I made it safely to my aunts' house. In fact, I've always been grateful to you."

"Grateful? How?" I'd forgotten how he looked at me like every word I said was the most fascinating thing he ever heard.

"I guess I had a really crappy high school counselor. Nobody ever told me about financial aid for college. If you hadn't left that message in the book you gave me, I would have probably spent my whole life cleaning motels and living with relatives."

"So then, you did find what you were looking for?"

"Eventually." I didn't tell him that it was only in recent weeks I even figured out what that was. "There was something else I was grateful to you for. It was because of you I stopped believing in the myth."

Under the artificial light that illuminated the parking lot, I saw him raise his eyebrows. "I shouldn't have done that to you. That was part of your cultural heritage and tradition. I should never have taken that away from you." I heard genuine remorse in his voice.

"That part of my cultural heritage and tradition was deadly poison. I had to let it go."

"Faith can be a powerful thing in a person's life, Des. I had no right to take that away from you."

"Trust me, my faith is still firmly intact. My faith was never in Adam and Eve, or the Garden of Eden. That is the part that stifles humanity and keeps women bound and oppressed."

"If it freed you to live the life you wanted, then I'm glad you stopped believing the myth."

"Tell me something, Michael." It felt odd referring to him by an actual name. "You said you had a PhD from Princeton. You could have taught at an elite university. What brought you back here to this Podunk community college?"

"A couple of things. Number one is I thought a rustic cabin on the shores of Lake Sutton was about as close to Walden as I could get in twenty-first century America."

"What was the other thing?" I was afraid I already knew the answer.

"I was looking for you. I wanted to find you. I wanted to make sure you were okay. I needed to know you really did make it."

"You could have just been a normal person and looked me up on social media," I joked, again jabbing his side with the book he had given me so long ago.

"Really?" he countered. "You go by Desdemona on your social media accounts?"

I marveled at how smoothly our conversation flowed. Michael and I had known each other a few months over twenty years earlier, but other than Connie and Trey, I felt like I'd never had a closer friend.

"Did you ever get married, Des?" Michael asked after a brief silence.

"No, but I am deeply in love with someone." My heart fluttered at the mere thought of Trey.

I am *deeply in love with someone*, I reminded myself. *What am I doing here with a ghost from my past, a past I have been desperately trying to put behind me?*

The sky was now a sparkling black velvet blanket covering the plain, and the security lights gave the pavement an eerie glow. I looked down at my phone. It was after midnight, and Trey's shift ended at eleven. Michael and I had stood there on that parking lot, talking for three hours!

"I'm sorry. I have to go. I have to go now." I shrugged off his jacket and threw it at him.

With no further explanation, I jumped in my car.

The Philosopher grabbed the door, hindering my hasty departure. "Just one more question." I looked back at him impatiently, and he continued. "Since you now know my name, shouldn't I know yours?"

I nodded apologetically. "It's Emily," I introduced myself to a man it seemed like I'd always known. "Emily Kirk."

I FOUND Trey sitting in a cozy alcove with both hands wrapped around a coffee mug. "Must have been a hell of a speech," he muttered when he saw me. Though his words were caustic, his expression was not one of anger or jealousy; it was concern, plain and simple.

I recalled how open he had been with me about his lingering feelings for Sarah, and I felt he deserved the same honesty. I'd never told anybody about my summer in that abandoned church, but now I told Trey everything. I told him about my daring escape from my parents' house. I told him about the old couple who let us do odd jobs in exchange for baths and food, and I even told him about the sex and drugs and the long talks about philosophy and life.

When I stopped talking, Trey had one simple, but profoundly complicated, question. "Did you love him?'

"By the time it ended, I thought I did," I acknowledged, rubbing my hand affectionately up and down the taut muscles of Trey's fore-arm. "but I really didn't. My feelings for Michael at that time were the confused emotions of a scared kid with a wounded soul."

"That's how you felt about him then. How do you feel about him now?"

All the way home from the college campus, I kept asking myself that same question. How did I feel about Dr. Michael Peterson now? When I asked the question of myself, I couldn't find the right answer, but now that I was confronted by the man I really loved, I knew the exact response.

"My feelings for Michael now are the same as they would be for a firefighter who plucked me out of a burning building. Respect, honor, and undying gratitude, but not love. At least not our kind of love. But Trey, if Michael hadn't come into my life when he did, I don't know where I would be today. I certainly don't think I would be here with you."

Trey looked relieved as he pulled me onto his lap. "I get it," he spoke softly into my ear. "In a very real sense, he did rescue you from a fire. That whole system your parents raised you in was about to go up in flames. He got you out of that mess before it consumed you. It's okay for you to care about other people, Em—even other men—just as long as you love me more."

"I will always love you more," I promised him. Not wanting to hide any part of my life from Trey, and unwilling to sacrifice my friendship with The Philosopher a second time, I pushed my luck a little further. "Would you be willing to meet my friend?"

Trey shrugged nonchalantly. "Why not? If he is in any way responsible for you being here with me today, then I like the guy already."

As the new trial date approached, the dreams intensified. Eve/Rose no longer waited for me to ask what she wanted from me before she bellowed her demand. "*REDEMPTION!*" She shouted with such force, the dry, cracked ground shook beneath my feet. I shot up out of bed, but Trey was not there to comfort me. He'd worked a late shift again. I must have cried out in my sleep, because I heard a light tap on my door.

"Emily? Are you okay?" It was Grace.

"It was just a bad dream." I replied, still struggling to catch my breath.

"Since you're awake, will you come out here for a second? I have something I want to show you."

I stretched, yawned, and rolled out of bed with about as much energy and enthusiasm as a sloth. Grace led me into an area of the house we had cordoned off for her creative endeavors. Several easels were covered with sheets. She never liked to reveal her work until she was completely satisfied with the outcome.

I never knew what happened to her artwork after she finished it. She showed us each painting when she perfected it, but then it would disappear from her collection. All her masterpieces were of people and they all seemed so real, I could almost imagine their heartbeats emanating from the canvases. I came to think of her as the anti-Madame Defarge. The Dickens villainess stitched the names of the condemned into her handiwork,while Grace painted the faces of the redeemed.

"You're worried you won't be able to testify, aren't you?" She offered me a glass of milk she'd already poured and I had the feeling she'd been expecting me to wake up in the middle of the night and join her.

I sighed. "Something happens to me when I have to see him. It's like I'm gripped with an overwhelming fear, and it's the most intense and paralyzing fear I've ever felt. I lose my ability to speak. That's how scared I get when I'm in his presence." I'd conquered my anxieties about abstract ideas, perceived threats I only envisaged, but The Beast presented a real danger, and I knew firsthand the full scope of his malevolence. I still trembled at the thought of facing him.

"Let me show you something," she offered. She jerked the sheet away from one of the easels and revealed her most stunning work yet. The painting was of twelve people seated in two parallel rows. It didn't take long for me to figure out it was a jury, but it wasn't just any jury; it was the seven women and five men hearing the case against The Beast.

"How did you paint that?" I marveled. "You weren't even at the trial."

"When you've seen one jury, you've seen them all," she casually dismissed my question.

I continued staring at the incredibly lifelike renderings of the jurors. "What do you see there, Emily?" Grace questioned.

"His constitutional right," I scoffed. "A jury of his peers."

"But they aren't *his* peers, are they? Not really. Not in any way that matters."

I leaned in closer and squinted, trying to figure out what she saw that I didn't see. Twelve people from varied races, different sizes, different hair colors. One was in a wheelchair; one had a jagged scar on the left side of his face, and one woman had the drooping mouth indicative of palsy or a stroke.

"Look into their eyes," Grace instructed. "You've always read their eyes." I wondered how she knew that.

I now focused my attention on twenty-four irises, some blue, some brown, some green. They say that none of us are ever separated from each other by more than six degrees. In a small town, it's more like two-and-a-half degrees. I hadn't realized it in court, but I'd seen these people before. I'd looked into those twelve sets of eyes. One woman worked at my bank. She used to bring her baby to work and I'd play with him while she completed my transactions. One man gave swimming lessons at the Y. I used to take troubled kids there because I knew learning to swim would help them gain confidence. I'd seen all these people around town, going about their daily lives. Grace was right. These were not Luke Detwiler's peers. They were hardworking mothers and fathers, people who'd withstood storms; they'd celebrated births and mourned deaths. They had known victories and losses, illnesses and health; they'd made horrible mistakes and had achieved great successes. They had experienced the yin and yang of human existence and had not allowed the bad to swallow up the good. There was not a soulless beast among them. They were human beings, each one a vital part of the magnificently flawed and hideously beautiful *Imago Dei*.

"Whose peers are they, Emily?" Grace asked again.

"They are my peers," I proclaimed triumphantly.

After that encounter, I no longer thought of Rose as the most enigmatic person I knew. There was nothing atypical about Rose. Like me, and like the rest of *Imago Dei*, she was a flawed human being, slowly finding her way in a world that wanted to destroy her. Grace was the real enigma, and I became obsessed with knowing her better and understanding her.

When she'd allow it, I'd sit in her little makeshift art studio and watch her work. She'd carefully situate her body between her easel and my line of vision so I couldn't see her masterpiece until she had perfected it. Her strokes were so wild and erratic it seemed impossible that anything other than streaks and smudges could emerge from such chaos, but when she finished, she always revealed an exquisite and unbelievably realistic rendering of a person or group of people. Most amazingly of all, she never used a single model, not even a photograph.

"How do you do that?" I asked her one day. "How do you paint such realistic images with nothing to go by?"

She smiled. "Practice, my dear. Years and years and years of practice."

I assumed she meant she had plenty of time to practice during the fifteen years she was incarcerated for the murder her son committed. Grace and I never spoke about her act of sacrificial love, but now I wanted her to know how much I admired her devotion to her only child.

"I know what you did for Trey," I blurted out, dipping one of her paintbrushes into a Mason jar of colored water. Cleaning the brushes was the only thing I was allowed to do in the art studio.

She stopped the wild, frenetic painting and stood perfectly still. "What? Do you mean feed him, change him, bathe him, love him? I didn't do anything any mother wouldn't do."

I grew a little impatient with her modesty. "You know what I'm talking about. I mean the way you took the blame when he killed his step-father."

She turned around to face me, her expression serious but not angry. "As I said, I didn't do anything any mother wouldn't do."

"I'm not sure that's true," I removed the paintbrush from the water and stuck another one in.. "Anyway, I don't understand why you did it. Trey would have been charged as a juvenile. As soon as he turned twenty-one, his record would have been expunged. You will be labelled a violent offender the rest of your life."

"Technically, you are correct. When Trey turned twenty-one, his records would have been sealed, and legally speaking, it would be as though nothing ever happened. However, my son would have finished out his youth in a correctional facility. God only knows what kind of subpar education he would have gotten. He probably would have been bullied and abused by older and bigger boys until he grew hardened and lost all that empathy and sensitivity you and I both love about him. He probably would have grown to resent law enforcement, and he certainly wouldn't be a police officer today. He would only be a sad shadow of the man we both adore. So tell me. Emily, do you think I should have done anything differently than I did?"

I shook my head. "You are an incredible woman, Grace. You pled guilty to spare your son a lifetime of pain and anguish."

"Emily, I was guilty. Not of pulling the trigger, but I brought that evil into our house, all because I got scared. My husband had died and Trey and I were alone with a whole lot of land to take care of. My fear is what put my boy in that horrible situation. In some ways, I was guiltier than he was."

"I certainly know what it's like to let fear make your decisions for you."

Grace resumed her painting, and I quietly exited the room, knowing the enigmatic woman had said as much as she was ever going to tell me about her sacrifice.

CHAPTER 33

*T*he courthouse loomed before me, a concrete barrier between my past and my future. If I ever hoped to reach the other side, I had to face what awaited me in that building. This time there was no escaping the reporters. They'd discovered the side door and they had every entrance surrounded. Short, pudgy men chased me with mammoth cameras riding on their shoulders, and skinny blonde women shoved giant microphones at my face.

"Are you prepared to make a statement, Ms. Kirk?" they shouted at me.

"We will make a statement when the trial is over." Karen Tobias pushed past them and reached back for my hand. She led me up the steps and inside the building.

"This is it," the prosecutor said when we reached a place of relative quiet and privacy. "The judge is losing his patience with both sides. There won't be anymore continuances, no more delays, no more second chances to pull yourself together. It's do or die time. Do you understand what I'm saying?"

"I understand, Karen, but I still can't make any promises. I don't know how my mind is going to react when I see him."

She sighed heavily, and then we entered the rotunda. Because it had been an extended period of time since the jury last convened, the first half of the morning was spent reviewing the scant physical evidence against the defendant. The new public defender, who knew less about the law than I did, recalled Rose to the stand and tried intimidating her into recanting her testimony again, but she remained steadfast and unwavering. She had no idea where her former husband was the night of Andi's murder, but he certainly was not with her, as he claimed he was. Mangy Dog was too much of a wild card for even the inept defense attorney to take a chance on, so he was not in court that day. After a short recess for lunch, it was my turn. Justice for Andi rested squarely on my shoulders.

The court officer announced the entrance of the jury, and we respectfully stood to honor them and their sacred duty. I watched them file into the jury box, a young man gingerly assisted an elderly woman with a cane, and one of the chairs had been removed to accommodate the wheelchair. There they sat, seven women and five men, a random sampling of *Imago Dei*, not the defendant's peers, but mine.

The judge began the proceedings by addressing Karen. "Counselor, you may call your next witness."

The prosecutor stood. She looked worried, but she managed to sound confident. "The State calls Emily Kirk."

I arose and began my walk to the witness stand. It seemed a mile away, and my feet felt like I had bathed them in wet cement that had now dried and hardened into heavy blocks, but I willed myself forward. As I passed The Beast, he again lightly tapped my ankle. This time I willfully looked into his empty soulless eyes. I needed to know I could do it without losing my voice. I stared him down, and I felt my voice rising in me. It pushed its way through my larynx, over my tongue, and across my lips.

Fist clenched, jaw locked, my determined glare fixed on my enemy, I muttered just audibly enough The Beast could hear me, but the judge could not. "Burn in hell, you son of a bitch."

I opened the little gate that led to the witness stand and stepped upon the oval shaped platform. The bailiff held the white Bible in front of me. As per his instructions, I placed my right on top of it.

"Do you swear to tell the truth, the whole truth, and nothing but the truth, so help you God?"

"I do." From the vantage point of the witness stand, I could see everything in the courtroom. Dark mahogany walls surrounded us and a giant crystal chandelier dangled from the center of the vaulted ceiling. It was a high profile case so the room was packed to capacity with reporters and curious onlookers. Most of the faces looked at me with warmth, kindness, and sympathy; but Jack Detwiler and an older woman sat behind the defendant, glaring hostilely in my direction, their eyes bloodshot and their mouths drooping in angry scowls.

I sat down in a high back gray office chair. Then Karen, after breathing a sigh of relief, approached the witness stand and began her line of questioning.

"Please state your name for the record."

"My name is Emily Kirk." I had never spoke my name more proudly or more forcefully. My identity had been linked to my voice. When I had no voice, I had no real identity. Now I wanted the whole world to know who I was.

"Ms. Kirk, on the night of July 10 three men broke into your apartment. You were violently assaulted and left for dead, and a child left in your care was murdered. As has been previously established in this court, one of those men was the now deceased Leonard Horton; one of them was Tony Detwiler, who pled guilty to assaulting you and is now serving his sentence in the Texas criminal justice system. But you said there was a third man in your apartment that night. Is that third man in this courtroom today?"

"Yes, he is," I boldly replied.

"And can you point to that man?"

Karen stepped aside, and I pointed to The Beast. "It was that man. It was the defendant, Luke Detwiler."

"Are you absolutely certain Luke Detwiler was the third man in your apartment the night you were savagely raped and Andrea Scoggins, a nine-year-old child, was viciously murdered? Can you say without any doubt that the defendant, Luke Detwiler, was that man?"

"I am certain beyond the faintest sliver of a doubt." My voice never wavered, and my confidence never lagged.

The prosecutor turned toward the jury. "Let it be duly noted that the witness has definitively and without hesitation identified the defendant, Luke Detwiler, as being physically present at the crime scene."

Then she resumed questioning me. "Prior to that night, had you known Mr. Detwiler?"

"Yes. I had known him about a year."

"Can you tell us the exact nature of your interactions with the defendant?"

"At that time, I was a social worker for Child Protective Services. I was assigned to investigate allegations that he had abused his children."

"So then there was cause for contention between you and the defendant?"

"I suppose he saw it that way. I just saw it as doing my job and protecting innocent children."

"Ms. Kirk, before the night of Andrea's murder, had Mr. Detwiler made any threats against you?"

"Yes, he had."

"Can you tell us when that happened, and what were the circumstances involved?"

"It was in March of that same year. I'd convinced his wife if she didn't leave him and get her kids away from their abuser, then she would lose custody and go to jail for allowing the abuse. The defendant was being arrested for beating his son when Mrs. Detwiler and I arrived at her house to collect her things and get her daughter. When the defendant figured out he was losing his family, that's when he made the threat."

"What exactly did he say?"

"He said, 'You take what's mine, I'll take what's yours.'"

"What did you interpret that to mean?"

"To me, it was pretty obvious. He thought it was my fault he was losing his children, so he planned to take something important from me."

"Like a child, maybe?"

"I didn't have any children."

"But the defendant didn't know that, did he? And when he broke into your apartment and found a child sleeping beside you, he could have reasonably concluded it was your child."

I hadn't thought about it before, but it made perfect sense. I always thought The Beast killed Andi because she was a witness, but that wasn't the only reason. He thought she was my daughter. I took his, and he took mine.

"Yes, I suppose that would have been the logical conclusion anyone would have arrived at under the circumstances."

"Now Ms. Kirk, while you were being brutally assaulted by the other two men, what was Mr. Detwiler doing?"

That part was still fuzzy in my mind. I tried to suppress those images whenever they surfaced, but now I had to replay that scene. I had to do it for Andi.

"At first, he just stared at her, with this horrible, wicked grin on his face. He was standing on my side of the bed, but when she jumped up, he leapt over to her side. She tried to get past him to go for help, but he was too fast and too strong, and she was small, even for her age. He grabbed her around the throat, and he just kept choking her." At this point, my voice faltered as I struggled to keep my composure. The judge had warned us that he would not tolerate any more shenanigans, and that included emotional outbursts. "Her feet must have been two feet off the floor, but she kicked at him. She fought so hard to live, but he was so much stronger, and she was so little. Then when she stopped fighting, he threw her body against the wall, and he looked back at me and said, 'You took mine. I took yours.'"

"And this whole time, the other two men had you pinned down, so you were powerless to help Andrea, is that correct? A child you loved like your own daughter, and you were forced to watch being strangled to death?" It was a leading question; the defense attorney could have objected, but he didn't.

"I couldn't even scream." It was now impossible for me to hold back the emotion. I collapsed my head on my lap and cried. Karen was merciful, and she ceased her interrogation. The public defender, who seemed to have gotten his juris doctorate from eBay, didn't even cross examine me. He could have asked about the lighting in the room, he could have asked about my subsequent mental health issues, but he chose not to question me at all. It was almost as if he had no desire to defend his client. The judge dismissed me from the stand. There were a few more legal formalities to go over, then the jury was sent into deliberation and court was adjourned. I exited the courtroom feeling somewhat like Atticus Finch, nobly exhausted and content in the knowledge that no matter how it all panned out, I'd done my part.

"As late as it is, I doubt we will hear anything from the jury tonight," Karen told us in the hallway. "Why don't we all go home and get a good night's rest? I'll let everyone know as soon as I hear anything."

Before we left the building, the prosecutor put one hand on each side of my face. "You, my friend, were stupendous up there. Rest assured, if we don't get the verdict we want, it will not be because of anything you did or didn't do."

We shoved our way past the throng of reporters and camera operators. Trey and I took Sarah back to her hotel and then we went home and filled Grace in on the day's events. I told her I didn't testify before the judge and I didn't testify against the defendant. I simply testified to my peers, and I told them exactly what I witnessed.

When we were alone, Trey wrapped me in his strong arms and kissed my forehead. "I can't imagine how hard it was for you having to relive that."

But I thought he had endured the much more difficult task. "I can't imagine how hard it was for you having to hear it for the first time."

He turned his head away from me and we spent the rest of the night in complete silence, but neither of us was angry. Other than affection, Trey often struggled with expressing strong emotions, and when that happened, I gave him the time and space he needed to process his feelings within himself.

Both Trey and I took the following day off work. We wanted to be free to rush to the courthouse as soon as we got the message from Karen. I ended up wishing I had gone in to work, at least for a few hours, just to have something to occupy my mind. As it was, I paced around the mansion, jumping out of my skin every time a phone rang or a text message came through. I usually handled the cooking, but I let Grace prepare breakfast. All I had was a glass of fresh squeezed orange juice, but I even had trouble getting the pulpy liquid past the labyrinth of knots in my stomach.

Trey seemed even more anxious and agitated than I was. He took his coffee and newspaper out to the veranda. Ordinarily, he would have asked me to join him; that balcony had become our special place for deep talks and peaceful moments. I wasn't hurt that he didn't invite me this time. No matter how much you love someone, or how much they love you, there are certain journeys an individual must take alone. I wasn't hurt, but I was concerned.

"I'm worried about Trey," I told Grace as I helped her clean up after the morning meal. "It's been over a year since we lost Andi, and I still don't think he has grieved properly."

"Grieved properly?" She looked indignant. "I didn't know there was a way to grieve properly."

"I guess there really isn't," I agreed. "There are supposed to be five stages of grief: denial, anger, bargaining, sadness, and acceptance. Of course, everybody goes through the stages differently, but I don't think Trey has allowed himself to feel any of those things."

Grace dried her sudsy hands on a dishtowel and then offered it to me. "What makes you think he hasn't felt those things? Just because he hasn't outwardly manifested his grief?"

"All I've seen is a few tears that he suppresses the minute he sees me looking."

"Let me show you how Trey mourns." She reached into the pocket of her paint-splattered smock and fished out a yellowed piece of typing paper. "Right after I was released from prison, I lived with my son for a while. During that time, Trey lost one of his best friends from high school. The young man died fighting in Afghanistan. For a while, I was like you, I thought something was horribly wrong with the way my boy mourned the loss of his friend. He got quiet and pensive, but he never cried or got angry. Then trash day came, and I was collecting the garbage to take to the curb for pick up. This piece of paper was on top of the trash in Trey's room."

She handed it to me. Curiously, I unfolded the paper and smoothed the wrinkles out of it. Then I read:

Ten Million Wars
They waged ten-million wars,
And they lost ten-million lives.
Made ten-million widows
Out of ten-million wives.
Ten-million mourning mothers
Still grieving for their sons,
And when all the wars had ended
Not a goddamned thing was won.

I gasped in astonishment. "That's excellent!"

Grace nodded in agreement. "You see, Emily? Trey grieves, and he does it in a healthy manner. He just does it his own way. I bet if you had searched through all the trash cans, you would have found a hundred poems about Andi by now."

My phone made a buzzing sound and vibrated on the coffee table. It was a text message from the prosecutor. Three words: "Jury is back." Trey must have gotten the same message at the same time because he came inside and grabbed his keys.

"Do you want to come with us?" I offered Grace.

"I told you I'm waiting for the sentencing phase."

I hurriedly kissed her cheek and replied, "Let's just pray there is one."

There was no media presence blocking the entrance. The reporters had not been informed when jury deliberation ended. I expected they would be there by the time we came out, because a crowd of onlookers gathered across the street and watched us rushing into the courthouse.

Someone was bound to figure out what was going on and alert the media.

"Any guesses?" I asked Karen when she joined up with us on the concrete steps.

"It wasn't a very long deliberation, considering all they had to go on was circumstantial evidence and one eyewitness testimony. Hard to say if that bodes well or bad for us."

The mood inside the rotunda was somber as the judge made his usual ceremonial appearance. Then we were ordered to rise for the entrance of the jury. I looked across the aisle at The Beast. The smug expression he'd worn throughout the trial had faded to one of grave concern; he repetitively tapped one foot on the marble tile. My testimony, if nothing else, had at least made him squirm, and that pleased me immensely.

The judge began. "Will the defendant please rise?"

The Beast scowled in defiance, but the man with the eBay juris doctorate pulled him up by the shirt sleeve.

"Madame Foreperson, please rise for the reading of the verdict."

A middle-aged woman with round eyeglasses and frizzy black hair stood and nervously straightened her skirt. The judge addressed her. "Madame Foreperson, has your jury understood the instructions as they were provided by this court?

"Yes, your honor, we have."

I grabbed Trey's arm and held it tightly, hoping our physical closeness comforted him as much as it did me. The magistrate went on, "And in accordance with those instructions, Madame Foreperson, has your jury reached unanimous verdicts as to the guilt or innocence of the defendant regarding the charges brought against him by the State of Texas?

"Yes, your honor, we have."

"At this time, I will read the list of charges against the defendant, Luke Thomas Detwiler. You, Madame Foreperson, shall respond with either 'he is guilty' or 'he is not guilty.' Do you understand these instructions?

"Yes, your honor, I do."

"On the first count, the defendant, Luke Thomas Detwiler, is charged with criminal trespass onto a private residence for the purpose of committing a felony. Is he guilty or not guilty?"

"He is guilty."

"So say you all?"

"So say we all."

"On the second count, the defendant is accused of conspiracy to commit rape. Is he guilty or not guilty?"

"He is guilty."

"So say you all?"

"So say we all."

"On the third count, the defendant is accused of conspiracy to commit first-degree murder. Is he guilty or not guilty?"

"He is guilty."

"So say you all?"

"So say we all."

"On the fourth count, the defendant is accused of causing injury to a child. Is he guilty or not guilty?

"He is guilty."

"So say you all?"

"So say we all."

"On the fifth and final count, the defendant is accused of the first-degree murder of Andrea Grace Scoggins, a minor child. Is he guilty or not guilty?"

This time more forcefully. "He is guilty."

"So say you all?"

The jury foreperson enunciated her words slowly and plainly. "So...say...we...all."

Trey dropped his head in his hands and wept bitterly. He didn't cry like a little girl, as the adage goes, but like a man. Like a strong, wonderful man who loved deeply and hurt profoundly, and had no socially acceptable outlet for such profound emotions. A man who wrote beautiful poetry he couldn't share with anyone, and who French braided his little girl's hair as a small token of his undying devotion to her, a devotion he could never quite verbalize. A man equally as robbed and cheated by the myth as any woman. I put my face against his, and our tears mingled, a river of grief flowing into an ocean of humanity. Since we lost Andi, Trey had cried the same leaky faucet tears I shed shortly after the rape, a droplet or spurt here and there. Now it was like somebody opened the floodgates of heaven and the rain came down, and it was a gullywasher.

Then the jury was polled, *Imago Dei* convicted The Beast, and court was dismissed. Karen told us the sentencing phase would begin in two weeks. She advised us to start working on our victim impact statements. Unlike the trial, where we were sternly warned against emotional outbursts, the prosecutor now told us to convey as much sentiment as we could muster. She was going for the death penalty, she explained. Luke killed Andi during the commission of another felony. That created aggravated circumstances, and that made the murder a capital offense. Those of us who loved Andi needed to show the judge and jury how much we lost when he took her from us, so they could comprehend the heinousness of his crimes.

Outside, the throng of reporters shoved microphones in our faces. One was so close to my mouth, the yellow foam covering the speaker tickled my lip. Karen gave a brief statement about how pleased we were with the outcome of the trial. The media representatives then turned their focus on the bereaved parents. Sarah trembled and frantically pushed the mics away. Trey guided her by the elbow, through the crowd; his other hand was on my back. "We have no comment at this time," he barked at no one in particular.

I invited Rose and her children to dinner, because I didn't think she'd feel like cooking after such an emotionally exhausting day, and I personally found cooking cathartic' the more people I had to serve, the greater the catharsis. I asked Sarah to join us, but she wanted to be alone. Her unbearable sadness was becoming physically evident now; she made no attempt to style her hair, and her face was pallid, with no makeup covering the droopy eyelids. I had told Michael about the trial, and when he called to see if the verdict was in, I invited him to dinner as well.

"Guilty on all counts," Trey announced to his mother when we walked into our house.

"I know," she responded happily. "It's already all over the news."

Much to my surprise, Trey and Michael hit it off immediately. When The Philosopher greeted me using the pseudonym "Des," I told Trey it was short for Desdemona, and then I started to explain the significance of the name, but Trey stopped me. He already knew that Desdemona was Othello's wife, falsely accused of betraying her husband; he even made the connection with the false accusations leveled at me by my father, my sister, and the church leaders. I stayed in the kitchen while the two men went into the adjoining alcove. I watched them skeptically while I prepared linguine and shrimp. Trey had regained his composure and made it clear that he was not interested in talking about the trial or the verdict, so Michael steered the conversation toward the subjects he was most comfortable with. I'd always assumed Andi got her intelligence from Sarah, but now as I listened to the quintessentially blue-collar cop go toe to toe with the ardent intellectual on everything from history and politics to philosophy and literature, I wondered if I had arrogantly stereotyped the man I loved. Trey hadn't gone to college, and they didn't teach some of this stuff in high school; they certainly didn't teach it at the police academy. He must have been self-educated. Equally surprising was the interest Michael showed in Trey's tales of fishing and crime busting. If I hadn't known better, I would have thought the two were old pals, and I was the one out of the loop.

When Rose arrived, all the attention was focused on Thomas and Harper. Rose's kids, I thought, were the forgotten victims in this horrific nightmare. As despicable and evil as Luke was, and although he'd abused his family mercilessly, he was still their father. He had once played a significant role in their lives, but they would never see him again. Rose vowed she would never allow them to visit him in prison. I didn't know how she explained their father's absence to them, but I knew neither of them was developmentally advanced enough to grasp the seriousness of the situation.

Thomas and Harper had grown accustomed to running freely

around the mansion because Grace had volunteered her services as their caregiver when their mother worked late, had an evening class, or needed quiet time to study. I worried about how Michael might respond to such rambunctious children. He once told me unequivocally that kids were not his forte, but he seemed genuinely smitten with Thomas and Harper, even patiently answering their questions about his tattoo and why he talked funny. Ultimately, it was Grace who grew weary of the children's antics, and she herded them off to her art studio where she allowed them to paint and draw.

The remaining adults lingered at the table and I removed four glasses from a cupboard, then opened a bottle of wine. Rose politely pushed her glass aside and explained, "I have an addictive personality. I don't think I should drink anymore."

"Did they tell you that at rehab?" As soon as the words spilled out of my mouth, I bit my tongue sharply as punishment for revealing an intensely personal detail about Rose in front of Michael, a complete stranger to her, but she appeared unaffected by my *faux pas*.

"No," she replied. "but I've known a lot of people who get off drugs, but then they turn to alcohol because they didn't deal with the root of the problem that was causing them to do drugs in the first place."

I was astonished at the insight and emotional depth she'd gained in the short period of time I had known her. Even her enunciation had improved, and her speech was more sophisticated. Michael was fascinated with her. I could tell by the way he leaned his head to the side and made eye contact with her, even when she ducked her head and avoided his gaze. If there was one thing I remembered about Michael, it was that he loved human stories. He listened intently as she recapitulated a lifetime of abuse and abandonment. She never knew her father, and her mother was an alcoholic. When she was barely a teenager, her mother started dragging her into bars and making her lift her shirt in front of crowds of boisterous, drunken men, who then threw money at her feet--money her mother greedily collected, and Rose never touched a dime of. She met Luke at one of those bars. The drugs he offered her mitigated the humiliation she felt so it was the escape from reality she fell in love with, not The Beast.

Whenever her words faltered, Michael urged her on with carefully worded questions, a gentle inquest from an empathic interrogator. She self-consciously knotted her hair around her forefinger as she became increasingly aware of his sincere interest in everything she said. After years of exploitation by practically everyone she knew, I was sure Rose was unaccustomed to the benign attention of well-groomed and highly educated men. She looked more uncomfortable under the scrutiny of his soul-reading glare than she had looked on the witness stand.

Eventually, Rose stopped talking about her traumatic upbringing and subsequent battles with abuse and addiction, and the conversation shifted to more lighthearted banter. Grace put the children to bed in a spare room and then retired herself. My three companions swapped jokes and told real-life anecdotes until well after two a.m. I stayed mostly quiet, delighting in the sound of their laughter. I always heard people talk about their "circle." In church, they called it "finding your tribe." I never knew what those phrases meant until that night after The Beast was convicted. I had a circle now. I had found my tribe

---

AT THE SENTENCING HEARING, everyone who loved Andi was allowed to give a statement regarding how her death affected them. We let Sarah go first.

Sarah Scoggins' Victim Impact Statement

Sarah was now a pathetic caricature of the glamorous woman she had once been. She bit her lower lip, took in several deep breaths, and began.

"My name is Sarah Scoggins. Andi was, is, and always will be my daughter. I wasn't one of those girls who grew up dreaming about becoming a mom. I didn't sit around thinking up cute names or going window shopping to look at all the adorable little girl outfits. I was too selfish for that." I never thought of Sarah as selfish, but then again, I never knew her before she had Andi. That little girl had a way of changing people for the better. "I just wanted to be beautiful and rich and adored. Having a baby seemed like an impediment to my self-centered goals, but that all changed when I fell in love with Andi's father, somebody who was the polar-opposite of me. He was as kind and generous as I was selfish and petty. Before I even knew what was happening, we were married, and our little Andi was on her way. From the moment I saw her first ultrasound picture, I knew I was meant to be her mom. That became my whole identity. All my selfish ambition just dissolved. I had something more important than myself to live for. I wasn't self-centered and petty anymore. My daughter filled my heart with so much love that I had plenty to share with the rest of the world. That changed me. It made me a better person than I thought I was capable of being. Things didn't work out between Andi's dad and me. In the end, I guess we were just too different, but we had this one perfect thing between us that bound us forever, and because of that, we never resented each other, and we never regretted our time together. Our daughter was like our little gift to the world. We knew someday she was going to do great things, and she would have. She was so smart and kind and giving and loving." Sarah had been staring blankly in front of her. Now she zeroed in on The Beast as she continued, "You see, when you took Andi from us, you didn't just steal her from her father and me. She was a precious gift to the world. You stole her from the whole world, and you deprived the world of all the enormous gifts she had to offer. People tell me I have to find a way to forgive, so I can start to heal, but how do you forgive the devil? And that's what you are. You are Satan, because only Satan could be so vicious, so evil, so heartless, so malevolent as to deprive the world of someone as special as my daughter. I wish I could find some way to forgive you, because this hatred that I now carry is killing me. If you had known me before you took Andi from me, you wouldn't even recognize me now. You didn't just kill my daughter; you killed the very best part of me, and I don't think there is any way I can ever forgive you for that. You didn't just take away my child. You took away my identity. I don't know who I am if I'm not Andi's mom."

TREY SCOGGINS' Victim Impact Statement

I had watched Trey work diligently on his statement, but I had no idea what he was going to say. Whenever he talked about Andi, it was usually some happy memory. I braced myself for his speech.

"My name is Trey Scoggins, and I am Andi's dad. Admittedly, I wasn't always as involved with her as I should have been. I could give you a million lame excuses why I wasn't more active in my daughter's life, but I guess the truth is, like a lot of men, I thought I just wasn't that important. I believed if she had food on the table and clothes on her back, then I'd done a good job as a parent. I'd made my contribution, and nothing more was required of me. I could give myself a pat on the back and rest well at night, because at least I wasn't one of those deadbeat dads who never paid a dime of child support. Things had started to change between Andi and me. I started realizing she did need me, and I was committed to becoming a better dad to her. I had made up my mind that if Sarah didn't move back to Texas, like she talked about, then I was moving to Boston. One way or the other, I was going to be with my baby girl. Right after I made that decision, that's when you took her from me. You robbed me of my second chance. Now I will live the rest of my life with the guilt of all the precious time I wasted when I should have been cherishing every moment. Sarah talked about not being able to forgive you, but I don't have to forgive you. You are like dirt that gets caked up on the bottom of my shoes. I don't forgive the dirt for being dirt. I scrape it off and move on, and that's what I'm doing to you. I'm scraping you off, and I'm moving on. You stole my daughter from me, but I'm not letting you steal my faith in God, my faith in humanity, or my peace of mind. Today is the last day I will waste one minute thinking about you, because like mud caked on the bottom of my shoe, you're not worth the mental energy it takes giving you a second thought. I don't hate you. I am not angry at you. In fact, if I was going to waste my time feeling anything for you, I'd feel sorry for you. Because you had a little girl, too, and like me, you failed to appreciate how important you were to her. The difference is I neglected my daughter because I got too busy, and I let time slip away, thinking I was doing the right thing by working long hours and making as much money as I possibly could. You gave up your daughter because of your blind hatred and your insatiable need for revenge. I would pity you because you will never know the joy of braiding that little girl's hair or having her climb on your lap after she comes home from school and telling you everything she learned that day. But you're not even worth my pity, because unlike me. your heart is so cold and empty you will never even realize you're missing anything."

GRACE SCOGGINS' Victim Impact Statement

Because I never met her until after Andi's passing, I never considered Grace's profound connection with her granddaughter. The woman who was usually lighthearted and jovial now appeared weary and overburdened, her wrinkled face contorted in emotional agony, her shoulders drooping from the weight of immeasurable grief.

"My name is Grace Scoggins. I am Andrea's grandmother. I thought a long time about how to put into words how much I lost when Andi was taken from me. I guess the best way to put it is I lost my right hand. You see, I am an artist, and Andi used to come sit with me while I painted. Even when she was very little, she had a great eye for detail. She could tell me exactly what was missing from a portrait, right down to the most seemingly insignificant element. I would add whatever microscopic bit she suggested, and the whole painting would burst into life. When she wasn't close enough to visit me, I used to send her pictures of my artwork, just to get her input. Now that she's gone, it's like I've lost my right hand, my dominant hand, the hand I relied on for everything. I can still paint, but it's much more of a struggle now, like I'm doing it lefthanded. I have to search long and hard for those little missing pieces that she could point out after one short glance. That's what I lost. I lost my co-creator. I lost my partner. I lost my right hand."

Rose Simon's Victim Impact Statement

Rose never knew Andi, but the little girl's murder impacted her life so greatly, she was allowed to give a statement. I never saw her more composed, and I never heard her speak more eloquently. She fixed her steely gaze on her former husband. Her body never trembled, and her voice never faltered.

"My name is Rose Marie Simon." She had resumed using her maiden name. "I was once married to this murderer, this filthy pig, this demon from hell. He did things to me that would have broken a much stronger woman, but I'm not here to talk about those things. Whatever Luke did to me, it was the result of my own poor choices. There may have been reasons why I chose the things I did, but they were still my choices. I'm here to talk about the way Luke's crimes have affected my babies. My kids didn't have any choices. They loved their daddy, even though he was mean and rotten to them. Their little hearts were so pure they just forgave every horrible thing he ever did to them, and they just kept right on loving him. That all changed after Luke killed Andi. I never told my kids what their daddy had done. I just told them he had to go away for a while because he had done something bad. But this is a small town. Parents talk in front of their kids. All the kids stopped playing with my babies, and they told them it was because their daddy was a killer. The other boys even started calling our son KK, short for "Killer's Kid." That's what you did to your own kids, Luke. Every day of their little lives, they are paying for what you did. Things are getting better for us though. I'm working and I've gone back to school, all the things I couldn't do when I was under your thumb. I'm even seeing someone, and he has shown the kids and me that not all men are cruel and mean-spirited. We have a good life now, or at least we're getting there. and that life will never again include you."

Emily Kirk's Victim Impact Statement

I gave my statement last. By that time, my vision was so blurred with tears I couldn't read what I had written so I wadded up my notes and spoke straight from my heart.

"My name is Emily Kirk. Technically, I guess I was the babysitter. Just the babysitter. I knew her for less than a year, before you took her from me. But I loved Andi as much as anyone in this room. I couldn't have loved her more if I had given birth to her myself. You ordered those two bumbling idiots to rape me because you thought that was the worst thing that could happen to me before they killed me, but then you saw Andi there with me and you realized there was something even worse that you could do to me. You thought I was going to die, and the last memories I would take to the grave with me would be of those two hideous faces hovering over me, and of Andi fighting for her life. Well, surprise. I'm still alive, and even though the memory of that awful night will haunt me until I breathe my final breath, those won't be my last memories. I have already made new ones and they are the best and happiest memories of my life. I have fallen in love, really for the first time. I have learned to love myself, something I never did before. I have a deeper appreciation for the world around me. You used to scare me, even before I knew what evil you were capable of. I would look into your empty soulless eyes, and I would lose my ability to speak. That's how much you terrified me. I thought you held my voice captive with some malevolent power you possessed, but I was really only a prisoner of my own fear. What I think frightened me the most was seeing what I was capable of becoming—what the whole human race is capable of if we lose sight of the good things in life and start focusing on the bad. We are all potential monsters under this thin veneer of humanity. The only thing that makes you different from the rest of humankind is you let the monster devour the human. You let hatred and anger consume you, and I was so very close to being exactly like you—empty, cold, compassionless—but I'm not that way anymore. I refuse to let my bad experiences define me. You don't win. You took Andi's physical body, but you didn't take her spirit. Her spirit lives in me now, and it gives me the power to rise above the evil you brought into my world, and the evil that I am capable of. You didn't win, and you never will."

No LONGER SMUG AND CONFIDENT, The Beast sat remorseless, angrily scowling at those who dared speak against him. The judge, who had been a bulwark of stoicism and professionalism throughout the trial, now tugged pensively on his silver beard and rubbed a few errant teardrops from under his round eyeglasses. The defendant was given a chance to speak, but he declined, so His Honor pronounced sentencing. He gave the maximum penalty for the crimes The Beast had been convicted of. Death. Just like that, Luke Detwiler's reign of terror ended. Or so we thought, but we soon learned malevolence is not so easily defeated.

OUTSIDE THE COURTHOUSE, Grace assumed the role of family spokesperson. The reporters wanted to know if we were satisfied with the death sentence, and if we believed justice was served. Trey's mother articulated my own sentiments. "We accept the judge's decision. We believe he ruled in accordance with the laws and sentencing guidelines applicable in this case. Therefore, we accept his decision. Satisfied? Are we satisfied that our precious Andi's killer will be put to death? How does anyone find satisfaction in someone else's demise? In the end, what difference does it make how, or by what method a murderer dies? Will his execution erase his crime? Will it for even one fleeting millisecond reanimate his victim, so she can return, no matter how briefly, to those who love her? Will it evaporate even one drop in the vast ocean of tears shed by those left behind? We humans like to arrogantly believe that we control justice, but true justice is not ours to dole out. We administer punishment based on our limited understanding of events and we tell ourselves that is justice, but we cannot even begin to comprehend what that means. All we can do is punish law violators, and truly Luke Detwiler deserved the harshest form of punishment allowed, but justice for my granddaughter lies solely in the hands of Almighty God. Whatever justice my grandbaby gets will come when the needle is taken out, not when it's put in. It's not my desire that anyone should die."

NOW THAT THE trial was over and Rose was firmly standing on her own two feet, Trey and I finally had time to concentrate on what mattered most—each other. Like much of our relationship, Trey's proposal was understated but perfect. He invited me to His Wednesday lunch date with Andi, something he had never done before. I packed a picnic basket I found in Connie's storage shed. Hoping I could persuade him to take the rest of the afternoon off, I included a bottle of *pinot noir* and two wine glasses.

The cemetery's caretaker must have been on vacation, because the grass around the cherub was taller than usual and dotted with wildflowers. Trey spread a blanket on the ground, and I plopped down on it as gracefully as I could.

"I know this is a weird place to do this," Trey started. "but I thought she should be a part of this. I think she would be pleased to know we found our way to each other, and we're happy."

"A weird place for what? A picnic?"

In lieu of an answer, he plucked a dandelion out of the ground and handed it to me. "Make a wish," he ordered. I'd never seen him smile more widely. I held the little weed close to my lips, shut my eyes, and blew on the fuzzy head of the wildflower. I wished I could feel that much love forever. When I opened my eyes, white specks danced in front of me like snowflakes, and Trey knelt before me, holding a heart-shaped helium balloon with a tiny box tied on the end. The box was opened, exposing a glittering ring that sparkled majestically in the sunlight.

"Is this what you wished for?" he asked.

"Yes!" I screamed the answer to the previous question, and to the one that would soon follow. "That is exactly what I wished for!"

"So, will you marry me?"

"Of course, I will! You knew the answer before you even asked."

"I just needed to hear you say it."

I threw both arms around his neck, kissed him passionately, and then officially answered his proposal. "Yes! Yes! Yes! I want to marry you more than I ever wanted anything!"

My fiancé removed the ring from the box and lovingly placed it on the proper finger

"Now that that's settled, let's see what you've got in that box," Trey laughed, and I opened the picnic basket. Immediately, our ham-and-cheese croissants and potato salad extended an open invitation to every gnat, fly, and ant within a thirty-mile radius. We swatted haplessly at the invaders, but they only seemed to proliferate, crawling up my jeans and feasting on every inch of bare skin they found on my body. Our romantic lunch ended abruptly when a wasp decided to join the festivities and I ran away screaming. Trey hurriedly packed our things and we decided we'd eat at home after we told his mother our news.

Grace seemed pleased, but not at all surprised, when I excitedly showed her my newly acquired jewel.

"I've been waiting a long time for you to officially become my daughter," she stated happily.

She couldn't have known how deeply her words affected me.

"I always wanted a mother. I mean, I guess I had one…," My voice trailed off, not knowing how to explain the situation to Grace.

"I know, my darling daughter. I know." She drew me close to her in a loving embrace. I reveled in her warmth, and I cherished the feel of her heartbeat next to mine.

When she released me, I vocalized the wedding plans I had already envisioned. "I want to get married at that little park in Trey's old neighborhood. It's cozy and intimate and perfect." I paused thoughtfully, and then continued. "The only thing is, I don't know who I want to perform the ceremony. I want it to be a person of faith, because I want to

signify that this is a union before God, but I don't know many preachers, and the few I do know, I don't like."

Grace's face lit up, and excitement filled her voice. "Well, daughter," she announced cheerily. "this is your lucky day. Didn't Trey tell
you? Back when she did her stint in the hoosegow, his crazy mama
went and got herself ordained."

I burst out laughing in astonishment. Once again, the enigmatic
woman had proven herself to be the rarest of all anomalies, a minister
with a fully functioning frontal lobe.

After the family celebration wound down, I told Trey I wanted to
see Rose and tell her the news, but I had an ulterior motive for wanting
to see her. In court, she mentioned she was seeing someone, and I was
slightly hurt she hadn't shared that information with me beforehand. I
thought we were becoming friends, and though I had never had a lot of
close female friends, I thought we were supposed to tell each other
things like that.

Rose and the kids were playing in the front yard. Between school,
work, and therapy sessions, Rose had precious little free time, but she
spent every second of her downtime with Thomas and Harper.

The children bombarded me with dirty, sweaty hugs that didn't
bother me at all. Rose told them it was time to get washed up for
dinner and after a mild protest, they acquiesced to their mother's
wishes. When they vanished inside the house, Rose inquired, "So,
Emily, what brings you to our neck of the woods?"

I flashed the sparkling diamond in front of her, and she squealed
joyfully. "Oh, Emily! You're getting married!"

I nodded my confirmation, and she went on, "Come inside and
have a glass of tea. I want to know every detail."

I followed her into the little starter house. It now reflected her
personality, somewhat cluttered, but still clean, with family pictures
displayed everywhere. We sat at the square wooden table where Trey
and I shared our first breakfast together. We could hear water splashing
in both bathrooms where the kids were preparing for dinner.

"Go on, Emily," Rose urged. "Tell me everything."

"I will. I promise, but first, I want you to tell me something." I accepted the glass of tea she offered me.

"Okay," she agreed reluctantly.

"In court, you said you were seeing someone. Why hadn't you told me about that?"

Rose squirmed uncomfortably in her seat, and she avoided my gaze.

"I wanted to tell you. You have no idea how badly I wanted tell you, but I didn't know how you would react."

"Rose, I am happy for you," I assured her, a little disappointed that she didn't trust me enough to be honest. "I know domestic violence survivors are usually advised to wait a while before getting seriously involved with anyone, but it has been over a year, and you're doing so well in every other area of your life. I see no reason why you shouldn't start dating again."

She looked relieved, but I got the feeling there was something she was still holding back from me, so I prodded, "Who is it? Is he someone you met at school?"

"No. I didn't meet him at school, but he does work there. Emily, it's Michael. I'm seeing Michael."

"*My* Michael?!" I vociferated.

"No, silly," she contradicted me. "It's *your* Trey. It's *my* Michael." She blushed and added, "At least I hope he will be mine someday."

Poor Rose, I thought to myself. She mistook Michael's kindness, empathy, and benign attention for romantic interest. It would be up to me, I realized, to straighten this mess out with minimal damage to Rose's still fragile psyche.

I AMBUSHED HIM. I waited for Michael on the parking lot of the community college campus, leaning casually against his "I am that subversive Marxist professor your mother warned you about" bumper sticker, so he couldn't get away from me. As he approached his car, he saw the disapproving scowl I intentionally fixed on my face, and his welcoming grin faded. At first, he ignored me as he opened the back door and threw an armful of books into the backseat. Growing weary of his coyness, I started the conversation. "I talked to Rose today."

"Then I deduce from that murderous look you're giving me that she must have told you about our budding relationship."

"You're not even going to deny it?" I was appalled. Admittedly, I didn't know that much about Michael, even though it seemed like he had been part of my life forever. I never dreamed he was the type of man who would take advantage of an unsophisticated, gullible woman in a vulnerable situation.

He directed me toward a gazebo, and we sat side by side on a cast iron bench with a lattice back.

"Why should I deny it?"

"She's your student, Michael!" I protested loudly, and he shot me an irritated look, as he glanced around to make sure no one was listening.

"She is not my student," he corrected me. "She is not in any of my classes, and I will make sure she never is. We are two consenting adults with equal power in the relationship. There is absolutely nothing inappropriate about us seeing each other."

"But it *is* inappropriate," I countered, but I wasn't sure why I found this peculiar coupling so distasteful. It made sense that Rose was ready to try romantic love again. Her kids gave her a foundation of *storge*, and I provided her need for friendship; she found self-love with her academic success, and with Trey's absolution of her involvement in Andi's death. She was ready to take the next step up the hierarchy of love needs, but why did it have to be with Michael?

"Why are you so opposed to our being together?" Michael questioned. "Is it the fact that we are from different ends of the socioeconomic spectrum?"

"Well, no." I muttered and wracked my brain for a sensible answer to his first question.

"Look, Des, I know she has baggage…"

"Yes!" I interrupted. "She has baggage! And that baggage has a picture of *Dora the Explorer* saying, 'Going to Grandma's.' She's a baby, Michael!" *She's my baby*, I wanted to scream. *I nurtured her! I*

221

did her two a.m. feedings when she wasn't strong enough to hold her own spoon! She was mine. I loved her, and I watched over her like a paranoid tigress shielding her cub from danger. Nobody was going to destroy her again, not even some well-intentioned, bleeding-heart philosophy professor who couldn't possibly hope to comprehend the hell she'd been through.

Despite all the self-awareness I gained since walking away from Janice and the old shack, I was still capable of surprising myself. I thought it was Michael's affection for Rose that triggered my jealousy, but it was really hers for him.

"She's a baby," I sobbed again.

"She's a twenty-eight-year-old woman who has endured enough and overcame enough for ten lifetimes. Are you concerned about the education gap and the age gap between us?"

"Oh, Michael," I groaned in frustration. "It's not gaps that separate you from Rose. It's *chasms*. Vast, unconquerable chasms. You have a doctorate degree from an Ivy League university. She is pushing thirty and still struggling to get through community college."

"What's your point, Des?" He sounded borderline angry. "You have a master's degree, and you're marrying a man who hasn't been to college a day in his life."

I hadn't noticed him staring at my engagement ring. "That's different!" I shrieked. "I'm not exactly Princeton material, and Trey is gifted in certain areas. He just knows things. He is my intellectual equal."

"Rose is not so inferior to the rest of us," Michael insisted. "The only thing that made me different from her was opportunity. The only thing that made Trey different was nurturing. As for you, my dear friend, the only thing that made you different from Rose was sheer dumb luck." He hesitated, shook his head scornfully, and then scolded me. "My God, Des, when did you morph into such an insufferable snob?"

I wasn't offended. Michael could never offend me. Even in those early days of our friendship, hiding out in what we dubbed Plato's Cave, our relationship had been built on brutal honesty. I expected him to call me out on my incongruences and hypocrisies, and I did the same for him. Besides, he was right on two counts: Rose wasn't inferior to anyone, and I was acting snobbish.

Soundly defeated by The Philosopher's reason and logic, I moved on to my next area of concern. "What about Thomas and Harper? Those poor kids have been through enough already. They need someone who is going to be all in, not in and out."

"Do you really think so little of me? Do you really think I am the type of guy who is just going to drift in and out of his children's lives?"

"You told me once that kids weren't your forte," I reminded him.

"That was a long time ago. Besides, Thomas and Harper have kind of grown on me. They're special kids."

"Yeah. I know. Michael, I just want you to be careful with Rose's heart. You're not Henry Higgins, and she's not your personal Eliza Doolittle who needs you to transform her into something she's not. If that's what this relationship is about to you, then I want you to end it now."

His voice was laced with incredulity. "Haven't you been paying attention? She started transforming herself before I ever arrived on the scene. Besides, I would never try to change Rose. I just encourage and support her personal growth and development."

We sat in silence for a while and watched a pair of squirrels scramble up a tree, chattering noisily as they ascended. Then Michael confessed something I don't think he'd even told Rose yet. "I love her, Des. I love everything about her. I love her commitment to building a better life for herself and her family. I love her courage in the face of adversity. I love the way she crinkles her nose when she laughs. I even love her goofy Texas accent, and that's something that always drove me crazy about you."

Ironically, I spent more time vetting Michael as Rose's potential mate than I had before I slept with him myself. Ultimately, I deemed him worthy, at least as worthy as any man would ever be of my beautiful, ever-blossoming rose. I always prided myself on my open-mindedness. I accepted my aunts' relationship, even when their love was still culturally taboo. Who was I to stand in the way of the happiness of my two dearest friends?

"Okay," I finally conceded, standing to leave. "You've convinced me. You love Rose, and at least for now, that's good enough for me."

Michael took my left hand in his and rubbed his thumb over the shimmering stone. "You know, when I came back to this area, I was searching for my one true love. Funny thing is, I thought it was going to be you."

"We were kids then, Michael. Just a couple of confused kids."

"And as wild and wonderful and unforgettable as young love is, grown up love is even better, isn't it?"

"Yeah, it is." So, he had loved me once. Or maybe he was like my aunts, and he only loved what I represented to him, a walking metaphor, the embodiment of all the reasons he rejected society. When he knew me as a young woman, I was poor and oppressed, a victim of the social structure he despised. I hoped that wasn't the only reason he loved Rose.

SINCE NEITHER OF us wanted an extravagant ceremony, we saw no reason for a long engagement, so Trey and I chose to marry that spring. I asked Rose to be my maid of honor, and she took the job as seriously as if I asked her to donate a kidney to a dying relative. She contacted the city parks administration and secured the venue I wanted. Then she called the florist and the caterer. The only thing she couldn't do for me was select the dress, so together we hit every bridal shop between Dallas and Austin in search of the perfect gown. I never thought I'd be the type of woman to get all giddy over shopping for a wedding dress; shopping in general made me anxious and irritable, but the time spent with Rose negated the drudgery of the activity. We giggled like school-girls at a slumber party. She held the dresses up in front of me, and then she made faces expressing her disapproval. One by one, each gown was rejected and discarded, until we thought the situation was hopeless and I might never find anything to wear on my big day.

We never found the perfect bridal gown for me, because it didn't exist. We came to that conclusion when Rose observed that she had never seen me in a dress before and I realized that was because I had not worn one since my parents used to force me to wear Janice's hand-me-downs. We stopped at a nice department store and I found an ivory pantsuit with a sleeveless top and cropped pants that only extended halfway down the calves.

"What do you think?" I nervously asked Rose as I stepped out of the dressing room. If she rejected my choice this time, I was prepared to fight her for this suit. I was exhausted and hungry now, and I was really in love with the outfit.

Much to my relief, my maid of honor agreed with me. "That's it! That's the one! It's so you, Emily!"

We selected a white neck scarf and a pair of cream-colored pumps that complemented the ensemble, and then we headed for home, music blasting and both of us singing along, butchering the lyrics and sounding like injured cats. The thought crossed my mind that if things were different—very different—this was a moment I would have shared with Janice, but I had learned that the nexus of family was not common blood but a common spirit. In that regard, I was enjoying the experience with my true sister.

ON THE MORNING of my wedding, I awakened with my heart palpitating and my lungs fighting for breath. My fiancé was much more of a traditionalist than I was, and he elected not to see me again until I made my grand entrance at the park, so he spent the night with his best man, retired detective Ron Tyler. Without him in the bed beside me, the dreams were more intense than usual. It wasn't only Eve/Rose who chased me across the fissures in the dry, cracked earth. She enlisted the aid of a hundred little girls who quoted Lord Byron and who knew why the sky was blue, and she called upon the fury of legions of mothers who stoically endured years of abuse but had now had enough. She summoned a coven of persecuted witches and a battalion of gifted intellectuals forced to do mundane domestic work. All those women chased me through the withered garden. Though their mouths were blurry, lipless circles, they screamed, as if by telepathy, their demands for redemption.

The sound of birds chirping outside my window soothed my frazzled nerves. Now that I was fully awake and listening to the avian serenade, I soon forgot my nightmares and focused on the joyous day ahead.

A springtime outdoor wedding in tornado alley required extensive consultation with a meteorologist, or at least, a reliable weather app. I kept a vigilant watch on the sky for a week before the ceremony. It rained a couple of times prior to the event, but no inclement weather was forecasted for the foreseeable future.

Rose and Grace fussed over me, making sure I ate a light breakfast and then helping me get into my unconventional bridal attire. They helped me squeeze the final button together; the elegant top fit more snugly than when I tried it on. Rose applied my makeup and Grace fluffed and styled my hair. When they finished, I stood in front a full-length mirror and marveled at the reflection of a woman I didn't recognize, a strong, bold, confident woman ready for love, but also prepared for battle if it became necessary. Only one thing made me feel like the insecure, self-loathing person who existed before I met Andi. I hadn't worn white since the first time The Round Man touched me, and I felt self-conscious, almost unworthy of that axiomatic symbol of purity.

"You are a vision of loveliness." Grace calmed me with her reassuring words.

"Yeah, you look super," Rose chimed in.

"Well, I feel a little exposed." I tugged at the low neckline of the blouse.

"That's what you have this thing for." Rose draped the scarf around my shoulders and tied it in a discreet knot. Finally, I felt like a true bride.

"Time to head for the park." Grace announced and ushered us out the door.

Most of the puddles from the recent downpours had already evaporated, but one still shimmered beneath the sunlight, right at the edge of my front lawn. I was facing it, digging my keys out of my handbag, when a utility truck passed by and hit the puddle with its huge tire. Instantly, I was drenched in stagnant rainwater. I clutched my chest and gasped in horror, as if I had been shot. Slowly, I lowered my arms and looked down to survey the damage. A heart-shaped brown stain covered my mid-section.

"Oh no!" I screamed, and tears spurted from my eyes.

"Get inside," Grace instructed calmly. "We have to get it cleaned up."

"There's no time to wash it," I sobbed hysterically. Why did things like this always happen to me? Even as a child, I had an uncanny knack for self-sabotage. Standing too close to a mud puddle in my wedding clothes was just the latest way I found of destroying my own happiness.

"There's time to get it clean. Go inside and take it off. They can't start without us anyway."

Numbly, I obeyed, knowing the task of removing the stain was more than I could handle on my own. I had no choice but to trust Grace to clean it for me.

I stripped down to my underwear, handed Grace the soiled clothing, and sat anxiously on a kitchen stool, wondering how the enigmatic woman would perform this magic act. She went into her art studio and returned wielding an orange object that looked like a marker or highlighter. I panicked a little thinking she was about to color over the blemish and make it even more unsightly.

"This little thing is the only reason all my clothes aren't ruined with paint smudges." I took a closer look at her tool and realized it was something called Tide-to-Go, a veritable first-aid kit for laundry emergencies. She spread my top out across the kitchen island and diligently scrubbed at the mud splatter. As she furiously worked away at the dirty spot, I thought about her meticulously wiping Trey's fingerprints off the murder weapon and replacing them with her own. She took his stain away, too.

After several minutes of fierce rubbing and scrubbing, Grace stopped, held the blouse up and smiled satisfactorily. "Now all we have to do is get it dry."

"It's too delicate for the dryer!" I moaned in defeat.

"I have an idea!" Rose interjected. She retrieved a blow dryer from the nearest bathroom, plugged it in, and turned it on medium-heat. Grace held the wet blouse up while Rose fanned the warm air over the garment. Soon, they had me back in my clothes.

Grace helped me with that last pesky button. Then she stepped back and admired her handiwork. "Nothing less than a spotless bride for my boy!" she exclaimed.

We left the house at eleven-thirty, precisely the time the ceremony was scheduled to begin. I tried not to think about what must be going through Trey's head. Surely he knew how desperately I wanted to marry him and only a dire wardrobe casualty would delay my appearance.

Michael waited for us at the park entrance. He greeted Rose first, and I witnessed the mutual admiration they had for each other. Then he turned his attention to me. "You look stunning. Des."

"So do you, Magnum," I joked. The free-spirited college professor wore a floral print Hawaiian-style shirt and a pair of khaki pants. "Are you ready to escort me to my groom?"

"It would be the greatest honor of my life." He crooked his arm and I looped my elbow through his. I heard my guests laughing and conversing, but they were hidden from our view by a row of evergreens.

"Give me a couple of minutes to get into position," Grace instructed us as she hurried off.

Rose handed me a bouquet of lavender orchids and white carnations. I nervously clutched the stems. Until this point, Thomas and Harper had been excited, but well-behaved. Now they were growing restless and whiney.

"Uh-oh. Better get this show on the road before I lose them," their mother warned.

Music started playing. I heard the traditional wedding march. It was a live band. Startled, I looked at Rose. "I thought you said we were having recorded music."

Michael grinned. "Actually, you can thank me for the entertainment. I bribed a few music majors with extra credit if they would perform this gig for us. It's my wedding gift to you."

"Thank you! It's perfect!" I tightened my grip on his elbow as a gesture of my appreciation.

"Well, it was cheaper than the toaster I was going to get you," he teased, downplaying the warm sentiment behind his thoughtful gift.

"Time to go!" Rose pointed to her children who were already working their way toward the groom's party. As ring bearer and flower girl, they were supposed to lead the processional. The maid-of-honor took a few quick steps to catch up, and then I started my walk down the proverbial aisle, which was really a narrow trail of lush green grass dividing two sections of cream-colored folding chairs. The end of each row of seats was marked with a vase of purple and white flowers. My shoes bogged up a little in the soft ground, but it didn't matter. I was floating on air. At the edge of the park, near the pond, Grace, Trey, and Ron Tyler waited in front of an ivory colored archway adorned with a gauzy covering. The city planted azaleas in the park that spring, and their colorful blooms added to the ambience. Wanting to savor the moment, I inhaled purposefully, expecting the sweet aroma of the surrounding flora. All I detected was the faint scent of cotton candy mixed with a tiny whiff of Chanel.

When we reached the archway, Michael removed his arm from mine and slowly stepped away. For the first time that day, my groom and I looked upon each other. Trey wore his ceremonial police uniform, the one he wore for promotions or award presentations. The irresistible crooked smile that melted my cold heart was plastered all over his face, and his pure blue eyes glistened with happy tears.

Grace stood in front of us and opened her beloved old Bible, the one with the yellowed pages that had almost every scripture high-lighted. She reminded the crowd, which consisted mostly of Trey's colleagues or mine and a few of my former co-workers from CPS, of the reason for our gathering. Then she paraphrased my favorite Bible passage from the thirteenth chapter of 1 Corinthians, known to many as "the love chapter."

"Though I may speak with the tongues of men and angels, but have not love, it's just a lot of noise. Though I may prophesy with all wisdom, but have not love, it's just a few lucky guesses. Though I may profess my faith in Christ, and I may observe the sacraments and follow the laws of Moses, but if I have not love, my Christian faith is just another vain, pointless, humanity stifling religion. Love is patient. Love is kind. It does not boast. It is not rude. It endures all. It conquers all. It is all. Love never fails. In the end, there are only three things that really matter; faith, hope, and love, and the greatest of these, as the apostle wrote so long ago, is love."

When the officiant finished her speech, Trey and I exchanged rings, recited traditional vows, and shared our first kiss as husband and wife. Then Grace instructed us to face the spectators as she boldly proclaimed, "Ladies and gentlemen, I now present to you Mr. and Mrs. Trey Scoggins. What Almighty God has brought together, no power in hell shall ever put asunder!" She made that declaration with such boldness and authority it sounded like she dared Satan to intervene in the union she herself had consecrated.

The chairs were folded and carted off. The music majors started playing a medley of love songs, and Trey and I shared our first dance. More accurately, he stood perfectly still while I clumsily gyrated around him. There was nothing clumsy about the way Rose danced with Michael. She twirled, glided, and pirouetted like a graceful ballerina performing a *pas de deux* with her lifelong partner. Recently, I discovered Rose possessed a treasure trove of hidden talents and untapped potential, from her home decorating and event planning skills, to her prowess in the classroom and now her dancing. I wondered how different her life would have been if, as a child, anyone had recognized those myriad gifts and nurtured them.

TREY OWNED a timeshare on the Gulf, near Galveston, because he sometimes enjoyed deep sea fishing. He'd bought it before Andi came along, before he was so strapped for cash all the time. We decided that condo was as good a place as any for our honeymoon. It took us almost all day to get there; Texas is an enormous state, and we stopped at every roadside attraction and tourist trap along the way. At times Trey grew quiet, responding only when I spoke first. I dismissed his aloofness as the behavior of a tacit man reflecting on a significant life change.

My first night as a married woman was blissful. Eve/Rose and her rapidly proliferating League of Voiceless Women gave me a reprieve from the terrifying dreams and I slept peacefully in my husband's loving arms, but when I awoke I was alone. I caught a glimpse of Trey standing on the beach, arms crossed over his chest, looking greatly grieved. Perplexed, I started a pot of coffee, filled a mug, and went out to join my groom.

"Regrets already?" I attempted to sound facetious, but I was genuinely concerned.

I offered him the coffee, and his warm smile eased my doubts. "No regrets, my love. Never. But there is something I need to tell you." Waves pounded loudly against the shore and the sea spewed its misty white foam into the air moistening the loose sand around our feet and turning it to mud.

"Okay."

"I didn't tell you yesterday, because when you look back on our wedding day, I want it of be filled with only the most joyous memories. Before the ceremony, I got a call from Sarah's mother. We'd always been close, so I thought she had heard I was getting married, and she was calling to congratulate me."

"That wasn't it?"' My stomach muscles tightened with trepidation.

"No." He sipped at the steaming hot liquid and gathered his thoughts. " Emily, Sarah's housekeeper got to work a little late yesterday, and she found Sarah on the living room floor. She had overdosed on sedatives and prescription painkillers. She's gone, Em. The last living connection I had to my daughter is gone forever."

An arctic chill ripped through my skin and snaked down my spine. I saw it coming months ago. Besides my own experience with The Whispers, I was a professional. I knew the signs of suicidal behavior. Every time she came down for the legal proceedings, she was a little more withdrawn and despondent. She became reclusive, only leaving her hotel room for court sessions. She neglected her personal appearance, something that had always been of paramount importance to her. I never reached out to her, never offered her any support. I never approached her about grief counseling. I never even gave her the number for a suicide hotline. In retrospect, I think I went into triage mode. I had a better chance of helping Rose who, despite her horrific past, had not succumbed to the dark forces of bitterness and cynicism, so I concentrated all my efforts on her. As a result, Rose bloomed while Sarah wilted. Andi's mother faded like the vibrant colors of the rainbow after the storm has passed by.

———

GETTING APPROVED for adoption is like getting vetted to meet the President. No stone is left unturned; no skeleton is left undiscovered. I feared my three days at Sunnyvale might negate my years of work as a children's advocate, but I had a small army of social workers and counselors willingly vouching for my competence as a parent, and Trey and I were soon put on a waiting list. We hoped to have a child within a year to eighteen months. Babies, however, don't care about formalities and waiting lists. Just like in childbirth, adopted children sometimes show up on their own schedule.

———

SHE DIDN'T HAVE AN ABORTION, that much I deduced from the squirming, colicky powder blue bundle she held in her trembling arms as if somebody had handed her a lit stick of dynamite. I only recognized my niece, Abby, from the pictures she posted on social media. She showed up on my doorstep one stormy evening when Trey was working late and Grace was at a church function. When I opened the door, tiny pellets of rain struck my face like liquid bullets, sharp and painful.

"Abby!" I cried "Come in! Come in out of this crazy weather."

"I'm sorry, Aunt Emily. I know I haven't seen you for a while, and

I know you and my mother don't get along, but I didn't know where else to go. My boyfriend kicked me out."

"You don't have to apologize." I showed her a place to sit, and then I gathered up some towels and blankets and put around them. I thought about that day long ago when I showed up at Aunt Lil's a virtual stranger with nowhere else to turn.

Abby sobbed and sniffled and judging from the redness of her nose and cheeks, I thought she must have been out in the weather for a while. The baby let out a deafening cry, and she held the little bundle out in front of her. "Please take him, Aunt Emily," she pleaded weakly. "I'm so tired. He cries all the time and I don't know what to do."

I gently took the infant and unwrapped the wet blanket around him, replacing it with one of my dry towels. I snuggled him close to me and his screaming stopped. He looked up at me and cooed contentedly. "Oh, Abby. He's so beautiful."

"I know he is, but I don't know how to take care of him." Her face contorted into an expression of sheer misery. "I don't know how to love my own baby."

"Abby, we can get you parenting classes," I offered. "In fact, we have parenting classes for single mothers at the crisis center where I work. I can get you signed up tomorrow." The baby started wiggling and fussing in my arms and I asked her for a bottle, which she dug out of a tattered backpack she used for a diaper bag. The instant I took the bottle from her, the smell of sour milk sickened me.

"You don't understand, Aunt Emily. When I asked you to take the baby, I didn't mean for a few minutes. I meant forever. I want you to be his mama."

My heart did a little backflip, but my brain quickly tapered the celebration. Sure, I wanted a baby, but did I want this one? If I adopted her grandson, would I be inviting Janice back into my life? I hadn't even started on the nursery, and I didn't have any of the things a helpless infant needed.

"Oh, Abby. I don't know about this. I'm not prepared. I just got married."

"Trust me. You're a hundred times more prepared than I am."

"What about your mother? Can't she take him?"

"I don't want him being raised like I was, and like you were, full of fear and self-doubt. I want him raised to be open-minded, tolerant, and loving. I don't want him to ever be ashamed of being human."

At first, I thought Abby was a scared little girl, making an impetuous decision. Suddenly, it dawned on me how mature and well thought out her decision was.

Grace burst through the door. She acted as if she already knew there was a baby in the house. She headed straight for him.

"Hold him while I fix his bottle." My mother-in law gladly honored my request. "See if she has a diaper. He needs changed." As an afterthought, I threw in the introductions. "Grace, this is my niece, Abby. Abby, this is my mother-in-law, Grace Scoggins."

While I scalded the bottle and replaced the clabbered formula with warm milk, I thought about how I would broach the subject with Trey. I knew he would be thrilled having a son, but we thought we would have a lot more time to prepare. A new baby meant tons of new expenses.

I didn't have to wait long for Trey's reaction. When I rejoined Abby and Grace in the living room, Trey was with them, holding the little boy and smiling more radiantly than I had ever seen.

"Emily, Abby tells me she wants us to adopt this little guy. What do you think?"

All my doubts were obliterated by my husband's confidence and jubilation. "I think I need to go shopping for a crib." I laughed nervously and kissed my the baby's forehead.

I put Abby in one of the guest rooms, the one I used when I lived there with Connie, and I kept the little one with me. When he awoke crying, I carried him to Grace's studio where she had a rocking chair. I fed him, rocked him, and comforted him. He wasn't a newborn; he was at least a month old, but I had heard stories about the sacred bonding ritual of skin to skin contact between mothers and babies. I lowered my top, stripped him down to his diaper, and I rested the squirming child against my bare chest. I felt the fuzzy cap of blonde hair covering his soft scalp; I touched his puffy cheeks, massaged his little feet and traced the contour of his pink lips. That night, while my loved ones slumbered peacefully nearby, I conceived my firstborn, not in my uterus, but in the safest and warmest corner of my heart, in that rich and fertile valley where the seed of all love must be cultivated.

Because I was a relative and the biological mother selected us as the adoptive parents of her son, the adoption process wasn't nearly as grueling as I expected. I used my social work connections to expedite the legalities. Our son was named Nicholas. Translated from Greek, the name means "victory of the people."

ROSE and her kids moved into Michael's rustic cabin on the shores of Lake Sutton, and we set Abby up in the starter house. I helped her enroll at the community college; she wanted to study computer science. When she visited us, if Nicholas was calm and content, she played with him, but she never fed or changed him, and she never consoled him when he cried. I was secretly relieved. She already had more than a nine-month head start on bonding with him, and I selfishly didn't want him becoming too accustomed to her voice or her touch.

By the time our son's first birthday rolled around, Trey and I were fully acclimated to parenthood, and like most new mothers, my life evolved into a whirlwind of happy chaos. Rose graduated from community college, and as our gift to her, Trey and I invited her, Michael, and the kids on a mini-vacation to our place on the Gulf. Since I wasn't yet comfortable taking Nicholas near the dangerous and unpredictable waves, Grace volunteered to keep her grandson.

I was unexpectedly subpoenaed to court on behalf of one of my counseling clients, and the court date coincided with our scheduled date of departure. Disappointed, I told Trey he should go without me, and I would join him the next day. I knew how excited he was about deep-sea fishing with Michael. Rose said she and the children would wait and ride down with me, under the condition I let them spend the night at the mansion, because she was scared staying in the secluded cabin without Michael. The men left, Grace took Nicholas to visit her friends in Ft. Worth, something she'd been wanting to do for a while, and I kenneled the dogs in preparation for the trip.

Rose allowed Thomas and Harper to stay up well past their usual bedtime, playing games and watching television, while she and I discussed her future, which was once again up in the air.

She wanted to pursue her bachelor's degree at a four-year university, but that required a lengthy commute that would cut into her hours of availability at work. Michael assured her his income was sufficient for their basic needs and her continuing education would be a worthwhile investment for the whole family. Though tempted by the kind offer, for obvious reasons, Rose was not comfortable becoming financially dependent on another man.

As we mulled over the perplexing situation, Harper appeared in the doorway and innocently announced, "Mommy, I saw Daddy on TV."

"I'll change the channel," Rose sounded annoyed but not terribly concerned. It wasn't unusual for the children to stumble across news briefs about their father. She followed her daughter into the den, and her response shifted from annoyed to horrified. "Turn that off! Turn it off now!" she ordered the children.

She summoned me into another room that had another television set and closed the door behind us. I couldn't imagine what triggered such a fearful response, but I soon found out. She clicked the TV on and found the local channel. A middle-aged man in an expensive looking suit stood outside the state prison where Luke was serving his sentence. The reporter spoke in a somber tone. "Our top story tonight —a prison van transporting a death row inmate to the hospital was ambushed earlier today and condemned murderer Luke Detwiler has escaped and is on the loose. Earlier Detwiler complained of a mysterious stomach ailment and was being taken to St. Francis Hospital for treatment when the ambush occurred. A tire on the van was blown out after being hit by a bullet from a high-power revolver. The guard accompanying the prisoner in the back of the vehicle jumped out to assist the driver, who was attacked by a man with a machete and a semi-automatic weapon, and that's when Detwiler made his daring escape."

The reporter's voice trailed off. I couldn't hear anything above the sound of my own pulse reverberating in my ears. I looked at Rose, pale and trembling, shrinking into a corner like she used to do when he threatened her.

"I know who did it. I know who helped him. It was Jack, his brother Jack." Rose spoke softly, so as not to alarm her children. "Now he's coming here. He's coming after us."

"How would he even know you're here?"

"He's had his minions following me ever since he got arrested. I see them lurking around sometimes. He always knows where I am."

I hugged her, suppressed my own fear, and rationalized, "He couldn't have gotten far. His legs would have been shackled."

She stared at me sympathetically, as though she pitied my blatant ignorance of the workings of the criminal mind. "Jack would have known to take bolt cutters," she pouted. "He's not like that idiot Tony. Tony couldn't figure out how to tie his own shoelaces without Luke standing there telling him what to do. Jack's evil, like Luke."

My mind reflected on the scraggly bearded man at the bar and how he callously stabbed Trey, like he was slicing into a watermelon, not human flesh. "We're safe here." I hoped I sounded more confident than I felt. "This house has a state-of-the-art security system. It worked like a charm the night Tony broke in here."

She forced a weak smile, but still seemed unconvinced. "I'm going to put the kids to bed," she said resignedly.

While my guest tended to her family, I checked the control panel on the alarm system. There was no flashing green light. *Wasn't there usually a flashing green light when the system was on?* I couldn't remember. It was one of those things I just took for granted it would always work when I needed it, and I never paid much attention to it. I heard breathing behind me, and I spun around on high alert. Rose stood there, pupils widened with fear and her body shaking uncontrollably.

"Emily, what security company do you use?" Her high-pitched voice trembled as much as her petite frame.

I had to look back at the panel to read the name of the company. "Prestige Home Security. They're one of the best in the business."

"Oh, I know all about Prestige Home Security. Luke used to work for them. He got fired for breaking into his clients' houses and stealing their stuff." She lowered her voice to a coarse whisper. "He knows how to deactivate the system."

"There *is* supposed to be a flashing green light," I muttered. That bone-chilling revelation coupled with Rose's ominous words triggered my stress response, and my adrenal glans started churning out cate-cholamines like nobody's business, making my heart thump palpably inside my chest.

"I'm so scared." By now Rose could barely breathe her words.

"Don't worry. I'm going to check the locks."

Fueled by sheer adrenaline, I raced around the enormous house, twisting locks and shutting blinds. *Why did anybody need so many doors and windows? Why did I ever think I wanted a house this big?*

When I returned to Rose, I heard her humming a vaguely familiar tune, a haunting melody from my distant past. What were the words? What was that song?

"Have you been to Jesus for the healing power...are you washed in the blood of the lamb?"

Strangely, Rose and I talked about almost everything else, but we never discussed our faith. Michael was agnostic, so I assumed she was too. Now with her life in peril she soothed herself with an old hymn, an eerie tune that only exacerbated my anxiety. *"Are you living fully by his grace each hour...are you washed in the blood of the lamb?"*

Stop it! Stop it! Please shut up! It was the song the church choir always sang after the pastor preached about hell. When I was a kid, those lyrics made me feel like Satan was right there beside me, and if I wasn't washed in the blood, whatever that meant, he was going to snatch my soul.

"Are your garments spotless, are they white as snow...are you washed in the blood of the lamb?"

The creepy music and the specter of the diabolical fugitive looming in my mind made my peaceful mansion seem more like a haunted castle. *Fight or flight,* I thought. *Flight sounds pretty damn good to me.*

"Let's get the kids and go," I suggested. "Trey's friend lives a few blocks away. He's a retired detective. You met him at the wedding."

I tugged at Rose's shirt sleeve and tried to move her forward, but she resisted. "It's too late," she whimpered, and I heard footsteps approaching somewhere behind us, too heavy for a restless child needing solace.

"Hey ladies! Guess who?" The voice was loud and menacing. He made no attempt to conceal his presence. Why should he? He had absolutely nothing to lose. He was already condemned to death. He could kill us and still not face a worse fate than the one that presently awaited him.

"Ro-sey Po-sey," he taunted her. "Daddy's home!"

She grabbed the phone out of her pocket, but before she could turn it on, a long skinny arm reached around and wrestled the device out of her grasp. The Beast threw the gadget on the floor and stomped it. It shattered along with our hope for survival.

My phone. We still have my phone. I have to get to it. Where is it? Where did I leave it? My God, why am I always so useless in an emergency?

"Mommy, I'm scared!" Harper cried out.

The Beast grinned maniacally. "Is that my little girl I hear? Is that my kids?" He walked toward the sound of the frightened child. "Tommy-Boy, are you in there?"

The little boy peaked out, and his demonic father reached for him. Rose threw herself between the two of them. "I will die before I let you near my babies!" she proclaimed with unwavering elocution.

"Suit yourself, stupid bitch." The Beast violently punched her and started once again toward his son who stood silently crying behind his mother.

Then I witnessed my first miracle. I saw a one-hundred-ten-pound woman morph into an immovable brick wall. She shoved Thomas back into the bedroom, slammed the door, and wedged herself in the entry-way, bearing her feet into the marble tile and clawing at the walls to brace herself. The Beast kicked, hit, and choked her, but she barely even flinched.

I still couldn't remember where I left my phone, so I had to think of some way to save her. Ever since my stay at Sunnyvale, Trey kept his guns locked up and hidden from me, but there was one he didn't know about. I reached into the coat closet and withdrew the shotgun Connie used to ward off Mangy Dog. The Beast was so hellbent on exacting revenge on his ex-wife for her betrayal, I wondered if he even knew I was there. I aimed the weapon and placed the barrel against his temple. I couldn't afford to miss. When he felt the cold steal, he stopped hitting Rose and glared at me. I released the safety and pulled the trigger. Only a slight puff of air escaped from the round end of the gun. Connie must have used the last of the ammunition on Mangy Dog and never reloaded. Defeated, I lowered the weapon and started begging for mercy.

That's when I witnessed my second miracle, and this one could not be explained away as the miraculous, but very human, power of a mother's protective nature. Eve/Rose extracted her legs from the globe where the blame for all the world's ills had been laid at her feet. She broke free from the barbed wire that bound her hands, pulled the electrical tape away from her mouth, and spat out the rotten, wormy apple that had silenced her for millennia. Now free, she stepped off the canvas and out of the frame. I sucked her in through every orifice. I absorbed her through every pore. I became her, and she became me. I was possessed by the spirit of a mythical character, an exceedingly pissed off one at that.

In a nanosecond that seemed like an eternity, she hijacked my physical being. She—or we—flipped the shotgun around, and its hard metal butt cracked against the skull of The Beast. He fell to his knees. As she prepared our stance for our second assault, she commandeered my vocal cords. With all the wrath and fury of a woman chained up in a withered garden for two-thousand years, she vociferated her battle cry. "REEE-DEMPPP-TIONNN!" We landed the weapon across the back of our adversary's head, and he dropped to the floor, unconscious.

Suddenly, I realized I was holding something, not the gun, something pointy, like a thorny vine. Metal shards pricked my delicate skin. It was barbed wire. We yanked Luke's arms behind him and bound his wrists to his ankles with the wire. Still using my appendages and gross motor skills, she grabbed a wad of his coal black curls and flipped him over. I didn't know what she was going to make me do next until I felt myself picking up the apple. We pried his mouth open with such force, I felt the mandible cracking. Eve/Rose and I weren't alone anymore. The League of Voiceless Women infiltrated my brain. I felt their pain and frustration, and I heard their long-suppressed cries for justice and equality. I spoke for every woman silenced by the myth when Eve/Rose forced the rotten fruit into the mouth of The Beast, and I shouted, "YOU EAT THE FUCKING APPLE, ASSHOLE!"

"MRS. SCOGGINS, please stop! You've done enough! We've got this!" It was only me now; Eve/Rose and the other women were gone, and I felt drained. A uniformed police officer stood over me, pulling me off a dazed and understandably bewildered Luke Detwiler. Several other officers surrounded us, staring down at the almost comical scene, the escaped convict strung up and stuffed like an unfortunate pig prepared for a luau roast.

"What the blue bloody blazing hell?" I heard someone mutter. It was Trey. The Beast writhed lividly but powerlessly in front of him, like a serpent whose venom had been neutralized.

My husband held me so tightly, I thought he might crush all my bones, but I begged him to hold me tighter. "How did you know to come home?"

"When a dangerous felon escapes, every law enforcement agent in the state gets notified. I tried to call and warn you, but you didn't answer."

"I lost my phone." I sobbed into his chest.

"Anyway, I called the station and told them I couldn't reach you. They had been patrolling the area all night because they thought Detwiler might show up here. When they found out neither you nor Rose were answering your phones, that's when they decided to come in."

Trey's colleagues dragged The Beast off the floor. They couldn't untie Eve's knots without cutting themselves, so they severed the wire with pliers and replaced it with shackles. "Back to death row for you," one of the officers informed the hapless prisoner.

Realizing Thomas and Harper were now safe, Rose succumbed to the pain of the beating she endured and collapsed in a bloody heap.

"Rose!" Michael shrieked as he pushed past me. He scooped her up gingerly, but held her securely, like lifting a sheet of fragile glass. I now knew he truly loved her as an equal and not as some pathetic symbol of a broken society. He rushed her outside just as the ambulance arrived.

"Somebody help her!" he called into the crisp night air.

I started chasing after them, but Trey stopped me. "I have to go to her. I have to make sure she's okay," I explained tearfully.

"Of course you do, but you're in no condition to drive. I'm going to take you, but first you have to tell me where our son is. Where is Nicholas?"

"He's with your mother. They spent the night with her friends in Fort Worth."

"Thank God," Trey sighed in relief. "Thank God he wasn't in the house." I was sure he was thinking about the last time The Beast broke into my residence and his child *was* there.

WE SPED THROUGH TOWN. At a red light, Trey posed the question I'd been dreading. "Honey, I get the rotten apple. It could have been pushed to the back of the crisper and overlooked for a few weeks, but where did you get the barbed wire?"

Not wanting to risk another stay at Sunnyvale by telling the truth, I coyly avoided giving him a direct answer. "Do you think you Eagle Scouts are the only ones who are always prepared?"

We sat in the waiting room, absently thumbing through magazines until a nurse approached us and said we could go in. I found Rose lying in a hospital bed, resting, and Michael sitting beside her, lovingly brushing the hair away from her face.

"Michael, is she okay?" I asked.

"Rose is going to be just fine." He grinned mischievously, and then added, "So is our baby."

"Baby?!" My exclamation woke Rose, and she laughed. "Why didn't you tell me you were having a baby?" I demanded of her as she groggily adjusted herself on the uncomfortable mattress.

"I didn't know," she defended herself. "I guess I've just been so busy with finals and graduation and work, and just plain being happy, I didn't even notice the signs."

After Trey and Michael exchanged a congratulatory handshake, Rose turned to my husband. "If it's a little girl, we'd like to name her Andrea, but only if that's okay with you."

Trey nodded, and his eyes glossed over. "That's more than okay with me."

The two men went out into the hallway so Rose and I could talk. I took Michael's place brushing the hair away from her bruises and lacerations.

"Rose, sweetie," I began hesitantly. "Last night, when Luke was at the mansion, did you see anything weird or unnatural? Anything you couldn't explain?"

"Honestly, I didn't see much of anything. I had my eyes closed the whole time, praying. Why? What happened?"

Not wanting to alarm her, I simply explained, "Let's just say I think your prayers were answered."

I TOOK a sedative that night so I could sleep, and it induced a disturbing nightmare. I dreamt I overheard a conversation between Trey and Grace.

"You didn't tell me it was going down last night, or I never would have left." I'd never heard Trey lift his voice to his mother before.

"That's exactly why I didn't tell you, son. You knew they had to do it alone. It's the only way they would ever know how strong they are when they unite."

The dream was shockingly real, but I knew it was just a dream. No way Trey and Grace knew Luke would escape, and if they did, they never would have left me alone.

I heard Nicholas cooing and babbling over the baby monitor. They were home, and it was after eleven o'clock. No mother of a precocious toddler sleeps that late, no matter what happened the previous night. I shot out of bed and ran to the nursery. My son played contentedly with a rattle and flopped around restlessly inside his playpen. I picked him up and cradled him close to me. Something about breathing in a baby's goodness erases all the cares and concerns of the adult world. Nicholas was dry, and he didn't seem hungry. Someone had tended to him while I slept.

As though she read my thoughts, Grace greeted me cheerily. "Good morning, daughter. I heard you had some trouble last night, so I decided to let you sleep in." She tossed my phone toward me. "I accidentally grabbed this thing before I left yesterday. I hope you didn't need it."

SOME PUBLICITY HUNGRY, bleeding-heart lawyer, who wasn't even from around here, temporarily raised a stink about excessive use of force in self-defense, and how if I wasn't a cop's wife I would be in jail. The only lasting consequence of Eve's vicious assault, however, was the good-natured ribbing Trey took at work about his "savage" wife.

IT DIDN'T SEEM right looking at that painting anymore. For one thing, it brought back too many horrifying memories of that epic struggle between Eve and The Beast. Besides, I knew she wasn't chained up in that withered garden anymore. Like Rose and me, she was free from her bondage. I gently took the frame down from the wall, wrapped it in an old sheet, and returned it to Connie's storage building where I found it. I only dreamed about her once more, but this time her message was not an ambiguous cry for help. It was a clear revelation of her struggle and her triumph, and I finally comprehended what she had been trying to tell me all along.

The legend of Eve was not so much a myth as it was a blatant distortion of fact. Sin, sickness, poverty, famine, and war did not come into the world through the actions of "one silly, gullible woman," as my father used to say, but through the trickery and deceit of an unfathomably evil and soulless beast. It is he who is accursed and not the woman. Eve stands exonerated and the curse is lifted from her daughters, and their voices are returned to them ten-thousand-fold.

ANDREA GRACE PETERSON made her debut three days before Christmas. Trey and I slid down city streets and skated across a thin layer of ice on Mt. Olive's parking lot to meet our new godchild. Winters in North Texas are not as brutal and unforgiving as the summers, but we still occasionally get a blanketing of sleet or snow.

I forgot to silence my phone when we visited the maternity ward and it rang while I fussed over Rose and the new baby. I didn't recognize the number so I rejected the call and turned off the device. When we returned to our car, I noticed three more missed calls from the same number. Slightly annoyed, I checked my voicemail. A woman introduced herself as a representative of the state adoption agency. In all the chaos that ensued after Nicholas abruptly entered our lives, Trey and I never thought to remove our names from the waiting list, and a newborn girl now awaited us if we were still interested.

We named our daughter Elizabeth. In Hebrew, the name means "the oath of God."

CHAPTER 34

*M*ichael took a teaching job at a liberal arts college in Massachusetts, near Walden. Rose could finish her education on the same campus and continue working and asserting her independence. Before they left, Rose and I took a long walk and ended up at the little park where Trey and I were married. We sat on one of the wooden benches.

"I'm going to miss you," I told her.

She rested her head on my shoulder. "Emily, you were my first real friend. You were the first person who saw any good in me at all."

I leaned my head against hers. Her hair, heated by the sun, felt soft and warm against my face. "Do you really have to go?"

She nodded sadly. "You know I do."

"Rose, I am so incredibly proud of the woman you have become. Watching you grow has been like watching a beautiful flower blossom after a long harsh winter. I am so honored to be your friend."

Rose wanted a road trip on the back of Michael's motorcycle, so Grace agreed to watch Thomas, Harper, and Baby Andrea while their parents traveled eastward in search of their new home. They wouldn't be back. When they found a place to live, a moving company had already been hired to deliver their possession and Grace would fly with their children to Concord.

I went to Lake Sutton to see them off. Michael had bought Rose a black leather jacket with fringe on the arms and back, and she wore it proudly. I helped her fasten the chinstrap of her helmet. She no longer needed my help with anything, but securing her protective headgear was one last thing I could do for her.

Michael started the motorcycle, and I heard the idling engine like I had so many years ago. Only this time it beckoned Rose. *Come on. Come on. Come on. Come on. Come on. Come on.*

I hugged my friend and whispered, "You hold on tight. He drives that thing like a bat out of hell."

Fond memories flooded my spirit when Michael shouted, "Where do you want go, my darling?"

Rose raised her arms triumphantly and replied, "Everywhere!"

She straddled the back of the motorcycle and they sped away. I stood on the sidewalk, waving and feeling like a mother sending her kid off for his first day of school, a sense of immeasurable pride tempered with a healthy dose of sadness, knowing nothing would ever be the same.

The first flower to bloom in my garden far exceeded my expectations. Rose became a pediatric nurse and she and Michael eventually married. He adopted Thomas and Harper, and we laughed about the combining of the names, the Simon-Petersons. To this day, I still communicate with my ever-blossoming Rose on an almost daily basis.

ABBY, the second to bloom in my garden, became an IT specialist for the government. We rarely ever see her as she travels extensively, but every year on his birthday, Nicholas receives a package from his biological mother.

With Ron Tyler's encouragement and support, Trey replaced his mentor as the lead detective for the violent crimes unit. The promotion came with a sizable raise that afforded me the luxury of leaving my job and devoting my time and resources to the starter house and its succession of residents.

One by one, the women came and went from the modest little home, each one adding a new and unique bloom in my glorious garden of feminine souls. Before I selected a woman to take under my wing, I always asked the same question: "Has anyone ever told you that you have great potential?" None of them ever answered in the affirmative.

A local news station once interviewed me about my work. They called the house a "dignity reclamation center," and I loved that description. Even the street address was apropos for my mission. 127 James Street coincided with my favorite Bible scripture, James 1:27: "Pure religion undefiled before God the Father is to care for the widows (disadvantaged women) and the fatherless in their affliction...." Any religion based on anything more or less than *agape* love is impure; it is tainted, and it is deadly poison.

THEY GATHERED in the town square, about fifty of them, I estimated, carrying colorful placards painted with quotes like "an eye for an eye" or "justice for Andrea." They didn't even know her well enough to know she preferred the diminutive form of her name, but they thought they spoke for her. They thought they knew what she would want.

Luke Detwiler exhausted his appeals in record time. His escape did not endear him to the appellate court judges and his execution date was fast approaching. Barring a last-minute stay of execution from the governor, The Beast would die by lethal injection on the seventh anniversary of his conviction.

Nicholas, Elizabeth, and I were headed home from the story hour at the local library when we spotted the protestors. My children knew they had an older sister who watched over them from heaven, but they didn't yet know the circumstances of her death. Nicholas was an avid reader, and he recognized the name on the posters. "Andrea. That was my sister's name."

"Yes, it was," I confirmed.

"Mommy, what are those people doing?" he asked curiously.

"Sweetheart, it's just a bunch of unhappy folks letting off steam."

At home, I relayed the story to Trey, and he said he had a similar experience at the post office. He ran into someone he had known for years, and the man asked him if we were going to witness the execution. When Trey told him no, the older gentleman became irate, even having the audacity to question Trey's love for his deceased daughter. How could we claim that we loved Andi and not celebrate the demise of her murderer?

The town's obsession with the impending execution grew unbearable and Trey suggested we all needed a vacation. We went camping on the shores of Lake Sutton. As Grace, Elizabeth, and I hunted sticks for marshmallow roasting, Trey and Nicholas assembled the tent. I overheard my son excitedly ask his father, "Hey, Dad, while we're here, will you teach me how to shoot the shotgun?"

My heart overflowed with love when Trey tousled the boy's hair and suggested, "How about I teach you to fish instead?"

Nicholas was satisfied. After all, it was *storge* he really craved.

THE DAY OF THE EXECUTION, Trey and I declared a forty-eight-hour moratorium on television, the Internet, and all other forms of news media in our house. We took flowers and laid them on Andi's grave and spent the rest of the afternoon playing board games with Grace and our children. The mansion was filled with so much love and joy, there was no room for hate and vengeance. After I put Nicholas and Elizabeth to bed, Grace, Trey, and I stayed up silently reading. At seven minutes after midnight, Grace shuddered ever-so-slightly, dropped her book and said, "Well, now that that's over, I'm going to turn in."

The next morning I went outside to water the hydrangea bushes while the children still slept. Grace already had her easel and canvas set up in the backyard and she worked frenetically on her latest project. I peered over her shoulders as she etched her name into the portrait. I don't know why I never thought of it before. I knew it was customary for artists to paint their names somewhere on their work. Heart and mind both racing, I ran to Connie's storage shed and flung open the door. My hands worked furiously removing the sheet that covered Eve/Rose, and when the masterpiece was revealed, I noticed something I had somehow overlooked for all this time. There above the auburn tresses that covered the woman's breasts was the one syllable name of the artist, "Grace."

I gasped in astonishment, but before I could react further, something even more extraordinary happened. The painting changed. It *evolved.* It was clearly Rose now, and only Rose. She frolicked in a crystal-clear pool beneath a sublime waterfall, an expression of unadulterated bliss plastered on her unblemished face. Even the title of the painting changed as I watched. The tiny white square of paper now identified the inscrutable artwork as "Redemption Rose."

I rushed out to confront the woman I now knew to be the artist. With her back still toward me, she never looked away from her canvas when she spoke. "Emily, do you still believe the only miracles are the ones we make for ourselves?"

I am certain I never told her that, and it didn't seem like the sort of thing Trey would mention, but intuitiveness was just another facet of her enigmatic personality. My mother-in-law had gifts and abilities unique to her. I never knew anyone more at peace with the world or more in tune with the thoughts, hopes, and dreams of those around her. Many western philosophers might call her transcended. I simply called her Grace.

EPILOGUE

The garden flourished again with one exquisite, ever-blossoming rose as its magnificent centerpiece. Crystalline streams flowed through the valley, providing life-sustaining water for the lush green vines, and healing the fissures in the earth. Though the yin and yang pendulum of human existence continued swinging its captive passengers back and forth, and they sometimes knew fear, they no longer feared themselves. They were not ashamed of their own humanity, for they now knew there was atonement for their inherent flaws and weaknesses, the things they once called "sin." Perfect love cast out all their fears, and by grace, they were redeemed.

Made in the USA
Middletown, DE
18 March 2019